SNAKE CITY

THE LARK CASE FILES, BOOK FOUR

CHRISTIAN D. READ

SNAKE CITY

THE LARK CASE FILES, BOOK FOUR

CHRISTIAN D. READ

SHOOTING STAR

SHOOTING STAR PRESS

First published in Australia in 2019
by Shooting Star Press

PO Box 6813, Charnwood ACT 2615
info@shootingstar.pub
www.shootingstar.pub

ABN 63 158 506 524

A catalogue record for this book is available
from the National Library of Australia.

Read, Christian D.
Snake City

ISBN: 978-1-925821-17-8 PRINT
ISBN: 978-1-925821-18-5 EBOOK

Cover illustration by Justin Randall
Design & Typesetting by Wolfgang Bylsma

ONE

I

'You've got a black hole in your brain.'

Doctor taps on the film up on his light box, white streaming through it.

Like it's something to care about.

'It's about a centimetre in diameter. Slightly smaller than a marble. Spherical. It's on your corpus callosum.'

Do you know what that means? Fucking no idea, me.

'Have you had any tremors? Limbs moving outside your control?'

'Nothing like that.'

'Problems in making decisions? Memory loss?'

'No.'

'Changes in personality?'

Shrug.

'What's ninety nine minus seven?'

'Ninety three.'

'What's ninety three minus seven?'

'Eighty... something'

'Hmmm.'

Doctor here made the scene a long time ago or he's not my doctor. Not Library but a magician in his way. Dunno how serious he takes it but I got photos of him, in my desk, in woods doing rites to Toth, god of medicine and magic. Figured to blackmail him, or something, one day, if needed. He's not a serious player but he's someone people like me can see and talk all open with. He wears his hair too long. Blonde, like a mane. *Fucking annoying.* His name is who cares.

He runs me through some sums, counting backwards, like that. Makes me squeeze his hands, makes me track a pen he waves in front of my face. Brain doctor stuff.

'You seem a bit shaky.'

'Nerves.'

'Lark, your corpus callosum... you *should* be having symptoms from a wound, an insult, like this. And you need about a hundred tests. You could have –'

I know where the wound came from. A bad spirit under the ground that took my life. It marked me and got in the wind. Where is it now? Who the fuck knows?

'Demon killed me, bought me back to life. That change the diagnosis or treatment?'

He just stares at me. 'Lark, I'm just... I hold to a weird religion. I don't know anything about demons.'

'Good move, doc.'

Figure we'll meet again, though, me and the creature. One day. That's some unfinished business.

That's how these things work out.

Sometimes, alone, in the dark, I can feel it as it creeps around the world in the dark, spreading disease and whatnot. Sneaking in to kid's rooms and eating up widow's grief and orphan despair.

Cruel motherfucker.

It liked killing me. Every now and again, it catches a taste of me like I catch it. And it gloats. Not with words but with emotions so vast you'd drown in 'em if you slipped. Seems curious about me in the way the cat gets curious about the mouse.

Cruel, cruel motherfucker. The Rabisu.

Doctor finishes his work and prints out a dozen bits of paper. Sign some. Don't use the name Lark, that's sure. Make another appointment but the card it's written down on is in the bin before two blocks are under my feet.

The hole in my brain won't kill me. And it won't slow me down too bad if it already hasn't.

Call it a wound because it is. But that's not its *purpose*.

It's a mark. A way for the Rabisu to find me one day.

Freed it from a spell and let it lose on the world. Had to, no choice to it. But a thing like that, doesn't exactly feel what you'd call gratitude. It'll never forget me. It'll work to hurt me just *because* it owes me one.

Demons, man.

Bastards, each of 'em.

Eleven in the morning. Time for breakfast. Ham and eggs and good, sweet coffee. If my hand trembles a mite as it lift the mug, there's no time to fret over it.

What's done is done and your scars mean something.

Get a text on my phone. It'll be someone from my office, asking if I feel like coming in today.

No. *Text messages.* Jesus Christ. The fuck do I want to get a goddamn text message for?

I I

The Library Chapterhouse is an old Victorian style apartment building. It's actually two, walls knocked out between them on the insides. But you wouldn't know that from the street. Magicians like to hide in plain sight.

Brownstone. Steps going up to a heavy red door. No marks to let you know this is anything other than an apartment building.

There's a doorman in a uniform who nods at me. Knew the old guy, before this guard, he did the gig fifteen years. Shaved ape who works it *now*, seen him four times a week for six months but he checks my ID before he enters the code to let me in all the same.

New security protocols. New faces. Things are moving on.

Inside, used to be all wood panels and brass. Old school. Kinda *elegant*, like. Now fucking Everett and his new school have changed it. Feels like a corporate headquarters. Guards on doors and receptionists behind desks in the lobby. Library done changed while I was out in the cold.

'Mr. Lark.'

Receptionist is the kind of beauty so bland you can't remember her when you're eyes aren't on her.

Show her my ID and she buzzes me through to the elevator. Used to be a rickety old thing, cage door you'd pull shut and it'd shudder its way up and down. Now it feels like a sports car and gotta put my ID card into it. Barely even feel like it's moving.

Wonder if I'm getting old or they really have stripped the place of what made it worth working for. It's all pretty and bland and looks good but has no traction, no grit. Like that receptionist and her white, white teeth.

Worked the Library ten years, then left after Jon snapped bad and Scarlet walked out on me. Worked by myself for a long time after.

Now they got me back here. Working for the man. Doing my old job in a new way and it's like watching another man hit my dog.

Get paid. Get an office. Get access to the books. The resources of a cult spread all over the goddamn world. So that's good.

But... Let's be honest with each other - The Library needs a cat like me and a cat like me needs the Library. Too many enemies to go alone, these days.

Part of me that feels like a crack in a wine glass. You see it. But you wanna drink, so you ignore it. And each time, it gets longer and wider and one day, one day, you know it's gonna shatter but what choice do you have?

My room, my office, feels like a professor's at a university. But bigger. Bookcases, a desk, covered in coffee cups, statuettes, more books, open face down or bookmarked. Window, opens onto an alley, for a good view of the rats playing in the stagnant water and skip bins. Four storeys up outta six.

Got a computer which is telling me about internal emails, which are good for ignoring. Close and lock the door behind me and collapse into my chair.

Got me a *job description* now, too. 'External Crisis Manager.'

Headkicker again is what that means. Sheriff. That's what I was for ten years. Took over from my old master, Mully. Fifteen years later and in the same place. But at least it's worse, now.

Black hole in my brain.

Someone slides paper under my door. Print out of the emails. Scarlet makes them do it so there's no excuse for me not to read what's as important. She knows that giving me a computer is like giving a wolf a hat.

Look the sheet over. Something about lions, which seems interesting. Scryers kept getting solar imagery and so field agents got sent out to do some leg work for me. The rest is just job type shit and there's no way to care about that.

Staff meeting at one? No. Karen's fucking birthday drinks? Fuck is Karen? No. No, no. *You really want a man with my meat hook personality trying to make small talk with someone called Karen?* Not a popular cat but at least I know that about myself.

Training at ten. *Can do that.* At least that's me talking about things that are interesting to talk about. Two hours.

Supposed to be all about me teaching theory and giving devoirs and inspiring a new generation of Acquisitors for the Library. That's what we start out as, field agents, finding and securing magic of any kind, though books are best. But that ain't my bag. Usually just take the new blood out on a gig, show 'em some pointers, and they learn real quick if they can cut it, or not.

Open Night tonight, Jesus fucking Christ. *They still fucking do that?*

See, we've always recruited when we can from the rich and powerful. Or simply gone in for patrons. It's an old move loads of organisations like the Library go in for. This might shock you but a collection of prophets, mystics and occultists aren't exactly the best at financial pragmatism and that.

Few years decided the organisation needed a lot more capital. Outreach to the gentry of the City. Bankers, surgeons, stockbrokers, trust fund kids, CEOs, celebrity types looking for some edgy press. The most boring people in the world. Coin people in a Wand world, coming for a walk in the weird, looking for masked orgies and something spiritual and weird, man. Something *real*.

Rich people come at our half-world like moths to fire. Same results, nine times from ten, too. Want to be a sorcerer? Wield powers over the hearts of humanity and the material reality? Need the *opposite* kind of mind from one that craves status and cash. Need to *kill* that ego to work proper magic.

Coming here, to us, they're just buying themselves a story to impress their neighbours and the other ladies who lunch.

Still. They bring in the cash.

Last on the list that seems made up wholly of shit *just* to mess with me – Preparedness meeting.

Fucking hell. The language. All toothless jargon designed to put the rubes at rest. They mean *scrying*. Divination. Part of the veil. Lots of the gig these days is a waste of time, waste of talent, but not the actual part where the Library acts as peacekeeper and adjudicator. Library is the biggest occult organisation in the City. Richest. Best trained magicians. Most contacts.

Also, we keep the peace. Make sure no chancer is hitting civilians or calling up what they can't motherfucking put down.

My work.

Knock at the door. Open it up.

Katanya.

III

She took over my gig when I was gone, exiled from the City for a year when some magic forced me out.

Come back and they give me a title and job and salary and all of it above hers. Truth is, she isn't as good as me and she knows it. My rep is better. Taught her, too. No shame, not bragging. She's clever and tough and dedicated to her hermetic style. But she's got a life outside this world. If she ain't as good as me, it's cause she ain't as *focused* as me.

Don't stop her biting at the fact she got demoted. She tries not to hold grudges but don't always succeed.

Thought we might have something once. But she likes women better. Went and married one last year. Shaved her head and got her woman's name tattooed on her knuckles. Leather pants and a black singlet and rings on her fingers chained to a bracelet. She weighs about as much as a cat and it's all straight line muscle. Biker leather tough.

'Boss asked me to talk to you.'

Her boss is Scarlet.

Scarlet. My ex, much a part of me as a sailor's faded tattoo.

Worked here for six months and never seen her once.

Figure that's how she wants it and figure that's for the best. Scarlet has a life and a daughter and a husband. Me? A black hole in my brain and what's coming to me.

'Training time. She wants to make sure you ain't skiving off work.'

She pushes past me, sits down on other chair in the office.

'Got anything to drink?'

Whiskey in the desk drawer. Two tumblers. Nods her thanks and slugs it back in one. Takes the bottle and pours again. Always did like a woman drinks before noon.

Something's on her mind. Take my own shot and wait. Katanya rubs her hand over her spiky scalp. Looked better with hair but she's not the kind of woman who's all that interested in what you might think of her choices, so my mouth is shut.

'The cadets are shit, man.'

Cadets. Military word I don't like. But that's what we're supposed to call 'em. Used to be called Acolytes but apparently, not everyone knows that word and we ain't supposed to call 'em that in case the money hears and gets upset.

'Always are. *Acolytes* are always hopeless.'

'No, seriously. They suck. One of them won't fucking learn how to fight. Says her path is a peaceful one and she just wants to protect people. And Anton is getting worse. He's a fucking risk taker and adrenaline junkie and shouldn't have been let through the front door.'

Say nothing. She's not here to talk about the future of the Library and the quality of recruits. She's just like me in that she finds teaching dull and no kind of challenge. She's Holy Guardian Angels to talk to and Gnostic Masses to officiate. Katanya works it Crowley fashion.

She goes on.

'Another one is so out of shape he couldn't do a single push up.'

'Don't reckon I could.'

'You in training?'

'My training was in magic, not fucking gym class.'

'I don't make the rules, Lark. Human Resources calls the tune.'

'Human fucking Resources. Jesus.'

She shrugs back at me. No point talking about it. It is what it is. And now our ancient lodge of sorcerers has an H.R. department, just as Plotinus, Dee and Ashamole would have wanted.

Warily, she asks, 'You ever thinking about leaving?'

There's a woman called Bernadette. She's looking for me. Until she's in the ground? Going nowhere.

'Not yet.'

'Me either.'

Finish the drink in silence.

'My wife would kill me if I lost the pay cheque anyway.'

'The things we do for love.'

She laughs but don't reckon she finds it funny.

I V

Whiteboard, long table, shit plastic chairs. Rooms like this make me want to be dead. Again.

Class is assembled. Professor Lark is ready to teach.

Prepare to learn.

Who's in today?

Sasha used to work for my old boss Mully. Someone got a hold of Sasha when she was a kid and hurt her and *hurt her*. Ritual Satanic abuse. It's something different where I live. Not something to spook suburban parents with stories of babies born in toilets. Think more getting possessed dozens, a hundred, times by a dozen, a hundred intelligences. Given visions of hell after some motherfucker's forced about a dozen psilocybin mushrooms down the throat. And the less *ambitious* abuse that's not much less acid in the soul.

She was a bright kid, trying to stay ahead of what lived down there in her past and howled and bit her. Don't think she made it back up. She's studying *ohmyodo*. Japanese sorcery. My own plundering traditions never went East, so fuck knows if she's good at it.

The first words Anton ever said to me was 'When I wearing my motherfucking magic pants I'm invincible!' Reckon he learned about Norse sedir magic from the internet. He works out like a fiend, came from MMA and won't live a year with his attitude. Might as well wear a shirt with the word CANNON FODDER on it. Stupid fuck. Short man with short man syndrome.

Karel comes from fuck knows where and can't talk about it. See, he's got no tongue. Someone took it from him. He signs but I don't. Katanya's learning. His English is not strong so when he writes things down, it can go tits up, communication wise. Clothes he wears, way he phrases, amulet he wears around his neck, figure him for Romanichal. Not sure about his skills and worth yet. He's got a knack for folk traditions. Finding things, fixing things. He's leucistic, too. Almost an albino. White but for the eyes, which are dark as murder. He keeps shells wrapped in a handkerchief. He calls them his *pocket gods*. I'm well curious .

Katanya starts the class.

Bettina used to teach fighting but that was pointless. She couldn't talk about what she did in a way you could learn from. My undead girl learned how to fight when the family men made her battle for coins since she was a kid. She didn't like explaining herself anymore than I do, anyways.

Lurk at the back like always. Katanya is explaining how to deal with civilians who've seen shit they can't explain. Never was good at the talking part myself. Jon dealt with it, he was always better with people than me. When Jon put on that goddamn mask, it swallowed him up. Teaching Darkness he called it, though most people called the fucking cursed thing the Hollow.

Lost more than a friend, oldest friend, then. Lost a partner. We worked great together.

Sasha asks how we should be dealing with cops. Katanya mutters some dark shit about how much she hates 'em. Everyone hates cops who ever dealt with 'em for real. That nice officer you met is digging his knee into a poor kid's spine for a bit of fun an hour later. But hating 'em ain't dealing with 'em and you'll probably have to deal with 'em.

They need some true knowledge, though.

'Don't.'

Kinda as surprised to hear my voice as the class is are.

Sasha turns and looks at me, raising up an eyebrow. She'd be a stunner if she didn't have the cold eyes of a madwoman. She's drowning in front of us. Maybe someone will help her one day.

Not my problem.

You think that sounds heartless? Maybe it is. But a man like me can't help a woman like her and it'd be a goddamn mistake to try. Who'd *be* helped? Her? With my lack of skills and empathy? Or me, for being able to look at myself in the mirror for another day.

Besides, if Mully couldn't pull her through, the fuck chance do I have? Mully gave her and me our starts and he was kinder than me by some way.

Was I always like this? Who cares? But there'll always be something in me that distrusts absolutely. Fuck... enough of this, eh? Anyway...

'Police don't like things that don't make sense. Makes 'em mad. They like people obedient and they like people sensible. Think they never smack around a drunk?

You get caught on a simple B&E, trespass, assault, most times, just take the ride to the station, call one of our lawyers, no sweat. Enjoy taking a piss in a room fulla strangers. Worst deal, you have to get yourself out of the cell. Shown you enough shadow magic, empty-handed magic, to make that easy.

Get mad-eyed on a cop, they'll kill you. Or beat the shit out of you, just because that's how a cop makes the world makes sense. Play smart. Yes sir no sir.'

Karel writes something down. Shows it to me.

DO WE FIGHT TO HURT POLIZIA?

Nod my head.

'You got to thrown down with cops? Choice made for you? You're a magician of the Library and you have business they can't know. You're *not* citizens. Do what you have to.'

Anton looks for a high five on that, but Karel ignores him and Sasha stares at him like she found his body in the water ten days after he died.

'You mean that?'

Sasha's voice is hungry and for something most unrighteous. All sorts of hungers there and none of them healthy.

Wait a moment. Stare at her. Yeah, there's something inside her that will not ever be repaired.

'...look. Alright. All of you. You'll see things that are... *fucked up* in this gig. Nothing is cruel as a magician who thinks magic makes 'em unaccountable. Sees people as experiments, toys. Sacrifices. Whatever. Citizens don't want to see what you'll see and that includes cops. You're not... you ain't accountable to police.'

'Fuck yeah!' Anton throws up some kind of salute again, like he's got a tic. Getting older, you never know what the fuck the youth is doing.

'But you're accountable to me.'

He snorts his opinion of this.

Dead in a year. I'd kick his arse out but don't care enough to save his life.

My phone goes off in my pocket. Bettina made me put in a tone just for her so as she'd get an answers. There's an address and one word GRAPEFRUIT. Her code for come now and don't fuck around.

'Class dismissed.'

TWO

I

Turns out, the address is for the zoo.

Late afternoon and the cops are out, speak of the devil. Which… don't do that if you can help it.

Bettina and her man, the vodou houngan Aristide are waiting for me. Bettina got a gig with the Library too. My insistence. She works her own cases and gets paid pretty good, which keeps her aunts happy.

Her and me, we don't care much about the money side of this gig. We're each other's. We still mainly double team it but she handles a lot of muscle gigs.

She's in a hoodie and chinos and shades. Get too good a look at her in the light, you can see the grey in her skin. Aristide tries to ride his Baron Cemetery image hard as he can but he sticks out like a leper in a hot tub in his totemic gear. We got him to take off the top hat and frock coat in public and now he wears ratty black suits and ties his dreads back.

Nothing will make him cut the fingernails he's lacquered into claws. Wears gloves though.

He nods at me. We didn't meet well and he's still sounding out how me and his girlfriend work together. *Could* tell him not to worry himself but that shit doesn't do anything. He's in it for good with Bettina, but me? He ain't exactly big on men and women chilling.

It'll shake out as it shakes out. He might come the voodoo

gangster with me yet.

They're at a kiosk under an umbrella, drinking bad coffee like goddamn tourists as people gather around the cops about thirty meters down a path that leads through cages. Slide in beside her and she offers a fist for jabbing. Only person allowed to do it with me.

'You were right.' All she says to me. 'Lions.'

'I thought you were wasting our time, man.' Aristide is still looking to match dicks with me, but he's figuring out I know what I'm about.

Part of my work is dealing with oracles. Fucking... Long-Range Tactical Department. That's what Elliot and his ghouls re-branded it, but they're scryers. There's a room full of crystal balls, tarot-readers, automatic writers. We hire 'em freelance or put 'em on the payroll and have 'em divine for the whole City. Been standard practice for the Library since Mully's day. He set it up in the 70s.

Last report I got, like in those mails, we got some solar imagery in their reports. Three different images of suns or crosses or like that.

Three results as overlapping? That triggers investigation. We don't check out crimes, we don't even stop them. All we do is be on the lookout for when our interests can be threatened or sated. Three is a sacred number, significant magically, mathematically.

So when three suns come up, three suns get the look.

The sun is...

Magic operates *symbolically*.

It'll never be a science because it's an art. The sun has a thousand of them symbolic meanings.

Astrologically, it means the higher self. Not a mystery why. Life giving, powerful, all that noise too. Latin word for gold, *aurum*, comes from Aurora, goddess of dawn. Used to put the Sun of Verginia, sixteen point starburst onto king's tombs. Alexander the Great's old man was buried under one. Suns and kings go hand in hand. Seal-symbol of the god's authority from New Mexico to Mesopotamia. Jesus and the sun? He's got that halo for a reason. Aztec heart sacrifice too, offered up to sun gods. Know what a monstrance is? That's the sun. Ra, Horus,

Apollo.

Those example are from the top of the head. Hit the books, literally, a thousand more would come out.

So, too big to really narrow down 'solar imagery' without real legwork.

Sent Katanya out to check if someone had been hitting up banks or whatever for gold but she's not found anything. Went down to some jewellers and dealers, sniffed around down with those cats but they don't talk to no one.

Lions are the king of the jungle. That links them with kings. Had no real reason to do it but sent Bettina down here on a whim.

You and me? Between us? Never thought it would pay off. But look like you know what the fuck you're doing, always, is pretty good advice to any magician.

'That's why they pay me the big bucks, baby.'

Bettina thinks I'm pretty funny but not the way you want someone thinking you're funny.

II

Wait a while for the crowd to thin out. Bettina and me can out-wait stone but Aristide's fried from a life of hell. He's patient as detonation tape, addicted to trouble. Keeps fucking off to get flavoured ice and literally poke the bears.

'Sweet tooth' says Bettina, almost an apology.

Yeah, sure, Aristide could be acting more pro. Not the time to get into it with her and don't want to nag at him like a boss might.

Zookeepers come to tell us park's closing but a sigil in the condensation off Aristide's stupid drink sees us left alone. Cops ignore us too.

Sun goes down and the zoo wakes up. Not expecting it to be so motherfucking loud.

Have to admit, zoos don't make me too curious. Animals that chill by day get ambitious by night, as it happens. Hyena hoots and monkey screech. Elephants and big cats. Whole bunch of others never did hear before.

Last time outside City, a demon killed me and burned through my brain. Don't know from animals. Would have been pleased never to see one again.

But I'm rarely that fucking lucky.

Cops set up mobile klieg lights and we head on over to where they've set up shop. Simple spells mean cops perceive us in their colours. Get the skinny.

As it turns out, I was right. This is the lion cage. They're missing.

Three males are kept here, separated from the females. Who the fuck steals three lions? Zookeepers are dead too. One vet and two assistants, one cop tells me, pointing out three figures under tarps. He's seeing his superior instead of me, thanks to a touch of shadow magic. Turns out, no one figured that out for an hour or two that the corpses were anything less than meat for the beasts.

Look over the bodies, lifting up a tarp and, no lie, seen a lot of corpses but wince at these. Stink of death doesn't get easier to deal with in time and these have been *well* chewed on. Looks on their faces, what's left, amount of blood all over the cage, they were mauled on alive.

No need to linger. Let the blanket slip. Go back to them if it's needed but not keen on the muck and mess of necromancy right now.

Bettina comes up behind me, too tense.

She lives off death. Flesh and blood and breath. But she's not entirely fond of that ghoul nature. She fights it off without too much struggle but she's twitchy with the scents of her sustenance all around but off-limits.

Wasn't always that easy for her.

Forensic techs in masks and orange suits all sealed up are at the bodies like vultures.

'In the mouth,' murmurs one. 'What's that?'

One hands another forceps and forces open the jaw, pulling hard against spasmed muscles. Get in closer and but the hoodoo on one.

'Hand it over.'

Magic's pretty good and you should do it if you can. The Tech, her mind recognising me as AUTHORITY, hands me what's in the mouth. It's a scroll. Grab some latex gloves from one of the techs and unroll it. Scroll. Just rolled up paper, good quality. In fine handwriting, trained and calligraphic, a poem.

Read it out to my girl.

'A god who lives on his fathers and feeds on his mothers ... who lives on the being of every god, who eats their entrails ... Pharaoh is he who eats men and lives on gods.'

'Fuck does that mean?'

'Dunno. Cool, though.'

Pocket it. Bettina helps me up. My hip goes out easy these days. Took a beating to it a few years back that isn't giving indications of healing itself up. Roll the scroll back up and if she notices the tremor in my hand, she's saying nothing. She then shows me her phone with a text message.

'The fuck now?'

Address and a code for response. That's one of Elliot's ideas. Keeping me on a leash. Making me work his way and his way is citizen.

'Dunno. Let's bounce,' she says.

We bounce.

I I I

Take the subway, the cross-town local west, to a good part of the City. A *nice* part. Where the teachers and nurses and restaurant managers live. Nothing flash. Solid apartments with nice people living nice lives in nice ways.

'Why lions?'

Bettina sits next to me, hood up, while I'm reading through *Demon-Mania of the Sorcerers* on my phone. Black magic books are pretty wild. Try one.

'Dunno. Yet.'

'That some human sacrifice shit?'

'Could be.'

'That's some straight savage balls, hitting up a major place like a zoo. All out in the open. Scandalous.'

'Or maybe amateurs going in on the horror movie tip. Or interrupted. Or whatever. We'll go back in a day or two when it's all sorted out with coppers. Then we'll do some hoodoo recon.'

'Coo'' She's learning French on an app. Won't help her with the creole her man speaks. Not much. Kinda surprised by how far she's taking it. Figured Aristide was just into her because he's a full on death fetishist and Bettina's blood runs cool. But he's still around and so's she.

'How's it all being? You and him?'

'He wants me to wear a dress. Just once. To dinner.'

'Heh.'

''Side from that, it's like butter.'

Nods at me, goes back to her study. Can see the reflection of it in her glass eye. *Like butter.* Smooth and good. We're the next stop so we start talking shop.

'Break down the case, baby.'

Out train rolls on and Bettina bobs her head, like she was listening to music only she can hear.

'Someone here called up Library emergency numbers for help last night.'

'Fuck it took so long to get to us? Ain't we the Emergency Response Team?'

She shrugs. *Emergency Response Team.* That's our official designation in the new boring Library. Apparently.

'Dunno. Lions is a big deal too, man. I don't assign cases. Just know it's a registered cult lodge. Some sort of Heathen Egyptian syncretic shit.'

'*Syncretic.* You been hitting the books.'

'Something like that.' She tries hiding a smile, glad her study was noticed.

Nice people. Nice lives. Ain't expecting the butcher's shop we walk into then.

I V

My line of work, ten bodies in a year is a *bad* year. Not happy with eight. Work hard to keep it from coming all to blood. Dozens of cults in the cities and the odd bad spirit, monster, whatever, hands get thrown. We try to keep peace, keep people talking, or just be scary enough to make sharp-knifed motherfuckers think twice.

Sometimes it all goes wrong and cult wars break out. Happens. My main job is to *cool that shit off*. Scarlet is chief negotiator, the woman every ritual crew in the City talks to. But you fuck up, you piss *her off*, she sends me.

Not always easy working for your ex but she keeps me at long arm's length and if she needs to explain something, she writes it up. Best for us both, innit?

Even then, even in this city that breeds magicians like spiders lay eggs, occult killings aren't common. For one, murder ain't so easy as all that. By definition, kill someone with magic, it's cold-blooded and most murders are just... like Burroughs said, 'anyone who owns a frying pan owns death.' Covering up a killing isn't a joke neither. Murder's a powerful magical act that leaves scars on the world.

And you kill someone, after, you best be able to handle blowback, payback, counterattack so you don't even *want* to get caught.

It happens though, sure. Humans dig killing humans, no doubt about it. But it's just not every day. We ain't homicide cops. So another bloodbath on the same night just ain't expected, which is what we're walking in to.

Anyways.

We're going to a simple space for hire over a dollar store. You know the kind of place. Buy pipe cleaners, tea towels and underwear made out of polyester and infection. Rooms up above it you lease out as flats or live in if you own the shop. Walk up squeaking old stairs and threadbare, ugly industrial carpet. Bettina opens the door first to secure it. As she does, stink of blood overwhelms us.

'*Mierda*. Come in.'

Look in. Gag. Hold it in. Tie a kerchief around my face for the smell. The lions can be looked at when the cops have fucked off indeed, but this needs attention right the hell now.

The room's been kitted out like any amateur hour operation. Banners hand painted hung on the walls and hung up with tacks with witchy point up pentagrams and stick figure style symbols, three of them side by side, waxing, full and waning moon for bellies. Corn dolls for God and Goddess on an altar.

Neopagans then. Not Heathens. Keep 'em straight, or it's like calling a Scot English.

Well, they *was* Neopagans anyways. Twice in one day the stink of an opened up human body coats the inside of my throat and skull.

They've been bound and gagged and someone's been at their organs.

Probably tried to do it when they were alive and conscious. Stupid idea. Child or pensioner, tied or not, try to operate on someone still alive they're going buck wild. Hit 'em with a paralytic if you're on the full sadist trip. Judging from the tears on the bodies from the ropes they're tied in, that didn't go down.

Two women, both in their fifties and an older guy.

Him I know.

Callum. Just some old druid type, beard down to his tits, liked getting into a white robe with no underwear on dancing around by moonlight. Robe's on him now but torn open down to the waist and underneath, good look at his ribcage.

Callum. Run through what's easy to remember. Part of a loose conclave of hippies who had some juice. Maybe a bit fond of the outdoor sex Working. But who never gave me any trouble.

Can't figure any reason for putting the knife to him. He didn't have what it takes to be a player and didn't mess with dark side shit that puts you in the way of this kind of murder.

The two women have that long, unwashed hippie hair look too 'em. Callum's heart's gone but they went in the side for the women. Then let 'em bleed out.

Three bodies mean the place is soaked with claret. Sticking to shoes as I check out the other body. Yeah. Poor slappers. Good news is, they would have bled out a lot quicker than Callum. Hope and Marie. Think that's their names.

'This is some serial killer shit, Lark.'

'Yeah.'

Look around the room for anything else but there's nothing for us. Broom in the corner, hand-made. Some ceramics. Deities in congress, as they say. Like that. Neopagans are pervs. Nothing special.

'Close the door.'

V

Detective time, man.

Hit the magic circle and then hit gnosis, the *no mind* mindset of magic. One pointed, low rez consciousness. Non ordinary reality.

Hell, you read this far, you know how it works by now. Can't do magic real easy except when you're experiencing Magical Consciousness.

Looking for clues, for hints, for images, through a sorcerous lens.

But this job has been ritually shielded. In the astral space, the world overlying ours, there's four faceless figures, tall, austere, that eat the past. Bound servitors put in place to hide what happened here from eyes like mine. I get some visions, some images, some hints at the past.

Callum opens a door. His eyes widen in shock. That's all can be gotten. From that moment, to their dead bodies, the memory of this place is torn away.

Serious mojo.

Spare you the wait and move this along. We find out the same thing has happened at the zoo. Same techniques.

Serious fucking mojo.

THREE

I

Elliot is angry. Think he's trying to intimidate. Which is kinda funny to me.

He's in a suit, no tie, pink shirt they tell me is rightly called salmon but its pink as an eye infection to me. His teeth are white as walls.

Best remind you concerning this motherfucker.

Few years back, me and my girl Scarlet split. Together ten years but the wheels came off. She stayed in the Library when I didn't. After they wouldn't let me help Jon deal with the Hollow, didn't see much point in staying. Wasn't real prepared for Scarlet to move on without me, but she did. Remade herself. This is a few years back now.

Library upstairs decides as they need cash and patrons. Went down like I said before. And in that recruitment drive, a man comes through the door called Elliot. Or Everett. Have troubles remembering. Got a black hole in my brain, savvy?

Anyways, Elliot come outta generations of wealth, his family name on park benches and subway stations, like that. The Library recruits him with a story about a life that's more *meaningful* than moving money around. He's a rich kid. Sometimes they get all misty eyed about *spirituality*. How there's some needs money can't fill. How sad.

Elliot starts up with Scarlet. Her old kind was dirtbags like me.

She did a one eighty on *that* shit. Listening to The Meteors with me in a futon in a k-hole to operas with French sparkling.

Marries her. Has... has a kid with her. Redhead swamp witch, my fever sex girl, dancing wild, buying prams now and picking pre-schools.

Told that's maturity.

But Elliot decides he's gonna be in the Library on day to day *operational level*. He's the kinda cat who has to call shots, even when he doesn't know how to aim the piece. Buys his way in, despite knowing goddamn nothing. Motherfucker just thinks this is all some kind of self-help thing.

Wants to run my order like a business too.

Let's just say – him and me have blood between us.

Wasn't working for the Library when we first met but a case with the Devil bought me close to Scarlet again. And Elliot and me, we... clashed. He came at me hard. Tried to put some thugs to beating me. No dice. Not much to do with him since then and, straight up, I gotta keep the static low. Rabisu is out there and a woman called Bernadette is out there. Looking for me. I need Library resources right now.

So... came back to work. Had to. And... Turns out, my office falls under his purview.

He loves that. He's alone there. Really alone there.

Fucked him up a time or two a few years back. Which, between the two of us, was kinda a highlight of life back them. Scarlet told me to stop. Stopped. Been years and she's still got a part of me so I do as she say, most times.

Keep waiting for that to let go of me.

But here we are and she's got hooks in me, still. A while back it was all romantic lost love. But now it just depresses me those feelings won't gutter.

Staring at Elliot across the long office table, radiating his naked contempt of a scumbag like me... feel that hold slip a little more. *She chose* him? *The fuck she want with me ever, if this is who she moves on to?*

Then Callum's snapped up ribs are in my mind and my goddamn stupid feelings aren't so important. Snap back to attention.

'Why aren't you interdicting these sorts of incidents!?'

Katanya sits next to me in the boardroom. Three men across from us. She stirs real uneasy. She's like me. Someone talks at you like this, they're stepping and need a beat down.

But it's his house now. Me? Staying quiet. Katanya coughs, then talks.

'Boss, we can only operate according to the information we're given. We're understaffed and ... there's gotta be fifty serious cults in the city. At least a hundred serious practitioners. Me and Lark can't –'

Elliot turns his back on her, looks at Foulstone.

The fuck did this prick do to get back in grace? Figured Foulstone for a traitor, myself. Low rent ghost molester. Necromancer. Still wearing fucking tracksuits out of the house. Still fat and looking like he needs a wash real bad.

Foulstone's staring at me like his eyes were guns and the gaze a bullet. Might say we have static. Give him nothing. Fuck him. My eyes fixed on Elliot.

Foulstone and me got into it a while back and I do not understand how he's back in grace.

'I'd mark his record down with incompetence, meself.' Foulstone's from London but he sounds like he's putting on a shit Cockney accent anyways.

Oh shit. Notice Blossom, the lawyer, is in the room, too. Ally of Foulstone's. Man with the personal warmth and charm of a serial killer's favourite surgical saw. But Elliot's still doing his tough boss routine.

'The fact is, the board,' which is what he calls the convention of accomplished sorcerers who run the Library, 'is running out of patience. They're uneasy with this latest act of violence. It's the third in six months.

To be fair, he's right. Three days after Callum's sad temple was raided and he and the women carved up, there was another body found. Some creepy bastards worshipping Pluto. Astronomer-necromancer.

'And not only that, other cults are starting to think we can't keep the peace in the City anymore! Their confidence in us is shaken. Under your watch! Well!? What do you have to say about that?!'

Katanya stirs in her seat.

Me? Shrug. Elliot fucking hates that and shouldn't admit it, but... digging it. He doesn't know how to deal with disinterest.

'Is that all you have to say for yourself?'

Shrug again.

'You're doing a shit job, Lark. You're weird and no one likes you but at least you were good at this work. Now you're just...'

Stand.

Turn.

Mully coughs as I do. One of the three men across the table from us. My old boss.

My old master.

Kind and smart, he showed me around when I was starting out. More than boss, if it's told straight. He started me out and gave me and Jon a chance just out the orphanage. He retired a while ago but they asked him to come in a few months ago. Figure he's being auditioned for a shot at the inner circle.

'Lark, please. There's... there's omens. We need you to talk to us. I understand your position and I understand you have some anger but we need you to understand, this... two serious occult crimes in back to back... I know, I know you've more than competent but we have to move quicker. Stay. We need to work together, all of us. This is bigger than...'

Stare at him. Cold.

'This isn't a factory. You know that. No guarantees, no deadlines.'

He glances over at Elliot. He brings his stare back to me. Gold flecked blue eyes, still vital in his face. Kind and compassionate. My true master and the man who, more than any other, shaped the path I walk.

On the other hand, he works with Elliot now. Fuck him.

Leave.

II

Fuck Elliot more, *for real*, though. We work to information we're given. And we ain't fucking cops with quotas.

Drinking alone in my office. Locked. There's been knocks and yells and the computer got switched off when it wouldn't stop fucking beeping messages at me. Phone too. Not in what you'd call a communicative mood.

Mully was right about one thing. These are all bad goddamn signs. Tarot spread for myself just to see if he's on the level. Don't use the major arcana. Just playing cards. Keep it low-fi.

Five of Spades. *Success by betrayal. Conflict.*

Cross it with two of Hearts. Two hearts coming together. Love. Or some other alliance.

Above, what's to come. Eight of cups. A long journey, away from happiness.

Next to me, what's here now, Queen of Clubs. *A powerful woman with a mighty will. (Bernadette? Growing cold.)*

Below me. Where I came from. Flip the card.

Throw the damn thing away.

The Devil.

Shouldn't have to tell you, ain't no goddamn Devil card in a regular deck of cards.

The Devil. My old friend. He'll never be done with me.

Hour later, there's a softer knock on the door. A woman and not Bettina, who'd slam. Open the door a crack.

Sasha. The little girl Mully pulled out of hell. My student now.

'I need your help.'

Go to close the thing again.

'Please.'

Something in her voice. Stare out at her.

'Please.'

She used to be alive, if wounded but whatever was down there in her past is biting her too hard. Looking at a house collapsed in on itself now. Black hole where a star used to be.

Open the door.

I I I

Bailed out of the office. We sit in a park on a bench. Same park Scarlet got married in. Well, nearly. Kinda fucked that up for her, though, not on purpose. Sometimes you get lucky.

Didn't stop her long, though.

But she came to me one night before she put the ring on.

No. Shake my head. Get that memory out...

It's good, here. A circle of white concrete in the middle of the green leaves that rustle in the wind. Curved park benches. Pigeons hob and bob, looking for a meal. Autumn days are winding down so the beams of warm light feel good on the face before the sun dies for winter. Some suit types are taking their lunch breaks here. Looks like the bodily resurrection of the dead.

Sasha sits, hands in her lap. Been here twenty minutes almost. She'll talk if she wants to talk. Just watch the citizens 'til she does. Get us hotdogs but she's a vegetarian. Of course.

Enough.

'Do you need my help, girl? You gotta say.'

She finally looks up at me, dark eyes filled up with conflicts that no one understands.

'No. You need mine. Help me and help us by your being smarter. You have to be smarter.' She sounds surprised at herself.

'That's always been true, lady. But you'll have to bring it home.'

'The Library. It's... you don't pay much attention but it's *bad*.'

'Yeah.'

'No! You don't pay attention like you should...'

Her hands twist and she looks at me the first time.

Play with a cigarette. 'Talk, girl.'

'Mully is old and he protects you from the others, but he's *old*. He's tired. And he won't be able to protect you forever. Elliot hates you.

You can't see it. You think you can but he wants to *hurt* you and you don't take him *seriously*. And he listens to Foulstone, who hates you too. You think they'll come at you like it was on the street. Like they'll *go* you. Or curse you.

But Elliot doesn't think like that. He'll come at you a different way. Office politics...'

All the people in the park look like puppets to me. Like they're not real, just things pretending as they were alive.

Say nothing.

'They're calling you *rogue*.'

'Sounds badass.'

'No. No! Listen! It means they can take you off duty. And I have to tell you. Elliot... people like me... we can see. He's not right for this work. He's put suck up like Foulstone into power and they're not good enough to keep the City calm.'

'Yeah.'

'I have dreams, you know, when I sleep. Snakes and worms eating the City. You're not *special*, Lark. You're rude and you're so shy you can barely talk to people at all,'

'Shy?'

'But you're not the same as Elliot. Katanya is good and Bettina is cool but you're like the veteran. We all want you to teach us better so we can do this work. Serial killer stuff going on and the guy in charge of it... Elliot's nice, he is, just not to you. He's nice but he's not right for the job.'

Sasha looks at me and for the first time, something lights up inside her.

'There are people that need stopping, Lark. There are people who need punishing. That's the job we need *you* for, not Elliot or Foulstone or Blossom. We want you to stay. We want to help do that.'

Maybe she's trying to touch me. Flatter me. Maybe she's thinking of the fucks who turned her childhood into a torture chamber. Who knows what bought this on, the little wounded girl opening up?

Like I can't see through her ideas about how to reach me. In the end, isn't sharing wounds just manipulation?

'But this attitude you have... you'll be fired. And we won't be trained. And the City...'

Alright. She's got herself a point.

Can't sulk behind a locked door. Can't get angry and cold. Got to put the brake on how much I hate teaching. I *need* the Library. Need the resources. Need the safety and the cash.

Has to be a better way of dealing with my problems than throwing down *for real* with my bosses, though. This wounded human has a point.

'Alright.'

She takes my arm and puts her head on my shoulder. Known her since she was just a kid, it ain't like that.

But does feel good, the weight of Sasha's bird bone body against me.

Bettina finds us a mite later. She always knows how to find me. Best fact in my life.

By then, got an idea of what to do next.

I V

The zoo at night.

They want results, we'll go in hard.

Getting in was easy as faking up a badge, telling the night staff we were following up on some leads, which should have told them we were fake as a lawyer's warmth. Didn't even have to hoodoo them even, just flashed official looking badges.

TV is ruining our children.

Crew is assembled.

Sasha is wearing a shawl and dressed in corduroy. Katanya in her black and Bettina in a hoodie pulled low over her eyes, standing apart from the rest. Karel, dressed in workman's boots and some hard-core band long sleeve, is watching Anton way you watch a mentally ill man masturbate on the street. If you're far away from him.

Anton, you see, needs to be told not to literally poke the bears.

'Hard-core motherfuckers, bears!'

The poor beasts are lured over to him by a simple charm and he presses fingers into their fat rolls, which they do not like and breaks the glamour. He lures them again, to start the whole thing over. You know, Anton once broke a man's jaw when the man suggested he not speak loudly in a movie theatre.

He's not my hire.

Don't worry about it though. He dies in a minute.

We come to the lion cages, still in police tape.

Teaching? No. Don't like teaching. But working with? That's different.

'No more classroom bullshit. This is the job. You're *doing* it. Want to learn how to work the Library, work for the Library. This is Acquisitions.'

Anton looks for a high five but no one gives him the satisfaction. Rap cage bar with my knuckles as we walk through the night time snarls of foxes and bison and crocodiles. Place really comes alive at night.

'Someone lifted lions and had them kill some citizens as they went. Nothing hoodoo in the cage we can use. Already checked it and they warded the scene. That shit takes time and is... localised. So we spread out seeing if they left traces anywhere else.'

Pat myself down but forgot to buy smokes.

'You hit gnosis and you search. Search entry gates, search access tunnels staff use, paths that lead to this cage. We don't find anything, we'll spread out wider. Do it in pairs in case of problems. Bettina?'

'Sup?'

Throw her my phone. 'Put this on walkie talkie, please.' She does and throws it back.

'Check in every ten minutes or so. Just need to know you're doing alright and where you are. Find something, call it in.'

Look over at Anton. Figure he should be told *no heroics* or something. But he won't listen. The fuck did he get on my crew…?

Katanya takes Sasha and they walk one way and into howl-crowded darkness. Anton and Karel go down an EMPLOYEES ONLY door. Me? Boss now, don't have to walk nowhere. Bettina sits next to me on the park bench opposite the cage. We stretch our arms out along it. She hands me a smoke. Put it in my mouth, don't light it.

'We gonna talk about why you're not smoking?'

You've got a black hole in your brain.

Say nothing. Don't *know* why. Maybe its health.

Sure.

'Being the boss is working out for us. We got *soldados* now, Lark. Living the good life.'

Just give her what passes for a grin.

Ten minutes exact, Katanya checks in.

'Nothing yet, boss man.' Catch on the word *boss*. Still bugging her, me coming in over her. Ah, fuck it. Deal with it later.

Three minutes after that, Anton gives as 'We're down in where they keep the food. Nothing so far. Karel's doing the scouting, man. He's going too fucking slow.'

Hand the phone to Bettina. 'He's supposed to go slow, fuckwit. And you were told just to check in.'

'Calm yo tits!'

Bettina's eyes go dark. Anton's ribs are in for a short sharp lesson. Breaks connections.

Two more check ins go ahead fine. Between the third and the fourth, start to hum *You Can Have Her* by Crazy Cavan. Bettina hates my music. She beat me all the way up when she heard me playing Hasil Adkins, so Bettina talks to shut me up.

'You're not doing so good with this new gig, hey?'

'Nah.'

'You seen *her*?'

Her. Scarlet. Don't even know what her life is anymore. Know it ain't for me, babies and pant suits. She left my way behind or she couldn't keep up, whichever way you wanna look at it.

'She's half a citizen now.'

'Yeah, she is, more than half. You *seen* her?'

'Not in months and even then, just in meetings.' Fucking *meetings*.

Animals howl, hoot and holler in the night.

'Don't want her anymore. Not who she is.' Light the damn cigarette. It tastes like shit. If the Rabisu-wounds hit whatever part of the brain likes Luckies, I'm fucked.

First time admitting that. *Don't want her.*

Cause that life of bottles and nappies and meeting teachers ain't for me.

But...?

She came to me and wanted back in to *my* goddamn life?

That's the question.

Perhaps it's just dude bullshit. Don't want her, no one else can? *Don't think so.* Maybe it just kills me she went on without me. We been over years now but she's still there. Why won't she go? Why won't this stupid fucking obsession leave me?

Maybe I can't stand to just be a memory she can't be bothered having.

Tattoos fade. Never vanish. Sit in silence a spell.

Phone crackles alive. Anton.

'Boss. Help.'

V

Anton's dead.

That was quick.

Told you.

Rest assured, he was a dickhead and it don't really matter that he's gone. Cheer up.

We track him down pretty quick. Following his path. Karel texts me to let me know he's still alive. Ten minutes later, we find a sign. It's easy for kids to understand so there's a big cartoon snake on it. The Reptile House.

House is just one long corridor under the ground. Walk along it, on either side, terrariums in the walls for you to look in. Get down there and the glass is all smashed out. Feelings of power here. Magic that affects the physical world is hard to do and rare and someone did it here. Waiting until Anton walked along the corridor, stupid and cocky, setting off a trap.

Glass broke outwards and the snakes came for him. They're all in a bolus, biting and biting the poor stupid bastard. His corpse, arms outstretched to the door, writhes and spasms as the snakes bite and bite at the back of his body. Bad way to die.

Later, I'll learn there's almost half a litre of venom in him. Snakes don't go like that. Not exactly a doctor of this stuff but there's no reason they'd mob the poor fuck and then keep going long after their venom sacks are empty.

Watch, real careful. Then, to see, I click open my zippo, sound loud over their dry scratching. As one, the serpents rear up to stare at me. Snakes are all white eyed. As if they were blind but seem to see just fine.

Not possessed but glamoured. In some hunting frenzy, made spiteful and eager to bite.

A spell has been activated here. Triggered by something Anton did. Not hard to figure out what went down. Someone comes investigating the Lions thing. Traps are laid not quite at the scene of the crime. Subtle, not right there with the lions but ready to go in case there was a sweep of the zoo. Someone, maybe, *expecting* an investigation. Who knows my basic M.O. Someone with the magic, snakes go wild, perhaps triggered by gnosis or something.

Behind us, a door opens. We spin, ready to throw down but it's Karel. He is shaking. He comes out of the bathroom behind us and even in the gloom we can see how wide and wild his eyes are.

Probably never seen anything like this shit before. Maybe never even been close to death.

Tries to write something but he can't.

He's alive because he listened to my girl and took it slow, though. So he's still ahead of the game.

He can't get through this, all the way through, then we have no use for him.

But shock is not failure and he can get a chance from me. Punches a wall a time or two to get himself together. Hear him breath in ragged and he comes back down to the door. Hands me a note.

CAME OUT OF THE PENS BEHIND US DEF TRAP I HID IN BATH

'The fuck is this?' Bettina is unhappy.

'Trap, like he said. Someone knew we'd be looking. Learning on the job went well.'

She looks at me. Can't read the expression.

'Should have been us, Lark. We could have walked through this but not the new blood.'

Say nothing. Dunno it's that simple but she's not happy Anton's body is cold.

Give it a bit. Karel scribbles something else and hands it over.

HELP HIM

Bettina sighs. 'He's dead.'

Karel hits me. Should say, Bettina lets him hit me. She's pissed. Guy can't throw a punch anyway and he mainly cops my ear. Turn away from him, like it ain't worth it, which it is not.

'Grab a snake.'

Poison won't hurt a dead woman. Snakes ignore her as she gets closer, quiet and slow. She grabs one by the end of the tail. It turns. Bite her four or five times. She hisses back at it. Dead, pain don't bother her so much no more. But she's not numb. She snaps the snake's neck, steps back out.

Take the body from her.

And she collapses.

Eyes rolling back in her head. Froth at lips.

V I

Pen knife in my pocket, slash as her arm and suck the venom out. That don't work on people and even if it did, she's got no blood, heart don't pump. Just pools there but it ain't venom, it's a spell that needs undoing. We're looking to create sympathy, a symbolic action. Occult poison means occult treatment.

Slash her arm open, suck it out and

By

Christ

It

Burns.

Healing magic. Shit at it. Never was what you might call nurturing.

Run through lists of medicine deities in my head. Aesculpius, Hermes, no no, don't know from them. Dian Cecht, Irish god. Gave Bettina's eye up to some fae fucks, so that ain't right. Ixtiliton, the black masked Aztec god. Maybe? Maybe. Heka, Egyptian goddess of –

Mind turns to fire on that one. A thought that sparks up in my head and I'm confused and feel like... anxiety

Wrap a warding circle around my thoughts, visualising black chains of ice. Calming, soothing and soon, thoughts again. Heka. Egyptian healing god. Something wrong with that though and so it gets put aside. Try something else, some other spell, some other rite.

A vision then, strong memory - me and Mully, working with angels.

Apocrypha studies, hunting the weird fringes of the myth that runs the West, showing me that a good magician works the margins, the hidden lore, the suppressed. Reading a book and can see the passage before me clear as seeing her spasm.

Raphael, angel of healing. Hunter of demons.

Spit the venom out and my mouth feels as if pure alcohol has pooled there. Cold heat and savage stinging. Remember that Raphael wasn't just a doctor but a fighter. Through a nematocyst mouth, through messy lips, recite a phrase from the Book of Enoch.

'Bind Azazel hand and foot, and cast him into the darkness: and make an opening in the desert, which is in Dudael, and cast him therein. And place upon him rough and jagged rocks, and cover him with darkness, and let him abide there forever, and cover his face that he may not see light. And on the day of the great judgment he shall be cast into the fire.'

Put my hands on her arm and think of wild celestial fire purging all impurity. Angel information, high and potent. Not a gentle healing but a wild storm of knitting flesh and a holocaust for malicious chemicals, going from drop to drop like lightning chaining and vapourising the ill. Make a fist, dig nails into my hand. The pain helps me channel the information, keeps me focused.

Bettina is undead. This is dangerous information released into her system. Angels and the risen dead don't easily mix. Control it. Guide it. Monitor it or it will rampage through her, burning, burning. It's like driving a car with no breaks.

Take another draught of my friend's cold blood. Breathe some of the venom down into my lungs. It's not so bad.

But, you know... *it fucking should be.* Realise the Rabisu is watching, licking up the pain and the venom and the death like a cat with cream.

Bettina grabs my hair at the back of my head. Pulls me back up from her slowly. Wipe my mouth with the back of my hand.

'I felt it. This trap was for... *me.*'

After that? Her eyes go dark and she's done for now.

VII

Heka.

A trap just for Bettina. Specialised.

Yeah. Have me an idea on what's occurring. Lions and snakes.

Just wish I'd put together that someone had sussed my methods quicker.

FOUR

I

Eighteen months back, was out of the City. *Geased.* Forced into exile by magical sacrifice. Died out there and came back, which cancelled the geas, the curse on me. Got me a reminder festering in my skull.

A black hole in your brain.

Out there, discovered that the Old Man, most powerful sorcerer of his generation and a bastard down to the marrow, had a kid. Name of Bernadette. Kid, hell, she's probably fifty.

She don't like me. See... she let something calls itself the Devil onto the world. Looking for an alliance with it. Marrying it. That's when she and me first crossed. I found the devil's old girlfriend and got 'em back together. Kinda. End of Bernadette's plans. She wasn't cutting in on Satan.

The Devil is still around. See him from time to time.

Fallout from that was I found Jon, my old partner, best friend. We got the cursed mask of him but it left him shattered, wretched, weak. He still had the skills but his body was kept strong by it. Removed from that power, he'd become wasted and feverish and ill, ill, ill. I figured he's be grateful but it didn't play out like that. He'd become addicted to the mask's power and sure as fuck didn't thank me for losing it.

Bernadette found him. Bernadette took him in. And she did it with the help a something called *the Sothic Temple*.

Cult on the Egypt trip.

Later, Bernadette would try real hard to kill me as payback for me getting her daddy dead and messing up her devil action. She's powerful, man. *Powerful*. And the only lead I had on her was she was connected with the Sothic Temple.

My job is knowing things. It's my *deal*. Give me a week and some books and what you want to know, you'll know. But the Sothic Temple weren't anything. A minor cult never caused any trouble. Never did *anything*.

Came back to the Library six months ago. About the first thing I did was to open a file on it.

Won't lie, didn't dig further than asking questions, checking Library records, old notes. Moving slow, cautious because... Bernadette is too much for me. The Old Man was no goddamn joke, not to anyone. And she's his heir. She's got a hell of a way with summoning wildly potent entities.

And she's got Jon.

Want him back, want him whole, so sooner or later, have to throw down with her.

Strikes me she's the kind of woman would waste him just to put the fire to me.

Sothic Temple research, though, it showed nothing interesting at all. Leader's called Todd Roberts. That, my friends, is the name of a man with a moustache and white shirtsleeves. An accountant for a software company. His actual job as it turns out. He's just nothing special at all. Most cats on the black magic trip build up slow but surely to the sacrifice and abuse.

But Todd and his whole cult have never given anyone a reason to be interested. Small, too. Maybe seven regulars attended the rites.

Lots of death stuff in the rites though.

Oh wait. Getting ahead of things.

Yeah, you might not know... *Sothis* is the ancient Egyptian word for the star Sirius. Sirius is a big player in that religion. The Sothic Temple is on the white robes and falcon-head masks trip. Worship Ra and Horus and Isis. Like that. Egypt was big on temples, big on rituals. Real big.

Sorcery was important as gravity to those bastards. It was in everything they did, from statecraft to cooking. See, sorcerous rituals powered Ma'at, which is... hard to explain quick but think of it like ... the correct order of the universe. Moral, physical, law. Without Ma'at and the sorcery keeps it going, the whole world caves in.

Temple seems like it's just a believer in Ma'at. Invocation of the gods. Group prayers. Re-enacted rites. Oracular visions. Fine, great, good. No problem. Knowledge from the gods is worth having. Beginning of time 'before duality', there's magic.

Heka. That's what they called it. Hekau sometimes. Literally means *magic* in the Coptic, Demotic, maybe just Egyptian, whatever language it is. Was more of a scholar, you'd be reading a scholarly work. This is the praxis, not the theory.

The activation of Ka, the vital force of the universe, life itself, *that's* what the various occult rituals of sorcery meant to that culture lasted itself a few thousand years.

Heka is the god of medicine as well as the personification of magic. A living spell. A humanised form of the vital force of the universe.

And, of course, snakes. What's more Egyptian than snakes? Weret-Hekau, a goddess of magic, cobras were her totem. But she was in the form... of a lion.

As was the great goddess of plague, war, medicine, Sekhmet.

Sothic Temple. Let them alone too damn long and here we are with snake magic, lion magic.

Time to work.

11

Aristide's joint.

An old basement he rents off a Dominican woman upstairs. She's strict Catholic, except for once a month, when Aristide Houngans it up for the islanders of the City and pays his rent. Decorated his place like you think.

Like Halloween every day. Be surprised how many skulls and black candles an adult man can own.

Bettina's on the couch, she wears an eyepatch around the house. Watching a show in which men with white, white teeth are trying to get married to a mean blonde who radiates madness. Just glancing at that shit makes me wish for immediate death but she digs it for reasons too mysterious for me. Sit down on a big black chair all painted up with bones. Newspaper on it. Terrorism. Man shot sixteen girls at their school. Presidents and Prime Ministers screaming. Some new disease, some new drug, some new gun, some new war.

Forget that noise.

'How you feeling?'

'Like shit, man. How you think? Fuck they hit me with?'

'Venom.'

'No shit.'

'Magic venom.'

'Ah.'

'You're not really alive but you've got... you're still in the world, you know? It made Anton's heart stop beating. Yours too but you don't need to live through it to get up again.'

She's quiet awhile.

'You ever get creeped out by what I am?'

'No. Do you?'

'Sometimes. Aristide helps a lot, though. He's kinda really super into the death thing.'

Look at a bookshelf on which eighteen skulls are presented.

'Could be.'

She grins, finds us some beers, turns off the television.

'Sup?'

'Listen. Got an idea. Bernadette. Was *her* set this up, I think. Her trap or at least, someone she's got working for her.'

'For real?'

'Maybe. Maybe I'm jumpy. Figure her for making a move. Lions have links to Egypt and we know she used the Sothic Temple to move on Jon.'

'Need to be sure with her. She's not playin''

Say nothing. Just nod.

Aristide lights a joint about the size and weight of a fat child. Offers me some. No. Last time I had one of his spliffs, felt like my legs turned to ghosts.

'You ever tell the Library about Bernadette?'

Shake my head. Library will freak, they know the Old Man has a kid and the kid is out for us. Except for Elliot. He won't know what it means. He won't appreciate Bernadette's strengths. Her skills. He'll hear it's some old lady and discount her entirely.

But also... when Bernadette came at me when I was away from the City... she turned a Librarian, sent him after me. She can do it again. Maybe already did.

'Not yet?'

'My call, lady. Got reasons.'

She turns away. 'I'm not coming. Whatever this is.'

'Yeah you are.'

'No she's not, Lark,' says Aristide.

Ignore him. He's nothing to do with me and her.

'All fucked up here, man,' she tells me, gesturing to the wounds in her arms that look like eyes.

'Just some poison.'

'Go fix with some battery acid, then we talk about what's *just*, motherfucker.'

Shake my head at her.

'Soft.'

'Fuck off. *Soft.*'

Stand up.

'I'll come tomorrow, Lark. Need another night in the dirt.'

But I'm not so sure she's not just trying to guilt me into playing by Library rules. Then again, maybe she is hurt bad as she says.

Aristide has coffins. Two on either side of the television and more besides. Filled one with the dirt from the park she got killed in. Peculiar kinda romance they got.

'I need you on this, lady. Bernadette's something.'

She turns away from me. Not sure what's going on inside her.

'And you'll have me. Tomorrow.'

Nod at her. She flicks a glance at me. Glances away. With the one real eye left to her.

Leave and put my ear to the door. Aristide is already whispering voodoo sexy death prayers. *To* her.

I I I

Don't clear this next operation with anyone. Work my shift during the day, head back to Aristide's at night.

Don't clear it because still not ready to talk about Bernadette and sure as fuck am not going to expose Jon to the Library right now. Elliot won't give a damn about ten year's service. Or appreciate how deadly that man is.

And Jon's still in this, some way. Can't face him alone.

But he has to be found.

Got one address for the Sothic Temple and so that's where we're going for a recon. Wait until midnight the next day and head on over to Bettina's. Her joint. When she's above ground, she hangs with her mother and aunts in a flat that always smells like limes, for some goddamn reason.

Knock on the door She comes out and can see she's ready for fighting.

Fingerless gloves. Pants tucked into workman's boots. Tight

singlet, sports bra underneath, not shirt, hair back in a severe bun. Simple engineer's jacket she'll have laced with brass knucks, a knife, like that.

'We run into your man, I'm a be *prepared*, you know?'

Bettina and Jon threw down once. Interrupted before it get serious. Jon had the moves and the reach and the quickness but Bettina had the muscle and the toughness.

Who was winning? Do not know. *Who do I want to win?* Both. Neither.

Problem is, fighters fight. Blood is up between them. They'll be looking for a result off each other. Need to keep that from going down again. Don't need the two of them killing one another.

Just nod at her as if to agree, keeping that concern to myself. She would not dig me fretting at her. We get ourselves into a cab. We roll in silence, her in the zero zone fighters can get in. Me, wrapped up in gnosis, preparing weapons in the astral.

On the radio, yet more war, terrorism, murder, rape, poverty, sickness. In the rear view, can see the tears in the cab drivers eyes. The world is breaking him. It breaks us all in the end. But this cat? He's done *now*. Watching him in gnosis is like a time-lapse of his coming suicide.

Dropped off a block from the Temple.

Stop in at the night time bodega and buy a pack of cigarettes. Don't want one now, which is strange but the habit of picking up a pack before anything is hard to break. Matches too.

Empty part of town, beneath an overpass.

Comes back in a flood. Remember being around here a while back, hurt and sick. Devil on my trail.

Doesn't touch me in the gnosis, don't feel fear or anger. My mind is serene as a horizon. But there's no *forgetting* this place, either. Up above on the overpass, night cars move about night time business. Sodium lights on the street flicker. Graffiti on the shuttered shops, the bodegas and liquor stores and fabric shops and gun stores and like that.

Warm night for autumn and old newspapers and food wrappers

move in the breeze, slow and purposeful, like they were hunting something.

End of the street, Sothic Temple's new address. New building. Moved about nine months ago. Cut ties with other cults in the City and went quiet. Not entirely certain this is their main sanctum either. Maybe a cut out, a decoy, but it's all we have to work with.

Magicians hide in plain sight. Just a glass door some steps behind it leading up. Secret place of a city, those doors that lead up. You might pass them every day for a lifetime and never see no one open them. Cities are always hiding things. You been everywhere you can in your town? Your high street? Are you the curious type? Or do you just mind your business like a good citizen?

People like me rely on obedience and incuriosity. The Sothic Temple does too. And you don't know what's happening because you just want to get through the day.

Walk close to the unremarkable door, in the gnosis, scouting the Temple. City spirits lurk around here. Rat gods. Rubbish elementals. Pigeon totems. Ain't no thing to be concerned with, the usual debris.

And the Temple itself? Nothing much going on there, no wards or protective spirits or even the bruised feeling you get from a lot of magic over a period of time.

But, you know?

There should be.

You do Workings, it leaves a mark on the world. Worship, sacrifice, rituals... it leaves a scar in the skin of the world. To any magician spies them, it's nothing serious. Churches, temples, mosques, all leave the same mark. So do arenas and music halls. Any place you step out of your ordinary mindset leaves marks.

The Temple's trying to keep the profile low. Fine. Even if they haven't been here long, there should be something and warding against *any* trace is a vast effort.

These cats really don't want to show up on any bastard's radar.

Fine, fine.

Bettina picks the physical lock. Even those there's no signs, we ain't just going in gangbusters. Assuming there's something going on here that we cannot detect.

Take a simple permanent marker and draw a sigil on the door. Leave a record we were here but some things can't be helped. Take too long to hide us completely anyways. Got to rely on twenty years of Worked and reworked wards to protect myself and my partner from them making us straight away.

First plan here was to mark the Temple's wards with an S.

See, that's the symbol of entropy. Measure of disorder in a system. Mark it and concentrate on it, maybe bleed into it, something like that. Introduce disorder into their defence and just walk in.

S.

Looks too much like a snake for me. Symbolism – it'll fuck with you. And something about serpents right now is spooking me for reasons you can probably figure.

Leave that be.

What gets up in snake's business? Was going over all of this when planning the job.

Think symbols. Think symbolically. Shapes that represent ideas, feelings, meanings.

Think of how to beat a snake in a fight that's symbols, not fists.

Your idea vs my idea: that's a magical battle.

Mongooses? No feeling for them. *Fuck do I know about mongooses?*

King Cobras hunt other snakes. What else hunts snakes? Bird of prey? Some live in cities but eagle, hawk, falcon... all too bold for me. That all feels like royalty and nobility symbols to me and there's nothing to connect too. To work with.

But, you know, birds that hunt snakes aren't always linked up with that sort of majesty imagery.

There's one bird speaks to me called the Secretary. Crazy looking thing, feathers on its head in a crest, looks well punk. That works for me. Proper name is the *Sagittary*. Sagittarius. A centaur, sure, but also... *a hunter.*

The Dreadful Sagittary appals our numbers. Mully quoted that to me once. Dunno where it's from but sounds cool.

Hunting. Hunters...

This is sorcery, my friend. The creation of *meaning*.

Back to the task at hand.

While back, raised a shadow of my hand into a servitor, an eregore. A spirit creature you can clothe in your own ideas. Do that now.

Give it a name and that name is a sigil drawing on the door. *Bespoke* spirit, small tulpa, made from thoughts and magic. Looks like a red crocodile, 'bout the size of your forearm, teeth and claws glowing green. Give it the wings and crest of the Secretary bird and the raptor nature of one, too.

It leaks into the world, manifesting from ink and will and thought, then vanishes into the glass like water and from there, into the walls, hunting serpents.

Wait.

Wait.

Out of nowhere a sudden wave of weakness takes me and I stumble.

Bettina looks at me weird. Shake my head at her. Not now. But it's the black hole in me, responding to the effort of the spell. She lets it drop and just holds me up while the world spins around me, like a vertigo attack.

'So what's this slapper want, anyway?'

'Bernadette?'

'None other.'

'Dunno. Not really. Payback for the Old Man, sure. She said as much. Payback for the Devil. She's been looking to work with hard-core entities. Her father was the same. He tried to summon an Archon. Become one.'

Got lucky with that, stopping him. Getting him killed.

'She after the same thing?'

'Not the exactly same thing but we know she was behind summoning the devil up.'

'Why she want the Hollow?'

That one, do not have an answer too. Maybe just to fuck with me. Maybe just to have someone spill on the Library. Just do not know.

There's a sudden feeling like pressure lifting and the vertigo fades.

'Try the door.'

She puts the lock-picks to it and it clicks open.

Leave some money for my tulpa to thank it, a few bucks from my wallet. It's not the cash they need, it's the giving up something you'll miss.

Open the door. Go up.

I V

Threadbare carpet and a flimsy plywood door at the top. The whole things smells like mould and damp rot. Head into the sanctum sanctorum. Which is pretty much just a common room of an upstairs flat. Decorations, though, is what makes it something else.

Drawings on the wall, in that Egyptian style, you know the type. 2-D figures in headdresses and robes, all shot through with hieroglyphs. Looks like the walls of temples you see in books of far off lands. Animal headed entities, about their divine business. Scarabs and fanned pharaohs. A barge sailing down a river. You know what Ancient Egypt looks like to us now, in our imagination.

So do the Sothic Temple.

'Photograph this.'

Bettina takes out her phone and does. Nod my thanks.

There's a stink in here but don't know what of, yet.

Find myself sighing. Too many days in too many bad and tired and sour rooms like this.

Maybe I'm depressed? Who the fuck cares?

Centre of the room, back wall, there's an altar.

Far ends of the later, jars, urns, put you in mind of the canopic, where they store the organs of mummies. Between those, three statues.

One side, a lion-headed woman.

Sekhmet, goddess of plague, war, healing. The other, jackal headed man. Anubis, of course, funeral god, judge of the dead.

The middle, cast in gold, fat and ugly, a snake rearing up. Bigger than the others. Coiled elaborately. Zig zags, really, rather than coils, angled not curved.

Apophis.

The Rabisu whispered the name to me. Talked about him. The primal destructor, Apep, called Apophis.

The Rabisu senses my thoughts and far away, wherever it is, purrs it's dark pleasure.

'You cool?'

Bettina's hand on my shoulder.

'What?'

'You went pale seeing the snake.'

Hands are shaking. Shove them into jacket pockets.

'Sure.'

She stares at me a moment. Gets back to her work.

Circle of cheap plastic chairs up against a wall. Hit the gnosis but there's not been much action here.

Doors leading off the sanctorum. Kitchenette with tea, coffee, a kettle. Almost laugh at how boring it is.

Another room, a desk in it, shelves lined with books, an office space. Collections of the *Book of the Dead. Dispute Between A Man And His Soul, Pyramid Texts*, which I read a long time back. Pharaoh threatening the gods with cannibalism. Check it out. *Enigmatic Book of the Underworld. Book of Gates.*

Take out *Pyramid Texts*. Throw it to Bettina.

'That poem at the lion cage in the zoo, pharaoh eating dudes.'

'Yeah, it was cool. What about it?'

'It's a quote from in here. Seeing it reminded me.'

Rifle through drawers but it's just receipts. Letters in the name of Todd Roberts. Discussions with other magicians working the Sothic trip. Sothis is important for lots of African religions, not just Egypt.

Dog Star cultist and Nommo-worshippers. Photograph it all with the phone.

Two other rooms. Changing chamber with robes hanging on pegs. And a bedroom. Four bunks.

Poster on the wall of some pop star kid, shirtless with shitty tattoos, zero percent body fat and the kind of haircut get you killed where we grew up.

Jon is the hardest man you'll meet. Saw him kick open a fire door one time. But his taste in dudes was always what you might call *suspect*. Liked 'em pretty and fit.

He's been here, though. Probably had these up just to fend off fucking boredom.

Someone *stashed* him here, then.

Drawer, go through them. Underpants, socks. Nothing serious. Then. Pyridostigmine pills. No idea.

'Look these up on your phone.'

'Not finished the walls.'

'Please.'

On the pillow, dark hairs. Jon's ancestry is Polynesian, African. These are his.

Take a few.

I have you Jon. I motherfucking have you.

Bettina calls my name. Come out. She's pulled back the altar cloth, opened up a drawer. Points at me to look in and so I do. Two lion claws. So that's what reeked.

'Alright,' nod. *The fuck are these slappers up to?*

'Muscle weakness.'

'What?'

'That's what the pills are for.'

'Cool. Thanks.'

Jon was weak as hell after the mask came off.

Bettina's phone rings. She answers.

'Shit, code motherfucking red. We gotta get in the wind and right now.'

Put Jon's hairs in my wallet like a creepy goddamn stalker. *Maybe that's how it is.*

Somewhere, the beat of black wings. The Rabisu watches me for a long time after that.

Her phone goes off.

'Another emergency.'

V

South of midnight and we report in to a butcher's shop of a scene.

Stroller Priests were a 17th century... not sect. Phenomenon. *Deal.* Back then, England had gone mental with a hundred different weird sects and cult and movements and schisms. One of 'em were Stroller Priests.

Stroll like walk. Cats would set themselves up as holy men, wander around the country, marrying people, holding scratch Services, blessing brats. All for free but some food.

Unfettered Hierophants, this crew is called. Modern take on that idea. Urban nomad types they call themsevles but to us, they was just called the hobo wizards.

Was called.

Looking down at bodies now.

Modern Stroller Priests. About half a dozen homeless or broke guys, who worked city magic down in the streets. Cigarette and chip packet magic. Rat and pigeon familiars. Street light oracles and crossing sign figure gods and sacred black mould rites.

Mad and dangerous. Not friends to anyone but the City itself.

Talked to this dead one a few times over the years.

Overture Street was how he called himself. Not long after the incident with the Old Man, actually. They were figuring out Wick, the tagger girl become Archon. True Goddess of the City. They wanted to talk to me about it. Word is Lark had something to do with it. Which, you know, was true. Weren't a secret so I gave him and his crew an interview.

Overture told me about divining the future from muggers as we finished up and talked a little shop.

'Shouldn't you be helping people instead of watching them get beaten? How's that good for the City?'

He dragged on a joint made from asbestos. 'City is a system. City operates on rules that aren't kind. Not ours to judge what the cells do in our body. Not ours to judge the cells in the City. Muggers mug. That's life here.'

He's dead now. Laid out with four of his brothers and sisters. His dirty old peacoat and ragged beard soaked through with blood.

We're in an subway station. After hours. Guard called this in to *us*, not the cops. Lucky break or someone wanted to find them. We bribe people all across town to call in weird shit to us first.

Five dead hobos with their throats slit, laid end to end like a goddamn snake is weird shit. They've been moved. Soaked as they are, five bodies all stabbed up? You'd be sick if you saw how much juice that was. But from one woman, Joanie Taxibless, that was her name … a trail of blood is leaking from her wound off the platform and down the track. A single serpentine trail.

More fucking snakes.

More dead magicians. This many, this close together. No doubt about it. Someone's targeting cults.

Jon's hair in my wallet. Hands itch. A shot at helping him. One last try. My only friend for the first half of life.

Tell my girl, 'Call Katanya.'

Bettina is resting up against a steel pillar. Eyes closed, breathing smoke slowly out her nose. This much meat, you know she's feeling the hunger.

Eyes snap open at that.

'Why aren't you doing your thing, man?'

'Katanya can do it.'

'Fuck that. This is *your* trip. This is *your* job. We got someone killing magicians like they was wheat on a farm. This isn't even serial killing, it serial genocide. Do your piece!'

Bettina is... well, you don't know what she means to me, you never will by now. But fuck it. Jon needs me. Turn my back.

'Call Katanya. I gotta find Jon.'

Walk up the subway steps and back to my joint.

'This is some weak bullshit, Lark!' She calls up after me. Don't care. Feels like my fists are gripping stars, so hot with the urge to deal out some harm.

FIVE

I

Came back to the City after coming back to life.

Last memory before leaving, figured it was forever, was in my old joint. Scarlet, coming to me her goddamn wedding night. And...

No. That's off-limits. Never mind that. Don't want to share that.

Anyways. Needed a change. Memories, man. Pay money for a surgeon to cut a few out if I could.

So anyway. Welcome to my new pad.

Basement of an old bank in Mockton, downtown. Bit upmarket than I'm comfortable with. Coffee shops and wine bars. Good bookshops, though. A jazz club, house band is some guys used to play with Taj Mahal. Not my scene but kinda different, mixes things up. Suits in the mornings and nights, khakis on the weekend. All the women go to the gym.

Nothing special here but not looking for special.

They sold off the bank a few year back, turned it into apartments. Basement was empty, so forged up notes in the name of a name that gets used for legit dealings.

Lark isn't my birth name but even so, it's my magical name. Got about three civilian ones and one of those dudes used the ancient and fearsome power of sorcery to scam his way into ownership papers of this joint.

It's wide open. Bed in one corner. Kitchen in another, one

of them floating benches. Books in cases and in piles. Stack em up high as my waist. Couch. TV. Desk, computer, notepads, phone next to it. Cement floors. Spartan. Dim overhead lights. No pictures, no decorations. Keep myself clean. A house free of symbols, of *meanings*.

One room, used to be the manager's office and it's the Sanctorum now. We'll talk about that soon enough.

Waiting for me by my desk is my shadow.

Shadow of my hand, given life. Walks around on two legs, little and thumb. Sometimes four, add pointer and ring. Middle's a head and neck. Inquisitive thing. Runs around the house kinda like a frightened kitten. Bettina watches it when she's around, plays with it like it's a pet.

Not a pet. It *works*. Part of what you might like to call my soul. Familiar. *Tulpa*.

Not powerful. Not a guard or sentinel. But useful.

It waves to me coming in, one finger limb, all nervous, like. Nod back. Once a month, sacrifice to it. Keep it alive and keeps it well disposed towards me. End of the day, nine times from ten, reactions you'll have with the spirit world are, underneath, *transactional*.

Two in the morning. Hungry but there's nothing in the fridge but some beer and gin.

Mix up a GnT and take to the Sanctorum. Armful of books with me.

I I

New workshop isn't what the old one was but that place was mine for years and this ain't but a few months old. This is the sanctum sanctorum. The holy of holies. This is the room where my practice is located, my sacred space. Where the sausage gets made.

Altar up on the wall, like a big arse shelf, on it, a few of statues of my favourite gods – Odin, Toth, Gwydion, the last a reminder how not to be. A beautiful one of Hecate Scarlet got me years ago, sensual and dark. Cloth doll of Marzanna, goddess of sorcery and winter for Slavs. San La Muerte, grim reaper intercessor.

Music stand to put instructions during complex rituals. Stereo for music, sometimes drumbeats for easing into gnosis. Candles everywhere because sometimes you got to really get into the mood. Yeah, motherfucker, they're even black.

Some of my oldest friends on that altar. *Ideas*, born before me, that will live on after. Immortal things that speak to what's truest in us. Living ideas that are in the world but not wholly of it. If you let them, if you want, they'll be real to you. As real as the moon.

Up in the rafters, hanging down, not yet truly... alive isn't quite the right word but you know what I mean... growing an Ultrascorpion. Home made murder spirits. Bodyguards. While back now, something killed them... what was that? The Devil? My memory is turning sour. *Black hole in your brain.*

Have to keep them fed with prayers and sacrifice and acts of comradeship. They're mine. I made them. Servant creatures of a god I made, the Omegamantis. Venom angels. But just because I made them doesn't mean they'll act as happy slaves. But not here to feed them, here for other work.

Finding Jon.

And to do that, have to bring the big guns. Have to make compact with a deity. Which isn't as dramatic as it sounds but isn't *nothing*, either.

Encyclopaedias of gods is what I bought in. Thumb through them. Egypt has loads of hunting gods and goddesses but not going near them. Let's see.

Flidais, Celtic hunting goddess and wild beasts. *Not quite my thing. Hippie vibes.*

Skadi, bow-hunting giantess of the north. Loki's wife. *Tragedy and sorrow. Not now.*

Goddess of hunting on land for the Inuits is Nujalik. *Better but still not perfect.*

Acteon is a Greek hunting god and of male animals. Image of him is that he's pretty good but that full on *dude* energy isn't right. Jon was never femme but outside of fighting, he was gentle. Took out the hate we were both raised with on the kind of cunts deserved it.

Turn the page and oh yes. ... she's perfect.

Bendis.

Hunt goddess. She's got a look I can dig. Cool boots and cloak and an ace fox skin hat. *Like her style.* Thracian. Northern Greek. Their version of Artemis, but Artemis is woman magic. Female associations. Not that she's *off limits* to men...but... OK.

Look.

Don't want to start a whole thing but magic is pretty traditional when it comes to sex roles. You feel you got a better take, your practice is yours, mine's min. Artemis myths are about the sanctity of women, the wildness part of them, the high black moon part. Which isn't to say a man can't or even shouldn't work with her. But it's a different dynamic than what's needed tonight.

Bendis is worshipped with night time races and torch relays. Coo'.

Get myself to meditating on that image a while. The ancients, playing with fire and doing dangerous things to please a moon goddess, animal goddess, dark and powerful.

She's the one. Feel her hunter's sense and her purpose and her fell power. To hunt is to seek with dread purpose and that's as needed tonight.

She's the one.

I I I

So there's a creature called a Preta.

In Asian cultures, it's the reborn spirit of a sinner. It has a hunger that can never be sated but each one of these motherfuckers? Cursed with appetites for filth. Humiliation that never ends. Made from *Akasha,* the stuff of space, so they're invisible. All they wanna do now is fuck with people.

Old monster. Old, old idea.

The traditions of Pretas are still alive, too. Modern tellings of the stories, all over Asia, they no longer want to eat blood or piss or jizz or whatever. Get themselves cravings for alcohol, for heroin and hash.

And people with addictions act like beacons for these bastards. Your kid's on horse, sooner or later, Preta will *feel* it, come to your house.

Jon was addicted to the mask, the Hollow.

First thought was to bind some Pretas and follow them to Jon. But they're savage things, burning with need and Jon might kill them anyway, if they find him. Give my game away. He learned bad things with the mask. Murder magic.

No. Want to find him? Have to be able to do it quietly and carefully. Can't just cast any old tracking spell. Not for Jon. This really *does* require the full evocation of divine powers.

Old ways of hunting goddesses doesn't mean much to me. No going out into forests to dance about like a prick, not running around Greece on a horse with a stick that's on fire. But there's ways and means, for the kind of cat like me who craves truth hard enough and I've got the hunger.

Begin, enter gnosis via meditation. Shirtless and surrounded by candles. Hot in here. Murky. Sweating. Good. Focus on that and feel my mind flat line until conscious though self-annihilates for a while.

Moon goddess. Hunt goddess. Think of myself gently stoned, weightless. A sea of moonlight. Imagine myself naked, bathing in a silver stream of moonlight. Erotic, light touching me sexy, teasing.

That's the moon to me. That's how she feels tonight. Playful. *Naughty.*

She was worshipped with orgies, you know, but that's not how I roll.

But this the moon and to deny it's sexual charge is pointless.

Floating upwards and upwards on that stream of charge argent light. To *her.*

Moving up into an argent world. A glowing, warm heaven, a lustrous division between earth and sky. It swallows me up and soon,

I realise I'm suspended and buoyed and bobbing on the borderlands between humanity and something vaster. Like a man waking from a fine slumber, it's soon apparent there's something... with me. Gather my wits.

A moment later, with a start, realise that I am in the presence of the goddess on the moon.

She wears a cloak and boots of silver. On her head, a vulpine mask made of platinum and silver. Her eyes behind it are violet. Erotic and maternal and unsettling. This is an unhuman presence, a tiger who is not hunting but cannot be tame.

It is proper to be humble before the gods. To understand that a human is just a thing of blood and bone and gone tomorrow but a God will exist long after us and beyond our ability to control.

Bow, cover my wretched nakedness with a hand.

Not here to try to get my end away. Men who shag moon goddesses tend to not walk away the same, if they walk away at all.

She doesn't talk but feels curiosity, amusement at this naked man come to beg.

Somewhere, far away, can feel my human body sigh in obscure kinds of pleasure. But it needs to work for me now so some attention is wrested away from the sight in front of me and my hands, distant, almost foreign, become a part of me.

'This is my libation to you.'

Half a bottle of gin.

Splash it out.

Incense, expensive shit. Light it. Charcoal flavour. Read once a while back the astronauts who visited the moon said the dust they trod back into their lander smelled of spent gunpowder or charcoal.

'This is my libation to you.'

Gods don't always speak in words. Feel her... her *grace*... shine on me, like, physically feel it. Somewhere, the hair on my body stands up. *Good, good.* You approach entities like this as you would a wolf you want to free from a trap. Carefully, correctly. Gotta get it right or it'll go bad.

What's bad mean here?

Madness. Death. An idea as powerful as a God is not dismayed by a human consciousness. There is no defence against an entity like this. They exist in stories for a million years and lurk behind every eye.

Careful. *Careful.*

'Your assistance is needed by me. I need to hunt. I need to course. There is prey to be grounded.'

A sensation like hearing a new song you dig a lot. She radiates that to me, letting me know it's cool.

Then that shit cuts out and feels like blood sugar crashing.

Need. Not words. But the meaning is clear. She requires things of me. From me. Either or.

'What is your desire?'

A sound like glass shattering. Not sure what that means.

'What would you have of me, Madame?'

What do hunters want? Grounded prey.

'If my hunt is a failure, my life is yours for one month. You will receive my service as if I were a priest in your service and will accept your devoirs.'

Nothing.

'*Three.*'

Number like that, three, more pleasing to her kind.

A chime sound. You ever hear someone play those high, beautiful, perfectly made chimes? How they ring out at a frequency you know is escaping the ears? Like that. The Platonic ideal of that.

'And should there be success, you shall be given silver in thanks. And the hunt will be made dedicate to you.'

Moonlight swirls around me, sexy and inviting and still playing.

Deal is made.

Bow my head.

Return to the world.

I V

Three months? Sound like nothing?

Library would crucify me. One of theirs compromised? No telling what the Goddess would want of me. Go live up a mountain, stare at her that entire time? Kill her enemies? Shag strangers for coins, a sacred prostitute or in *hiero gamos*? Don't exactly groove on that action. Work against other gods and spirits already in alliances with?

More serious than it sounds, man.

Means finding Jon is a heavy play now. Have to find him. Need to find him or I'm out of the game for a long time when the only winning move is to be in.

The spell will work. When we come at Jon, we'll do it like the huntress God's own hounds, quiet and assured and stealthy as twilight.

But when we find him? Even wounded and diminished as he is, Jon can't be discounted. He don't need muscle to kill.

One final bit of business before that hunt starts up.

From the altar, five bullets. Got them from the morgue, dug fresh out of a corpse. Been putting this off.

Pick up my phone.

Five missed calls from Bettina. Three from Katanya.

Oh no. I am in trouble. Jings. Fret. Oh dear.

Fuck 'em. Later.

Make my own call. A woman I met a while back in the course of my business.

'Kira?'

'Lark.' Her voice ain't warm.

'Need that favour.'

'It's fucking after midnight, man.'

Say nothing.

She sighs.

'It's still warm. If you can be here in an hour, we can get it going.'

'Aces.'

Hang up. Call a cab. Part of the reason this part of the City is alright by me is how easy it is to get around. Home. Take a syringe and a vial been saving just for this Working. Blood comes out. Jon's hair goes in.

SIX

I

Lot of use for gems, rare metals in the scene.

People make their own ritual tools and weapons. Their own panoply. Jewellery, wands, athames and … like that. Some cats like me make ritual chalices from beer cans, conscious of the territory and not the map. But more like to keep it classical and classy. Impresses the rubes and gives the whole thing that black magic orgy scene in the 70s movie feel.

Kira gave us a call when she found she'd been short-changed by someone buying her gear.

She's into smithing. She can make jewellery, sure, but she prefers working heavy.

Her magical practice is the creation of beautiful objects from metal and stone and gems. Want a sceptre or a crown? Go to her. An amulet, periapt, ring, she's the one. She gets it right every time. Her rep is solid.

Black market is vital for her business. Think running a regular jewellery business is pricey, imagine what it costs to not only source and import larimar and painite, but shit that's been mined only under certain zodiacal signs, or never seen light, or was never touched by men's fingers. Magic bans and geases are weird.

So, you can imagine, she has fucking insane overheads. Kilo of gold, and gold's just basic, costs her five grand. One day, some cat contacts her with three kilos. He'll sell to her for four a pop. *Sweet deal.* She hits her bankroll, thinking to save a few grand.

But wait! Shit's just tungsten, coated in gold.

She goes to find the dude and, turns out, he's pulled the same shit uptown too.

And some rich motherfucker who wants some payback more than they want their cash back, well, went and *cursed* the chancer. He suddenly developed himself a real bad case of depression and gaffer taped his mouth and nose shut. Then he ran out into the street to die bad in front of all the nuns and lovely pre-school kids.

Killing the dude... whatever. Try and grift a magician, fuck you think is gonna happen? Killing the dude in public? Bad form. That's when me and Jon got called in. We had to find who cursed the dude and explain to him why that shit was bad form.

We found Kira, liked her for the hit job, investigated her and bought her in for questioning. She didn't seem the type, though. Solitary practice, always a bad sign, but she had a lot of ties to the regular world. Married and pregnant when we met. She knew and we knew she didn't, like they say, *fit the profile*, and let us know it was bullshit loudly and with pretty good swearing.

But you know? There's not a person on this planet wouldn't do harm and more harm than that, right day, right place, right push.

Not one.

Learned that a long time ago. Let her be insulted and figured the rest of the case. Helped her restore her rep afterwards though and even got her some of her cash back. We built up a kinda respect after.

Her front is an mechanic business she runs with her brothers after her dad set it up in the 80s. Second generation Black Irish. Three brothers and her, all with darker skin and eyes like sharks. The brothers are all citizens. Well, citizens to us. They're fucking crims to the bone, and stupid besides. They make fun of the forge she's got set up in a far corner of their workshop. Cars overhead on those big jacks, walls lines with shelves, work benches full of car parts and tools. Smell of oil, petrol, metal. She tells her brothers she sells on to those cats dressed up like knights on the weekend, or that she sells her shit to the internet.

She's waiting for me, playing patience at a card table. She's tiny, barely five four, hard muscle under a singlet, thick trousers, hair under a bandana. Vulpine face with flashing eyes dark as a hound's. Katanya fancies her. Forge ready and equipment laid out. Watches me warily. Carefully, not saying a word, I take off my leather jacket and do a quick spin. No weapons on me.

Kira's brothers have all done time. A lot of the cars here won't exactly be owned by them. This is low hood shit but it's her house and her rules.

Notice she's got a pale mark on her finger where a ring should be. Maybe she got divorced or maybe she's just wanting to get to work right quick and prepared her hands for hammering.

'Alright. Say what you need and I'll make it. If it's possible and you aren't on some madman's tip. But we're done, OK? After this, I don't owe you or the Library any favours. '

'Sure.'

'What do you want?'

Hand her five bullets.

'Are these... are these spent bullets?'

Say nothing. *Fuck do you want me to say? Of course they are.*

Take a book from my pocket. Tell her the page. She looks and finds a sigil, a magic diagram.

'Amulet made from bullets killed some cats. Put that on the front of the amulet.'

Kira looks over the book. Snaps it shut.

'Sure, man. You want any spells said over it?'

Hand her a vial. My blood.

'No. Just need you to prepare it. Ritual-like. Don't mean to tell you how to do your job, but if you can, cool it down with this after you've fired up the forge. If you don't work that way, just let it soak in it.'

'Yeah, I'll use heat. You don't have like AIDS or any shit do you?'

'No. Be back to collect it tomorrow night.'

'Tight deadline, Lark.'

'You don't want to be quits, can walk away now.'

Her hand closes over the bullets.

'I'll figure it out.'

Nod. Walk out. Catch some sleep on my couch.

Shadow puppet watches the world outside the window, keeping me company while the television bathes me in pointless, stupid light and horrors from the outside world.

I I

Around lunchtime the next day when Katanya knocks on my office door. 'Boss wants to see you. Now.'

'Which boss?'

'The one that'll piss you off.'

The boss is Elliot, then.

Two ways this can play out. Make him come to get me or go see him.

He comes to me, is that a strong move, or me just being petty? Dunno. Can't be fucked finding out.

But... Sasha's words are with me. That this internal bullshit *matters* and that going along to get along isn't necessarily a loss. Which, you know, feels like losing,... but sometimes you gotta give up a pawn.

In the elevator up to manager land, Katanya looks at me. She's dressed smarter than usual. Button shirt over something like a black bolero jacket, hair slicked back, the usual severe eye make-up done sharper.

'You look good today.'

'I knew we were in for an arse kicking. Figured if I looked all power dykey they'd keep it relaxed. But don't talk to me. You fucked up last night, Lark. I'm not your goddamn junior to call in when you don't feel like taking the call. You fucked up.'

No I didn't.

Doors open and we hit a conference room. Old days, hashed out shit like this differently. Stand in a dark room on a pentagram and voices would bark at you from the dark. Now, there's motherfucking *protocols* to follow.

Waiting for us, Foulstone.

Cannot fucking believe he found his way back here, still. He's wearing a suit looks like it's made of little boy's school uniform pants in 1930. He strains at it like a sausage overfull of meat. Guy is a skilled necromancer but no one even seems to know what he did to make upper management. He stares poison at me from septicaemia-coloured eyes.

It's the other guy, Blossom, who needs paying attention to. Tall, thin, round glasses and a regulation haircut and sober dark suit. He nods to me and even gives Katanya something you might call a smile's ghost.

In my experience, the ones who hate you fuck up their moves against you. What animates malice destabilises their play. They get all emotional. They want you to suffer and to know who made you suffer. They move too quick and are easily scouted and dealt with.

Blossom? Whatever plans he has for me will be execution of duty, nothing more. Shine a flashlight through his skull, the light out of his eyes would be cold, cold blue.

Makes me nervous. He and Foulstone came in together a few years back and he just seems... invisible.

Elliot is there too. Hair slicked back and in a tie with flowers on it. Good watch and nine hundred dollar shoes and a white gold wedding ring.

He's hungry for whatever is about to get served up. You can see it on his face, avid and schoolboy cruel.

We sit across from them. There's another woman in a suit, specialist Librarian. Older. Hair in a bun. Name of Igle. Bought her across from Holland but she looks North African to me. Berber-skinned. She works as a priestess of Eirene, peace-goddess. Concord magic. Statue of the goddess on the table. Water in bottles.

Riles me up that she's here. They're expecting a scene. Fuck it. Let's just get on with it. Play the hand dealt me.

Igle opens up the meeting. Foulstone tries figuring out a way to squeeze bullets outta his eyes. Elliot's real excited and Blossom's about as emotive as glaciers.

'Mr. Lark,' starts Igle.

'Lark.'

'Lark, last night, we received an official complaint about your conduct in an investigation.'

Say nothing.

'You were called on an emergency investigation and abandoned it to conduct non-Library business. This is against your terms of service.'

Terms of service. Fucking... what?

'This can be punished by an official reprimand and potentially expulsion from the order of Librarians.'

Say nothing, let them work. But then something bad slips into my head.

'The charges against you are fairly serio- '

'Who made the charges?'

Then Elliot's face cracks open like a fruiting body.

'Bettina.'

Say nothing. Surge of anger but that's just reaction. Bettina isn't shopping me out to upstairs. She's not dobbing me in. This is something else.

'Where is she?' If she ain't here, there's a reason for that.

'We, er, didn't need her testimony in person.'

That makes it make sense. She don't know I'm up here. Which means she never made no complaint.

'She got mad and blew up at me. Right? Not formal. She blew off some steam and a ghoul of yours told you and you took that for a chance to bring me up on charges. She doesn't even *know* about this shit right here, does she? You're looking for a wedge but you ain't got nothing. She never made no goddamn *formal* complaint, did she?'

Maggots is maggots and Elliot is a maggot.

Foulstone laughs ugly. Elliot blinks. Got him in one.

Blossom? He leans forward.

'Lark. I think the procedures here today are overstated. And you are correct, Ms... I'm afraid I don't have a surname for her. Ms Bettina has not made formal charges, no, so this is not a formal hearing. However, what she has said warrants *enquiry*. You did leave an Urgent level investigation, after all. It behoves you to answer very clearly regarding what happened.'

Bettina. These snakes will use you against me if they're allowed. Not even mad at you, baby, but Goddamnit.

'None of you served with Jon.'

'That's not the -' Elliot sputters.

'Shut the fuck up.'

That's outta line but there's no more *time* for this piece of shit. *Hated you for Scarlet but now hate you on my own.* Blossom notes something down but the rest stare at me. This isn't how you're supposed to talk to a boss.

Stare at Elliot like there's money behind his eyes.

'Listen. Actually. Listen. Jon... my partner. You don't know who he is or what happened to him. Before the mask went on his face, never met a man who could take him in a fight. He was world level Ultimate Fist, Heart/Mind/Hand technique and Eight Direction Palm style fighter. Seen him kill a man by taking the qi outta him.'

Need a smoke. Hate talking this much. Sip water.

'After the mask, it taught him dark side shit like no one's heard of. Murderspirit whispering him evil secrets that lodged in his head. Elliot, you think you know. You think of him kind of like some thug got off the leash but he's not. He's a fucking *angel* of killing.

Now it's gone and he's alone and sick and fuck knows who's out there waiting to use him. Learn from him. Fucksake, don't you understand? He's a bomb and he's ticking down. Even if we didn't owe him anything, *which we actually do*, we need to find him because he's a threat like you don't even know.'

Under the table, Katanya's leg touches mine. Thigh to thigh. Trying to help me, maybe. The fuck knows?

Silence.

'Whatever stupid title you wanna give my job, doesn't matter. I'm the Custodes of the Library. Head of Acquision. Security is *my call*. Until he's found, Jon's a priority. Magician serial killer or no.'

Elliot blinks at me. Can't remember the last time spoke this much and damn sure never to him. Foulstone snorts and snot comes outta his nostrils. Why isn't he talking? Cunt usually likes the sound of his own voice. He nervous? *Maybe*. Note that for later.

Back to silence. Curl up into it like a snake.

Blossom notes something else down on a legal pad then talks.

'So, we can assume your defence is simply that you had a higher priority?'

Nod.

He takes off his glasses. Pinches the bridge of his nose. Elliot is almost slavering.

'Mr. Everett.'

Your name is Elliot Everett? Elliot Everett talks to me.

'Yes. Yes it's true, Lark. You have sitcom.'

What? Situational command, must be.

'But you're being formally told to suspend the investigation into Jon the Hollow. We disagree with your assessment and feel he's no threat to us or of significance to our operation.'

Say nothing.

'Do you understand? *He's not your concern anymore.*'

Talking to Elliot's as useful as chewing stone. Stare into Blossom's eyes. He just feels empty. Something... get a cold feeling from him. Need to know more about him. He's not just a lawyer or whatever. He's... got some moves.

Elliot loses his temper. Bangs on the table and all.

'Do you fucking understand!?'

'Please acknowledge you understand.' Igle, uncomfortable. She taps the statue of Eirene and the testosterone drains away from Elliot, can almost see it.

Foulstone looks happy as a piss fetishist with a full nappy.

Blossom likes nothing and Elliot thinks he's won something and not graciously. Katanya snorts her disgust. She's not entirely in my corner but she knows garbage when she smells it. Dick sizing don't mean much to her.

'Do you understand, Lark?' Foulstone's voice is almost a children's sing-song. First thing he said. He seems under stress to me.

These stupid fucks... in the old days, in that room in the pentagram, truth spells worked. Should have kept it that way. Go along to get along. Fine, fine.

'Yes. Understood.'

'Then you'll call off your investigation of Jon?'

Nod. Elliot smiles at me. Like I got in trouble with Mother for something he did. He figures he won. Knew the Library was in poor hands. Now it's clear - Elliot's not just incompetent. Fucker's dangerous.

Oh, Scarlet.

'Meeting adjourned.'

I I

Back to Kira.

'This is a weird job, Lark.'

Shrug. No such thing as weird out here.

'Not... malevolent but... dark. Deathly. Necromancer shit.'

'Sure.'

'You gonna tell me about it?'

'You wanna sign up for lessons at the Library? We give lectures.'

Kira kinda laughs. She works indie.

We sit at the card table by her forge and she pours bourbon for us both. No real taste for it. Age bourbon in sherry barrels and you can taste it. Want to drink cooking wine, drink cooking wine. Still, sip away. She slides what was commissioned over to me, wrapped in a chamois.

Pick it up. Unwrap. Examine.

'Hell yeah.'

Medallion. On a chain. One side has abstracted Saint Skeleton.

Grim reaper. South American folk saint, keep you safe from death and cops and that. Bandit intercessor. Medallion made from the bullets that killed a Christian man.

Was careful in the morgue. Picked out the right cat for the job. Religious type. Russian gangster, tattoo of Christ on his back from arse to neck. Good enough for me.

San La Muetre is not Santa Muerte. More like a bad spirit than what you'd consider even a folk saint. Angry. Slow to help humans but venal. Easy to bribe. Save you against death and witchcraft and that, but he's a criminal saint. Pray to him to get less time Inside. Pray to him so the cops won't rumble you. Pray to him to help you kill your enemies.

This is a bad trip. Cultists dead and the shit in the zoo... whatever the deal is with Jon. Can feel it all souring. Elliot well keen to fuck me up and Bernadette doing some shit.

Most times, need a spirit ally, make one. Tulpas and eregores and that. Need something else, need back up, need skills that I don't have and can't imagine ever developing.

Drain the bourbon.

'You're happy?' Kira is eager to be done.

'Sure.'

She nods once, face straight but pleased her work is appreciated. Slip the medallion, size of a coin, marked with a skull, over my head. Like the bag you put on a guy you're gonna execute.

I I I

Some days go by. They often do.

Door to my office is locked as work gets done. Write up some reports overdue. Do a training session. Funeral for Anton. He's got no people and no friends so we just have him burned up real quick. Dunno much about him and don't care but he worked Norse *seidr* and Vikings cremated so that's probably best. Keep his ashes in my office to remind me of... something.

Used to bother me that, sometimes, people just didn't mean a goddamn thing to me. But there's a black hole in my brain and a life after death, so go on into it, Anton. You just didn't count for anything and you're lucky you were remembered enough to even make into this account.

Spend some time in the Library proper. Just those cool ladders to get you up to the top shelves and twenty thousand books that fill up a whole storey of the sanctum. Stay away from Sothic stuff and anything interesting. Figure Foulstone will be having my reading habits watched. Websites, emails. All that shit.

Elliot don't want me at the Library, that much is clear. Fuck him. Give him no excuses. Do my work, quiet. Let him think he's in control. Authority is important to a cat like that. His arse will need to feel he's on top.

Nights at my place are different. My time is still my own.

Egypt magic. Heka. *Got my own goddamn books, motherfuckers.*

Fill up pages of notes. Study. Television on, drinking coffee, not whiskey.

One night, get the shakes. Black hole in my brain.

It ain't going away and not sure how to fix it.

Sometimes, have Rabisu dreams as it flies on dark wings. Idly track it as can, from images I see and landmarks I spy. Wherever it is, spikes of old diseases. Smallpox. Typhoid. Measles. The old infections. Yaws and Yellow Fever.

Bettina's mad at me. Don't hear from her. Make no move to get in her business. She'll work it out in her own time and she's got herself a boyfriend these days. Who begrudges their pal getting laid?

Days are slow and nights are slower. Read. Write. Days go by without speaking to humans. Doctor calls for follow ups but he's got no cures for me so what's the point?

Then the moon goddess sends me a dream. *Here we go.* First got the idea for this off a wizard by the name of John of Morigny. He used a book called the Ars Notoria to summon dreams to give him wisdom.

Worked, too, according to his memoirs. Until Jesus turned up to tell him these dreams were black magic. Which is, you'll agree... kind of a paradox. But I had no Jesus. For me it was that goddess.

Anyways... dream of a shadowy man in a shadowy place. The first place ever saw the Sothic Temple in action. Old wine cellar where Bettina fought Jon. Where first saw that Jon was *gone* and that, without me, he was never coming back. Maybe it's him and maybe it ain't but goddesses don't work to human logic.

Can't remember why we were there.

Memory is getting unreliable now.

Black hole in my brain.

I V

Bettina meets me there, dressed to throw down. Hoodie and camo pants. She says nothing. Just comes up to me like she was just in another room. No questions, no snipes. No recriminations.

This is the old part of the City.

Devil got called up here once.

Built up over plague pits from the 1600s. Basements and subbasement. Low, black, chthonic power.

Sure.

Down we go, through the broke basement of shop and down through that. Old wineracks all smashed up from the fight that no one's cleaned up.

We move slow. Slow and quiet and careful but certain. Back against the walls, down a small stairway. My mangled hip groans at the pace and the basement coldness. Then.

Man's voice. Drifting up from even further down.

'It is to you, in this dark place, we offer up this gift. As you wait beneath the world, to devour, we send this down to you. As you approach from the void, we welcome you.'

Bettina turns to look at me but in the hood, she's nothing but darkness.

Nod at her to keep moving.

Down the stairs and then down another.

Achingly slow we move and the voice becomes clearer..

'Your enemies are light and darkness and we stand against both. All illumination shall die and darkness will lose all meaning. The world shall return to what it must be. Take a due of pain.'

Crying, not from the man doing whatever rites those are. They love their clichés. Pain and darkness. It's a little kid who's crying and what's more badass satanico than hurting children? It starts to scream.

Fuck.

'Go.'

Bettina springs into motion like a bear trap. She leaps down the stairs. Follow up.

'Fuck!' is yelled out from bellow. All he's got time for as she's on him real, real quick.

Come down the stairs and Bettina's throwing punches at a shadow.

Drawn all over the walls, snakes and upside down ankhs and a symbol called shen mark. Shen mark... kinda looks like an Omega symbol but without the break. Protection magic. He needs it. The air here is thick with vicious psychic disturbance. Demons are watching. Cruel intelligences. Nothing to see but can *feel* their lavish hungers.

No.

Wait.

Looking gives them form. Hyena faced things made from darkness, eyes mad, tongues lolling. Vulture eyed monstrosities. Move my hands in quick protective patterns and their energies dissapate.

But Bettina's gone and ruined the sorcerer's day and the rite is failing. Dragging my eyes off them collapses their reality. The demons can't stay which is *a serious fucking relief.* They'd be sons of bitches to banish empty-handed.

Turn my attention to the material world.

Lit by those gas lamps you take camping so we can see a kid tied up in tape, pliers and knives at the ready on a cold stone floor. Looks like the magician already started in on an earlobe.

Chanting man is in a white robe, white hood but his flesh is insubstantial shade. The man getting ready for this butchery bullshit is made of shade, the shen turning him immaterial. Bettina's throwing hooks at him.

Passing through him but making trails of smoke around him.

He falls back. Even though he's not solid, can tell he's no fighter. Intimidated by her.

'The fuck are you?! What's this to do with you?!' But she's already back in the game.

She brings a knee up, would have gone halfway to breaking his thighbone it could connect. Throws a combo. Nothing special. Basic but effective always, the jab right at his face he can't help but flinch at. The right cross to hurt him and the left hook to open him up to more. Then another right to smash his jaw to shards. But it's not happening. He's not flesh right now.

He gets it together, slaps at her. Weak move but all he needs is to touch her. She hisses and leaps back. Smell of frost in the air.

Shadow man makes a sound like he's fucking happy. Moves in at her but she's too quick. He'll never touch her. Give him this, he figures that out fast. Goes to run.

Motherfucker, you're going nowhere.

Snap my zippo open and spark it.

Stare into the flame.

Hurts my eyes, sudden light in the gloom, but that's as what's needed. Nothing without a little pain is worth a damn. You know that. Hold it closer, so close to my eyes my finger touches my nose. Vision floods yellow. Nothing but light. Too much. Sluicing into my eyes, nerves screaming from it all.

Shut the eyes. Open them sharply.

Nothing but white. Blinded by it. Pain moves inside my eyes from too much light. Fed too much into them.

The paradox of an overlit eye is magic. Power. Needed information to engineer a Working and my gaze has too much information now to even work.

Skull full of light magic that floods from me, banishing the shadow.

There's a sudden low laugh from Bettina that, ain't gonna lie, I kinda love. And then screams from the man which are almost as good.

Take almost a minute to get vision back, lost to phosphene hazes and cruel patterns. The magic wants it due and takes it out of me with a minute of needles in my orbs.

No shadows exist in light and my spell stripped his spell from him like fog in a storm.

Bettina leaves him a few teeth lighter and he won't be posing for photos soon but she knows how to do it without executing a motherfucker. He can walk and talk when she's done. She leaves him on the ground while she checks the kid. It's started crying and crying but who can blame it.

Still, no time for a child.

'Get it out of here. I'll take care of this... human.'

She grabs the kid and nods at me, moving on real quick and the shrieking sounds it's making fade as she goes up.

Turn my attention to the magician. He's up against the wall, legs spread out of in front of him, lap full of his own blood and teeth.

Sit down next to him, my own back against the wall, like we were just two guys.

'Well, friend. You have to know what comes next.'

V

They never want to talk at first. Dunno why. No one resists long. Just not how shit works. But they always front like *no man can break me*. Pride. Fear. Whatever.

What's your name, where are you from, what are you doing here, who do you work for.

Nothing at all. Just him with his hands across his mouth,

groaning from pain.

'Alright. Listen. You can talk to me, or you can talk to *her*. She can punch her way into an armoured truck and, man, she fucking hates cats like you.'

He's white robe is a mess but he turns to be and tries to spit blood. Globs down between us.

'Fuck that bitch.'

Snap open the zippo. Set his robe on fire.

Cotton burns pretty good and a lingering spark of light magic helps it along. He screams and pats it down and puts it out quick. Got him on the sleeve hem where's there's not much blood. Burnt hands he holds under his armpits, sucking in air. While he's doing that, light up his hood. Doesn't burn as quick. Blood dampens it. His hair burns but he pats that out too, smacking his own head real hard.

'Just gonna get worse, friend.'

Snap the zippo open again. Love that sound.

He flinches.

Looks up at me. Without his hood he's just some cat. Balding, ring of hair over his ears. Shaved face, weak chin. Thirties. Hard to tell in the camping lantern light.

'You can tell people you resisted now. All burnt up and battered and shit. You never signed up for no goddamn torture, right?'

He nods.

'My name is William.'

Alright.

VI

Grab the fuck by his hair and hit the Black City.

There's other worlds. You've felt them. A walk in the wood or the bush and suddenly things feel... strange. Passing by an alley at night and you know it's a real bad idea to go down there. Kids vanish and they're never found again, no clue, no lead. You walked past a soft place, a threshold.

There's other worlds. We make them with our mind and our bodies can follow. Sometimes they take us.

The Black City is a dream of the City, its spiritual photo negative.

Can't drag this fucker along the street, all burnt and bloodied so we take a shortcut.

Plan is, show this fucker to Foulstone and Blossom and Elliot. Prove the Sothic Temple is something we needs be dealing with. He's obviously on that Egypt tip.

Enter the Black City and move along chiaroscuro roads. Scratchy, vast abysses of streets that seem almost animated. Towering, shadow buildings arching overhead, tendrils and tongues of the stuff they're made from licking out of their outlines.

Faceless creatures, mannequin citizens, staring at us as we walk from office building windows, cowering if noticed. Now and again, ghost cabs and buses, black as the inside of your mouth, flow along like liquid shadow. Walking down main streets and avenues, broad and cold and black.

And the moon, perfectly black in a grey white sky.

There's a scent in the air.

Musty. dry.

Reptilian.

This is new.

Walk shadowless across the Black City. Always creepy. Always weird. Something about this place makes you crave looking over your should. Feels like something is breathing hot on the back of your neck. The black hole in my brain... can feel it... *pulsing.*

Somewhere, in the world, a monster feels me. We're linked. The Rabisu is thinking of me. This affects the spirit stuff the Black City is made of.

The pigeons of the Black City fly overhead in unnatural flocks, making occult symbols with their bodies. Swirling into spirals, alchemical meanings.

Something.

Something.

Is watching.

There's a sound. Hissing.

Put my back against a building wall. Those licks off it at my back feel like painless whips.

William struggles. He's coming out of the beating Bettina gave him.

'Something's here.'

Put my hand to his palm, knock the back of his head against the wall.

'Shut the fuck up.'

Hissing. Where? There it is. Against the wall. In the wild glyphs of taggers, my name.

LARK

With a quickness, summon up defences. Whirling barrier of ideas and emotions. My mother holding me down and trying to put hot glue in my eyes, age eight. That becomes a lumbering golem rushing up from the street. Watching Jon win his first kumite. A thunderclap of force in my fist. Mully telling me my mind was sharp, age sixteen and my pride when he said that, first time ever, something sliding into me that changed me, purpose. Turn all that into a warm shield.

'What?'

More tags write themselves, white against the building's black.

SOMETHING IS COMING

'Wick?'

The tagger girl got turned into the City's archon.

OBVIOUSLY

'This the right time to get smart?'

YES

'What's this something?' Tell you the truth, should treat her with more respect. She's something vast *now*.

I DO NOT KNOW THEY HIDE FROM ME

'Need more to help you.'

HARD TO NARROW DOWN TO TALK TO PEOPLE THAT

MAN KNOWS GIVE HIM TO ME

Stomach goes out from me. Fear shoots into my fingers.

She wants him but I've a need too.

'No.'

GIVE HIM SOMETHING COMES IT WILL HURT ME

'Wick, no. We'll help you. You know that. But we need this fuck. To talk to *us*. You're too... you're too big for this, now.'

Truth is, though. she's an archon. Cosmic being. Bigger than gods. Something can hurt her, can't see what we can do about it. Then again, she's a rook and who knows what she's perceiving. Not that it matters now.

GIVE HIM TO ME. Words spell out on the road in front of me.

The Black City goes blacker. The pigeons pour down from the sky and fly overhead in a circle around me, thick and black. Slow, too. Slower than should be possible. Black except for the streetlights which suddenly burn like klieg. Pressure grows now, like in a fast elevator, vision starts to swim.

Not gonna risk my life for this fuck but *I want him.*

'Come on. Wick. You got to know we can do what needs doing more precise than you.'

GIVE HIM GIVE HIM GIVE HIM GIVE HIM writ out in the lights from the black buildings.

Drop out of the Black City. Just let the spells that take me there fade. Not toying with Wick all pissed.

She reaches for me as I'm going. A hand of smashed black glass. Annihilating white light. But she's too big. Her mind is as big as everyone in town. She's trying to catch fleas in a fist and react with nerves as big as city blocks.

Fade away before she can react. Come to outside a bus stop. The working girls notice us but they know the score and mind their business. Then the weight of who Wick is now, the price of me defying her, crashes down.

Shit. Fuck. Shit. Eloquent motherfucker, me.

Have to make it right with her *somehow*. And soon. But for now, get this fuck to somewhere safe. Her consciousness looks for us and the streets are her tongue but we are just too small.

SEVEN

I

Move this William fuck along on a frog march Jon taught me. It's late at night, make it look like helping a drunk friend. Call Bettina but she's not answering which is fine, she's busy.

Leave a voicemail telling her we're heading to the Library's offsite detention centre. Clearly, part of me was thinking of it because we're real close.

Down an alley and through the back of a shopping mall entrance. You know the type, arcades all lining up between two buildings. Food court and fountains down the bottom. Close up behind glass now but we're not going in. We're out the back with the rubbish and the loading dock and stuff like that.

Malls, shopping malls, are riddled with doors that go somewhere - ain't never are quite sure where.

Hit a security door with a keypad, the password I know. And from there, down into the sub-basements.

Rush of heat and air conditioning machines down there, fans moving with that *whop whop* sound. Warrens of anonymous concrete tunnels and closets and storage. We move through bland walkways and flickering fluro lights till we hit rear of the nest. Security guard outside a plain blue security door marked PRIVATE sees me.

Nods. He's seen me before.

'Open the door, man.'

'Just need your pass- '

'Open the fucking door, man!'

Offended but taken aback, he does.

Waiting for me, on his cane and in a white suit, is my old master.

Mully.

II

First, the offsite. Where we are. Why here?

Hide in plain sight. Good rule, good plan. Magical thinking.

That simple PRIVATE sign keeps most people out. It's a warding glyph, no doubt, even if we hadn't put sorcerous intent into it, it's still a warding glyph. Some people like to obey rules. Most do to spare themselves hassle.

But behind it, ten cells where we keep the worst of the worst who we can't vanish, can't magically... neuter. We don't keep 'em at the Library for a lot of reasons. Deniability. Safety.

The cells themselves, just locked rooms inside, looks kinda like a changing room. Simple doors with simple locks. But warded to fuckery and back. Every inch of the doors have script on them. Did a few myself but the Library's been using this place since the 80s, when I was just a kid. Mully's work is on the doors as well and some others, dead or gone.

Norse runes, Yantra script, spidery Arabic symbols and evil eyes, Solomonic Seals, Chinese Wu symbols, heathen hearts and polite pentacles. Personal idiosyncratic Alphabets of Desire. Each coded so only Custodes like me can open them.

Mully I don't say boo too. But he walks with me as William gets pushed down the hallway and into the cell. Just boring cement rooms with nothing in 'em but a bucket and room to lay down. That boredom breaks you.

Close the door behind him and say the word to lock it behind it. *Clauditis.* Classy Latin.

Cruel as fuck, the cells, small and hot and cramped but we don't keep 'em long. Besides, William here wouldn've knifed up a kid and be hiding a pair of tiny shoes if he wasn't enjoying my hospitality, so try to keep your mercy in your pants.

'Lark, come. Let's talk.'

Mully smiles at me and fury sparks up deep within.

I I I

Mully's eyes are blue flecked with what I'm telling you is gold. The security guard, all pissed at me, is given instructions on feeding William. He logs it all and we bail out. Mully walking after me on a beautiful cane. He's in a cream suit and holds a white hat.

Bettina texts me back that she's trying to get the kid home. Good.

'We really should talk, Lark.'

Maybe we should at that.

So now we're at a diner at five in the morning. My former master drinks tea and makes a despairing face as they bring him a hot cup of water and a bag. A red neon lamp casts light over the both of us. OPEN LATE flashing on and off. The waitress is so tired, her hair the colour of dishwashing water, with a scar from the corner of her mouth to the corner of her eye.

'Honestly...' he says, dunking the bag into the water like a man doing surgery on a mutant.

Sip my own coffee. His long fingers play with his hat. He'd never wear one inside and sure as hell not to eat out. Old school, every inch of him.

'Mully, what do you want?'

Don't bother to ask how he knew where to look or when. Cat is about the best you'll meet, outside of the Ascended Masters. He looks at me with those eyes that are kind but twisted with toughness. Feels like when crows on the branches stare down at you. He's not a nice man, he's a good one.

'Senior fraters at the Libraium Temple are making reports about you, Lark.'

'Elliot. Foulstone. The other one, what's his name. Who fucking cares?'

'I do. I'm concerned for you.'

'Don't need concern.'

'See, here's the thing. I rather think you do.'

'Handling it all.'

He sips at the tea and sighs. Like he thinks he'll have to do something the hard way.

'I had your job for decades, Lark. And I must tell you, I must be frank... *there's always fools*. Incompetents. They frustrate and they annoy but they are not all to the job there is. They come and go. The Library is ancient, Lark, and it is powerful but these money men without a syllable of poetry inside them have always been a necessity to it. And if you fail to navigate them, you'll be alone and without allies.'

'Been alone without allies before.'

'Yes, where you were doing exorcisms for gangsters and cartomancy for rich widows. And after that, alone in the forest, prey for ancient monstrosities. Not only a waste of your potential but a danger for your life, soul and sanity. Will you burn your books and break your staff if they cast you out again? I feel you must, to forsake this life. Because you have too bloody a history to work alone. '

He's... not wrong. But don't like hearing it.

Shrug.

'Lark. You were a fine apprentice and you need no assessment of your magical skills from me. I shall always find your style... eccentric, but effective. Universalism seems...'

'We've had this discussion. You're grimoire down the track.'

'We have. I'm not here for it again.'

Mully comes at the world pretty strictly Hermetic Western tradition. He's no magpie like me. There's never been a serious issue about it. Think he just likes to tease me about a lack of rigour.

'But your distrust, your anger, your frustration with people who see things differently from you... these must be cooled. You have to be better with people.'

My mother holding me down and trying to put hot glue in my eyes, age eight.. Torturing a child in a basement.

Say nothing.

He sighs at me. Reckon he knows what's going on behind my eyes.

'You must leave Jon. He is beyond you and helping him will endanger you. And then the others... these madmen and butchers we deal with... if you busy yourself only with your personal business, they will remain safe and free to indulge their ghastly whims.'

Say nothing.

'Oh, Lark. I'm not telling you to smile and shake hands and picnic with your co-workers. I'm asking you to put aside anger and pride. You are a magician. Your ego. *Self.* These must always be fought, that is the primary goal of the magician. You know this lesson. To war against this dense coagulation of ideas that make up our minds. I am asking you to lead as you have been lead. To teach. As you were taught. And whatever irritations you have must be fought.'

He's right.

'Mully. No. They'll do it my way. Show them they're wrong and I am goddamn *right.*'

'This isn't about *Scarlet,* is it? Proving her wrong.'

I don't know.

'No.'

'It's not even her anymore, Lark, even if you're lying to me. She's long gone. Just a memory of happiness. Love cannot be clutched or horded. If you still fight for her, you fight for a name written on water. Let her go.'

But there's something inside me that can't. Something that's beginning to rot. Something that a year or two ago you could call love, lost love. You could squint at it, call it heartbreak but now is sucking me down. Twisting me up. A cancer of the emotions, metastatic.

Say nothing.

Stand.

'Lark, don't go… I'm not here to scold or upbraid. Bettina feels the same. Yes, she came to me and if you think *that* other than an act of love, you are very much mistaken. Don't put your obsession with loyalty on her.'

Stare down at him. His gaze holds mine. For what seems a very long time. Then… he sighs and shakes his head.

'You could never be told anything, could you? Just… just work with them. Not for my sake or theirs but for *yours*. For your magical practice and for the people you can help.'

He's wrong. *He's as wrong as poison.* Never do what they tell me. Never let the scum have their way.

'No. Go to hell.'

I V

I never saw him alive again.

V

Go home, wash up, go to work.

Log in the prisoner. Well, wait until it's after the morning meetings so it doesn't flag for a few hours. Do it by the book, all protocol and shit. They'll come at me over it but not until tomorrow when upstairs checks the worksheets. There you go, Mully. Playing by rules.

Do my shift. Strengthen some wards on a client's house. Go over the scryer's reports. Talk to a private detective on our payroll, used to be a cop.

Training session after, down in the conference rooms. Except it's just Sasha and Karel now. Not much point.

Karel hands me a note.

WE GO FOR DRINK AFTER WORK YOU WANT TO COME

I am asking you to lead. To teach. As you were taught.

No.

Then back to the mall at about six, grabbing some shit I'll need and down into the prison.

Everything is making me goddamn angry. Realise my whole day was spent pissed off. But got a bottle of whisky and two glasses and that improves a man's mood.

No matter the kind of ugly fucking duties he's got in front of him or the kinda scum he's gotta drink it with.

Open the cell door. Stinks of piss. Security man, he comes to clean it. Take William, would-be child killer cultist man, who is sore as hell with a face looks like squealing meat, to the interview room. Hand cuff through a ring in a desk, two seats bolted to the floor. No mirror window to look through, this isn't the police. We do things private.

Pour him a shot. Pour one for me. Hand him one other thing I got. Just a sandwich.

'It's yours, man.'

William, who was gonna torture a kid to death, feel I should remind you, nods thanks and wolfs at it, bent over the table. Give him some water and then show him the whisky.

Normally, good cop bad cop with Bettina. But could be Mully's onto something. Read not long ago that you use *empathy* to get a suspect to talk. Technique so good it actually went too far, got too many false confessions, made frightened people so eager to get into the copper's graces that they'd say anything. Cat's gonna try keeping that friend in the room, even if it means copping to what they never did, so they ain't left alone with no friends.

Plan and prepare. That's the first step. Know who you're dealing with. Sothic Temple is probably like other cults that work the dark side. They find freaks, losers, guys who post on the internet how women are all slags and black people can't read. Those cats. Not strong people.

Engage and explain. Jon was always good at the rapport thing and Bettina has a low key likeability when she wants it. The trick is to make them feel like *you're not such a bad cat*. Don't overdo it but, hell, you're just some guy, in a room with another guy, not an agent of law or punishment.

Here we go. Let's try to fly solo. Being a likeable regular Joe. Me, a man with a personality like a serial killer's basement.

'Look, sorry about last night. My partner... you know how it can be. She over reacted.'

'Where are we? How'd we fucking get here? The path we took...' Local accent. City boy.

'Oh, that's... kinda one of the secrets of the Black City. Once this is all done, can show you how to get there. None of your crew use it?'

'Never fucking heard of it.'

'Ah well, different crews have different... specialities, you know?'

'Yeah.'

Pour two glasses full of whisky. Plastic cups, don't need glass in my eyes.

'Sothic Temple. That's the Egypt trip, right?'

'Yeah.'

'Love all that stuff. Horus and that. Mummies, like. My job is to talk to other organisations. Help me understand yours, William.'

The Dale Carnegie move. People like their names said out loud.

evil portent, bringing heat

And fevers to suffering humanity

Sothos has a rep and Egypt wrote prayers to it. Let's see if he knows it.

'It's the brightest star in the sky. I think that Sothos is the Egyptian word for Sirius.'

'Sounds right to me, Bill. Or do you prefer William.'

'William.'

'So it is. William. You reading like the *Pyramid Texts* and... Never mind. We'll talk shop later. I'm just into this stuff, you know?'

But he doesn't seem the type to want to talk classics from the clubbed dog look he shoots me. Or the huge occult history of that star he worships.

'An Egyptian year is a Sothic year, that's what's up.'

Maybe I was wrong.

'We worship the old gods and we work their magic and hold to their calendar. It's powerful shit man. Heka and all that. I joined them, I didn't know much about this stuff. My old cellmate upstate, he was part of them.'

'What's his name?'

'Er...'

'S'alright man. We can come back to it. How'd you get involved?'

'My old man was real religious. Old time. I hated the old fuck but I missed some of the Revivals when I got older. You been in Revivals?'

'Sure,' tell him true. 'Even went to snake handlers one time. Wild shit.'

'Yeah, we did that when I was a kid. Didn't much care for a lot of stuff in the church but when I told my cellmate... well, he told me about *his* church. Seemed like bullshit but you listen to anything inside.'

'It's boring, right?'

'Like nothing fucking else. But it's a lot worse when it ain't boring.'

'Heard that.'

'Then... he told me about this sex magic shit. Women just lying there with their tits out on altars. Run a train on them if you wanted. And I thought that was something I could get involved with. *You* ever see shit like that?'

'Aw, man,' say it like I was a little shy but disgust makes my neck sweat. 'This is magic. Things happen.'

'Yeah. So *that* happened. Hooked up with them and got involved. At first, just figure it for a weird new religion. Learned some magic. You know about that shit.'

Nod. 'Yep. All real.'

'Then, you know, I'm level. I cursed my landlord. Cocksucker said I was late four weeks. Fuck you, lucky you get paid at all, bitch. Suddenly, he gets bit by a rat that goes all feverish and then, get this, he gets a fucking brain fever from it. His slapper wife takes over, but she's easy to scare off. So I figure, *it all works.*'

Typical kinda story.

'How long ago was this?'

'Five years ago I joined.'

'You must know Jon.'

He blinks at me. 'You… you know that freak?'

Swear to Christ, want Bettina here to finish as she started on his face.

'Yes, of course. *He's* who we want. He's what this is about.'

'What for?'

Think a moment. Stare at him real careful. His pinched mouth, his dull eyes. Jon's name made him warier.

'You've met him. Want a motherfucker like that all out there in the street?'

'Don't want a motherfucker like that at all.' He snorts. Snot in his nose. Pour a drink.

'He's all involved in *your* organisation. Someone *put* you close to him. You tell me more, can take him out, leave you guys unharmed. You get out of here, and on the downlow, Library owes you, William, you, a favour for the assist.'

He goes for the whisky on the desk. Hands are greasy. Hands that held knives…

'Yeah, yeah, ok. Can't drink with my hands like this.'

'Sorry.'

Uncuff one of his hands. Knew this was going to go down. He still can't make a strong move with one hand chained up and I'm too far if he rushes me.

'Thanks.'

That *thanks* is important. He's grasping what seems like kindness like a drowning man clasps hands.

That's *engagement*. Move it on to the proper meat of this. The *account*.

'But gotta know what goes on in there. Got to know who fucked up and bought in a freak. Got to know who to hold to pin all this shit on.'

'Fuck man, this is holy stuff, you know?'

'Yeah. And it's *respected*. But listen, William. My gig is to take out bad motherfuckers. Not a *cop*, not here to punish anyone, just here to make something stop. You know Jon, though... he's not normal. Get rid of him and got no problem with the Temple. *Or you.*'

Which is what he wants to hear. Forgetting he would have killed a child. Fucking maggot like this is always escalating. Always looking for more. He woulda killed a little girl for some power. He has *his* though and now he'll rat.

He talks more about how the magic gave him advantages. Charms on women to help him get laid. Lottery ticket wins. Sacred power and he used it for hundred dollar payoffs and squalid lays.

'Then, Todd got promoted to leader. Never had much to say to him before. He was just some citizen, you know. Shirt sleeves and a moustache and glasses, you know the type. But turned out, he had some ideas.'

William tells of a change that took over the Temple about three years ago. Rites to Isis get darker, seedy gangbangs and desperate group masturbation. Rites to Seth, God of darkness and deserts start up.

Add it up. Would have been around the time we were dealing with the Archon and Wick. He finishes up with this -

'Yeah, we found this fucked up porno dude, you know? He wanted his dick cut off so we did it for him! Fucking wild!'

They love the torture porn, the dark side cults. The lonely and the weak and the mad. Turn weak people into *things*. Devices for the magic. Seen it and seen it and seen it in the last ten years.

(Don't think of Bettina's eye. The eye I let get taken from her in sacrifice when I needed it.)

And then, into this evil saturnalia, comes a woman. Todd tells the cult she's major. *A Cheriheb*. Proper priest, initiated in the highest rites.

'Describe her.'

'Fifty. Not all that hot but a... way about her. Brown hair, short.'

Good enough for me. *Bernadette.*

'She... look, man. Some dude getting his dick cut off. That's fucking funny, right? And it worked for us. We got strength from it. Money started rolling in. I got women I wanted, not just settled for. I had these dreams, man. So... like... *beautiful*. I know how faggy that sounds but it was incredible. Used to go to sleep at like eight at night so I'd have 'em. Just feeling... *so great*. Gifts from the Gods. But she started telling us about something bigger than gods. Something older.'

Lean in.

'What was it called?'

'Apophis.'

Apophis. The primal chaos. The great serpent, enemy of Ma'at, the cosmic commonweal. Dweller in the Tenth Region of Night. Each dawn, the sun would travel under the world and the snake would try to swallow it. Only Ra, his sorcerous, violent Eye and Seth, the devil god, could fight it off.

'You worshiped it.'

'We did. But man... it's...'

Cell door slams open.

Elliot. Face ugly with hate.

'Release this man at once.'

V I

'Fuck I will.'

With him are two fucks. Dunno names or deals, but both are muscle for sure. Elliot's gotten himself a *gang*. Both dudes in suits, one who looks like his face, under a buzz, will burst from the blood in it about the same time arms will burst his suit jacket. *Juicer*. Can see the steroids in the shape of his face, the smell of his sweat.

Kinda pointless for real body work. Fucker like this'll throw six punches and be gassed. But the muscles impress rubes.

Other is a piece of work. Black leather overcoat and boots to his knees. Half moon fucking glasses and a complexion like milk and a shaved head. Again, Elliot goes style over substance.

'This is you directly contravening orders, Lark.'

Stand up straight. Get in close to my *boss* and muscle steps in, dragging Elliot aside like a ragdoll.

Look up at the juicers and stare. He's got four inches on me and probably thirty kilo of muscle.

He thinks it's a showdown, me versus him giving the eyeball. Don't play those games.

Picture a brain full of poison, shoot it down my optic nerves. Think of the *ale* rune that protects against poison, conjure it up as if it were there, floating between us. Flip the rune upside, literally reversing the meaning. Wanna get good at magic? Know things. Know things like that. Disgust and anger and my bad mood day, all that gets channelled into the rune, shooting it like electricity through a circuit. Venomous information in my brain hits him.

He steps back like a wasp stung him in the eyes.

Then Milkface counter-spells me. Wards he's put on the muscle wake up. Sloppy work but muscle gets it together and looks over at Elliot taken aback. Slowly look over at Milkface but he's concentrating. Countering me made him work.

Nothing to worry about from him. Jesus Christ, a long black leather overcoat. Can smell the album covers on him from here. Kind of dude advertises his corporate ghost hunting business. But no time for him.

'Elliot. This shit is *important*.'

'I don't actually care about how important it is, Lark. It's about your *obedience*. You've overstepped yourself detaining this man. Consider yourself on probation.'

Look aside, getting my thoughts together. Thinking of Bettina and Sasha and Mully, who all told me to accommodate. Look back.

'Why is he off limits?'

'He's involved in the Sothic Temple and that's linked to Jon, isn't it?'

'Yeah. But he also tried to cut up a kid.'

'You're not the police, Lark! You're not fighting fucking crime!'

'You still think you're at a fucking day job, don't you? Fuck, man, you're wearing a tie down here.'

'I'm wearing a tie worth a week of your rent, dickhead. The fuck did Scarlet ever see in a man like you. Well, she's got some bad habits, I suppose.'

Say nothing. He's faking an opening. Scarlet's name is bait. Fucking obvious.

Muscle man has his shit back together.

'Answer the man. What she see in you? Fucking pussy.'

Hit *gnosis*.

Milkface has warded him, sure. From *direct* harm.

My spell has linked me and Muscles up. What you call in *sympathy*. So don't try to hurt him. Just open myself up to him and go wandering in his mind for a bit. Impressions flee through me. Fan 'em like cards. Looking for things to exploit. Fears, doubts, shame, like that. He's het up, ready for a fight, which means his mind's open as untreated wounds.

Yes, yes, here's the first. Big guy, stinking of booze. First person view of dad or stepdad or someone with a belt working the strip while his mother screamed for mercy. The drunk hits him, hits the mother too. Anger, grief, hate. *Grief.*

And something colder too. Not natural. This is a memory but it isn't a childhood recollection. It's something recent.

Haunted. *Fucker's haunted.* Explains how he came to Elliot's attention. Witnessing something muscles saw real recent.

'Milkface here tell you about me, juicer?'

'The fuck you say to me?'

'He tell you it's nothing for me to summon up your father's ghost before sun rises?'

'They warned me about your voodoo shit.'

The link is good. A sudden surge of fear rises up in him that doesn't show in his face but shows in his heart. The heart I'm staked out in. *Mother screamed for mercy.*

'What?'

His face gets redder, which is a neat trick. But there's dread in his voice which is what I'm needing.

Milkface says, wild, 'He's fucking with you, Mike!'

Tell him, 'No, Mike. He's not. Your old man's back, isn't he? You volunteered to do body work for this man because you need help with a ghost.'

Never let the link die.

'Ask around. Ask what Lark can do. Then ask if I'm the kinda man to let the ghost of your old man at your mother.'

Muscles is done. He looks over at Milkface and Elliot almost in a panic. Elliot's eyes are bugging. He can't even lie good in pressure like this. He's feeling it fall apart like that last time he stepped up to me. He doesn't belong in this world. Not an inch of him. He thinks of me like a jealous ex he has to deal with. Unruly, subordinate too.

Slow it down. Take a breath. Look at Milkface like I had something to say, but then never cared to say it. Try Mully's way now.

'Elliot. Let's play this with cool hands. There is *need* to question the fuck in there. This is about the job and nothing else.'

'No, there's not because *I told you* there isn't! I am giving you a direct order. Cease and desist this right now.'

Bettina's the angel on my shoulder. Her, Sasha, Mully. Telling me to go along, to get along all three. Stare at Elliot long. Never noticed he's got green eyes.

He blinks. Looks away. Good.

Sound petty? Him backing down? This all seem dick sizing to you? *The fuck it is.*

He'll remember it. He'll be a little ashamed of it. It'll make him easier to deal with if he's acting from a memory of when he went weak sister, just a bit of him. But enough.

'You wanna pull rank, rank's pulled. But what happens after, it's on you.'

'No it's not! This is all on you!'

Spittle flying into my face.

'You're the boss, boss.'

Leave.

EIGHT

I

Woke early next morning.

Into work.

Hate in my hands but that won't do me much good. Try and find some ease in routine. Read the news. Killers and rapists and wars. New diseases and someone fucked someone they shouldn't. Temperatures rising, seas are boiling.

The world is bleeding out.

Open emails but they're so boring. Some acolyte got my internal address and wants an answer about what I'm doing to control the demons who seem to haunt his skull in what's, for once, a metaphor. Reply to someone making an actual request for an opinion on the City of Pyramids and the Night of Pan, but that Thelema trip is not my speciality. That shit's a religion and got no use for that.

At least it's a question about something worth my time, though.

Worth my time.

Wheels spinning, now. William's off limits. Jon's still out there. And now Elliot is acting like the Sothic Temple as a whole is nothing for me to fret over. *But why?*

Knock at the door.

'What?'

Bettina opens the door. She's in a black turtleneck and grey trousers. Holding two coffees.

'We got to talk about last night.'

'What?'

'I got a call to come down to the holding cells. Elliot his own self. Told me it was a point of order that you, a field officer, had made an arrest. They needed another field officer to sign him out all by the book.'

'Point of order.'

'Rules is rules to these types. Made me overrule your decision, so it was protocol. Let the prick you had go.'

'So a fucking kid killer walked?'

'Yeah, but I tailed him. Aristide can track him if you need him. We got an addy.'

'But he walked. My prisoner. A Custodes prisoner.'

Never grow hot, me. Something in my head goes real cold, though. Say nothing more. Hate is seething around me and that makes a man dumb.

'Had to do it. Wanted you to hear it from me.'

Not mad at her. Library's a sweet gig for her. Money coming in and access to food, gig for her boyfriend.

'Sure. I dig it.'

'He had the fucking crazy, that one.'

'Kid killer.'

'I was there, man.'

'Yeah.'

'You shouldn't have gone after him, Lark. At least not the way you did. Something's spooked 'em. The Library. Ever since the lions, it's all gone squirrely.'

Nod. That's true. Elliot's been at me.

Desk phone rings. Blossom.

'Mr. Lark.'

'Just Lark.'

'We'll need you to meet with us in the Formal Convocation Chamber. In fifteen minutes.'

That's serious. That's... Upstairs.

'Sure.'

Hang up.

Bettina hands me the coffee.

'Got to go Upstairs.'

'Shit.'

Yeah.

I I

Quiwe Bensaa is a name you might like to know.

He lived over in Finland. Four hundred years ago. Cat was a
Sami shaman. Knew the old trick of Finnish magic. Catch the wind in
the knot of a handkerchief, let it out when your boat needs moving on,
catch more wind later. Record says his praxis was to wet his feet in the
ocean he was sailing in, then throw a pig overboard. Sailor comes to
him. Asks for wind. Quiwe says *sure* and does his pig thing.

It works.

It works too good. One day, he's doing his bit same as normal
but this time the breeze that should just be enough to move a boat over
lakes turns into a storm. Five people on the boat die. They get back to
land and the Sami stands trial. Guilty. Burned to death. Historical shit.
Look it up.

Two things that story teaches.

Be *real* careful who you do magic for, and why.

And that even something you've done a thousand times before
can go tits up in a sea of failure.

Thinking about that when the Convocation opens.

I I I

This is Old School. This is when Dad comes homes.

Up the elevator with a private code that gets me to the top
floor of the quiet brownstone. A professional man in a suit behind a
desk puts the metal detecting wand over me in an anonymous office of
lacquered floorboards and no windows.

Used to be a goddamn demon did this job. Proper *Psueudomonarchia Daemonum* demon. Nothing you could see, just a bad though in dark room that made sure you weren't gonna try some shit on some of the most powerful magicians on the earth.

For once, feeling underdressed in leather jacket, blue jeans and boots. This is meeting with the Masters.

A door opens into a back room and out comes Melina Velasquez.

She's four foot eleven with a severe bob haircut, pearls and a lavender suit. Her eyes are like a crow's. She stares at me a moment with kind of gaze a microbe might see if it looked up from its slide. Haven't seen her in years. She's probably the finest numerologist in the world and top five in notarkion, gematria and isopsephy. Took a lesson with her maybe five years back and she knows her business. She's one of the few people knows my real name. Had to give it to her and she analysed it and put me in contact with a terrifying thing you might call an angel. Spent a week in a mental hospital afterwards. Jon bought me a box of chocolates and some mittens. He was afraid I'd have an attack and wank in front of the nurses, he told me.

Silly bastard.

'Lark.'

'Madame.' Serious respect for her. Not playing, not sucking up. She couldn't hold her own in a fight but what she knows… Read a paper she wrote once, though. Claims she had sex with God, which was not expected, given she comes across like a therapist who thinks you suck.

'Please come in.'

Been here maybe half a dozen times in the last thirteen years. Most times, just being in the room to clarify incident reports on heavy juice cases. Made one after the Wick case, for instance. And the devil.

Circular room, three storeys high. Skylights shoot the place full of sunbeams. Around the room, lining floors two and three are the Rendition Books. This is where we keep what we want for ourselves that we don't let the public see. Crowley's *Idylls of the Abyss*. Found in a safe and stolen by us in the 60s. The Varaszlo's *Sarkany*. Chan's *Five Poison Tracts*. Nothing in circulation. Nothing you can buy or borrow.

Grimaldi's *Satanas Patefacum*. Don't go on the internet for that shit. You won't find it and fuckers like me are why.

Then again, you won't cry your mind out with tears made of your own brain, so, you know, did you a favour.

Floorboards are black and reflective. In the centre, chased in silver, a circle and within, septagram. Holy magic. Around the circle, twelve high chairs, tall and dark and beautiful.

Velasquez takes a seat.

Just me and her. Stand looking at her.

'We will be joined by *Perfecti* Vimbo in time. Please sit, Lark, this is not an interrogation. We need to understand a situation among our soldiers.'

'Never a soldier.'

She waves a hand, dismissing me. Which, have to say, sits badly. But got bigger problems. Vimbo is coming.

Sit two chairs down from her. She looks at me a while, stare back. Thinking things through.

'Elliot tells me you have, in his words, been insubordinate.'

Shrug.

'Lark, I'm not like the others. I know that every time you talk to anyone you feel strange and off-putting and out of place and ill at ease. But if you have a place, it is here. We must talk freely.'

Ill at ease. And bored by people. Sasha said it was shyness but that's for people who want to go along to get along but can't.

Fuck it. All in. Might not get this chance again.

'Elliot's a fool. He's *money* and he's promoted above his station.'

She tilts her head. Looks at me with those bright eyes in a web of wrinkles.

'Yes. He is.'

Gotta admit. Didn't see that coming. Maybe this won't be that bad.

Yeah. Sure.

'He made a call last night and, Madame Velasquez... straight up. It was a bad call. Sure, he's in charge but.. it is dereliction of my duty to obey him on this. He ignores a very real threat.'

She drums her nails on her leg, bony beneath her skirt. Her polish is purple. She rolls a hand at me to go on.

'The Hollow is a dangerous artefact. It is *dangerous*. Jon, my former partner, has learned from it. Come at it straight for you now - loved him like a *brother*. Want to save him, yes. But bigger than that, we need to know what happened to him and why the Sothic Temple wants him.'

'The Sothic Temple?'

'Looks of it, just a regular crew. But... you read my report on the Old Man?'

'Yes, of course.'

'He has a kid. A daughter.'

She looks at me very carefully.

'The Old Man has a daughter.'

Nod. Keep talking and maybe they won't ask why that never made no report.

'Seems so. She's got issues with me. OK, sure, whatever. But even if it's personal and she wants to take me out, she's a serious player and she's *at least* aligned with the Sothic Temple. Guy last night, he hinted big time she's running the joint. She's got Jon and she's got herself a cult who put the spooks on me.'

'I see. Go on.'

This is where I need this talk to go.

'Temple? Started out as just a cult, same as three dozen minor arcana in the City. Was heading down and going dark and then she came in, took over, played at high priest. Also, and we gotta assume this is related, murders in other cultists. Stroller Priests and... and...'

Forgot the others. *A black hole in my brain.*

Velazquez goes real quiet. Then she stands.

'I believe you. I do. But.'

She raises her hands out, palms down, turns towards the circle.

'*Subjecto, voluntati.*'

In this place, magic can work freely. Not just in the minds.

This is a ritual place. All here is non-ordinary reality. Here, magic is objective, not subjective.

In the circle, bound by silver, there's something like a heat haze.

'We need you to be honest with us, Lark.'

Kick my head to one side like a dog read a poem.

'Think I'm running some kinda game? On you?'

She turns to look at me, hands making ritual gestures. She's so good she can concentrate on me and the rite at the same time. Like it weren't nothing.

'No. No, Lark. I think in your own way you are an honest man. Do you enjoy your work here?'

'Fuck does - Sorry, Madame. How is that relevant?'

'Don't you think someone in this line of work should take pride in what they do?'

Shrug.

'You don't feel joy in beating the snakes out of the cane?'

Think for a bit.

'Joy isn't the word.'

'Pride?'

Think for a bit.

'Suppose so. Satisfaction, maybe better way to put it.'

'Do you feel any pleasure in this work? This dealing with madmen and violators?'

'Pleasure... Pleasure's a cigarette after a coffee. Pleasure's a girl's kisses hot on your lips. Pleasure's a book that rearranges the furniture in your head and secrets well won.'

'So not pleasure?'

'No, Madame. Not pleasure.'

'Then why come back? We know you sought surcease from this Bernadette's attacks on you with the Library as defence but you could have made a case to take yourself out of the field. You could have simply come and lived here in sanctuary. You *in fact* came back to your role as sheriff and you bought capable agents with you.'

Shrug.

She keeps staring at me. Don't spook, not from a stare. But there's something in her word...

Shit.

Enchanted.

Feel it inside my nervous system like a strike on the ulnar nerve. *Damn she's good.*

No wonder I'm spitting straight truth. She went right through my defences and enchanted me. It comes out like a drunken rant.

'Lady, it gets done by me because I'm good at it and it's work that needs doing and there's books here that I'd never see otherwise. Knowledge that can be gotten too without dealing with the spilled mess that's *people*. Sure I wanna save Jon. Kinda need to. Can't hack him dead. Just can't... it would wound me in ways that I don't want to suffer. Can't just let him walk alone and even if he can't be saved, he deserves better than being a chew toy for freaks.'

'That's very commendable. But isn't it you detourning Library resources for you own ends?'

'If you like. But in this case, my needs *are* the Library's needs. It was me that stitched the Old Man and this is fallout comes outta that. Jon got the mask on his face because of our work together. Ms. Velasquez, men and women in my position are going to make enemies for us all. This is just how it got dealt and now we gotta play the hand. And I don't like talking this much. Sorry, but you hit me with honest hoodoo.'

She nods. 'It is time to see your worth, Lark. Your true mettle. I very much hope you are a true man.'

With a final flourish of her hands, the heat haze grows worse. Stare at it until my eyes feel like they're drowning, like there's something inside 'em, worms or some damn thing.

Close em. Rub 'em. Open 'em.

Standing there, in the circle, Vimbo.

IV

Vimbo's one of the most beautiful humans ever had in my sight.

She's my height, hair in neat dreadlocks. Long dress to the ankle of a dozen colours and patterns that leave her muscular arms bare. She looks at me and have to fight not to step back from the power in that haze.

Told you before, *I ain't new to this*. Got some tricks and moves of my own, some skills with magic.

But Vimbo's something else.

Projecting here over fuck knows how far and can't hardly tell she's not flesh. And a look in her eyes. Feels like being in the pen with the tigers who done skipped a couple of meals. She fills up the room with her potency and you can tell she's barely contained by it. Moved past humanity in fine ways.

Perfecti.

Ascended Master.

Secret Chief.

Deep down, under everything else, sort of hope to be her one day. Free of attachments to earthly things. Sudden though irrupts in my head. *Wait. Is that true? To leave the world?* But no chance for self-reflection.

'Lark. Nice to see you again.'

No time to follow that hound.

'Not sure we've met.'

She frowns.

'No, you shouldn't, should you?'

What? What?

'Excuse me?'

'I have only a limited time, sir. Fight confusion. Ms. Velasquez here is uncertain of what kind of loyalty you hold to Raibhurai.'

Her musical accent makes the word beautiful. *Library*. Nigerian loanword? Maybe.

'Are we still on this?'

'Surely you have some allegiance, this is not in doubt. But what kind? How far does such loyalty extend? We need to know about you, Lark. There are bad omens all around and our attentions are thin. We need to know things about you and one thing most of all.'

'Sure.'

'You don't seem moved by this.'

Shrug.

She looks over at Velasquez who simply nods her head.

'You must speak to me, Lark. I am not some local manager of a chapter house. I am Vimbo and my word echoes loudly. My authority has few limits. You have been a fine factotum for Raibhuarai over the last decade or more and we are pleased you have returned. But we must know you are committed to the cause, which means working with superiors. Even those you clash with.'

Say nothing.

Watching her eyes film over with grey. Not grey. The colour of television static. Pearlescent. She stares at me with the attention of a vivisectionist.

'You want me to talk true. You want me to lower defences.'

'I do, Lark. We need to understand your position. There is more to this than some romantic rivalry or the egos of our patrons. There are rumbles in the earth, Lark. There's is smoke in air and dogs howl.'

Sudden craving to light a dark. but not here, not now. Wishing for a drink, too, mouth dry.

Nothing for it.

There's no scheme can get me out of this. If Vimbo is going to trust me, which is needed if I'm going to throw down with Elliot and Foulstone and all those dullhead fucks, just have to give in.

Wards spent twenty years building and rebuilding. Wards as much part of me as tattoos. Some have not been dropped in those two decades. Velasquez charmed me - this is *surrender*.

'Need a minute.'

She smiles and tells me take time.

This is like undressing. This is an unwanted, needed intimacy.

Life of meditation is all keeping me calm as the barber's razor kisses my throat.

'We begin,' she says.

Her very gaze is annihilating. Pins me down and flays the untruth from me. Klieg spell eyes cut through dark untruths. Could not more like than could wish myself to death right now. Her mind opens me up like a surgeon opens a patient.

'Say your piece, Lark.'

'*Perfecti Zimbo*. This is my word as a Custodian of the Library. You get the sense for when it's black and black and *black*. Lady,' risk calling her that.

Lay out the case again. Bernadette, her links to Jon and the Temple. She holds my gaze at me with them grey eyes, shining. When I'm done, she and Velasquez look each other in the eye.

Vimbo waves her hand and shows me something. A vision in my head. A memory of something that never laid eyes on.

A sheep on an altar, feet tied together. An Indian guy with dreadlocks and a beard down to his waist, eerie face paint, is in a temple is stroking it's head. Take some time to look at where I'm seeing. The rich colours and arches put me in mind of some Hindu holy place. Statues around it but they are no Gods I know.

A hook above it, set into the roof.

He slits its throat. Watch it kick out for a bit but whoever this cat is knows his business and the hot jet of blood is strong and it doesn't take long to die. He hangs it up on that hook when it's all the way dead and with a curved knife opens up its belly.

This is extispicy. Haruspexy. Divination in the entrails of animals. This is old magic. The position of the organs reveals what's going down. Never tried it myself but pretty sure the bad omen is obvious.

Inside, the sheep's organs are withered. Black. It should not have been alive. The Sadhu recoils. And he belongs to an order that rejects the world and embraces filth. He reaches in and pulls back his hand.

Inside the sheep, coiled up in viscera.

A snake. A dead snake.

The Sadhu lifts its rotted head and bites him, animating real quick. Spit flecks up at his lips. Starts to convulse with a quickness. Falls to his knees, fitting.

The vision ends.

Vimbo's gone.

Velasquez is staring at me.

'We believe you, Lark. There are omens. The man who died from the bite of a dead snake was a seer of considerable insight and look where he is now. All around the world, bad snake omens. You are right. Elliot is wrong. You will be given assurances of our esteem.'

Then.

'We are done, Lark.'

Gather up my wards like gathering up clothes in the shameful light of dawn.

NINE

I

Seems good, right? Upstairs knows my moves are the right moves. Only problem is, upstairs is *upstairs*. Elliot and Foulstone are down with me. And the call to let me do as needs doing is going to *wind them up.*

They can't come at me correct no more but they can come crooked.

Thing is, though... ain't that simple.

I have a note from the doctor.

Didn't go to school on the reg. Bit different in the group homes me and Jon grew up. But one year, some asthmatic glasses kid got out of doing P.E with that excuse. He was a natural born victim. Ugly, spazzy, uncool. Just meat in the zoo. The gym was a crucible for the poor doomed fuck. You know the kind of shit kids do. But this one time, he came in with this note for the teacher. Four forty five minutes, he was safe.

They put him in hospital after school that day.

Certain kind of humans see disobliging their hungers as provoking. Certain kind of human thinks you've gone to authority, they'll come at you like blunt knives.

Got to figure Elliot Everett for the kind of fuck who'll see it that way. And to tell you plan, don't much want to be the kind who has a note anyways.

Resolve to stay off radars.

In my office, finger that amulet Kira made for me.

Get a phone call.

I I

Another dead cult gets passed on to me. Bettina meets me at a
burned out burger joint where they met. Old friers and melted plastic
tables and the stink of ancient grease. Normally, anyways. Right now,
there's blood and the stink of death.

Gloomy Satanic occultists met here. Pentagrams drawn in
carbon soaked walls. Looks like someone burst in on their crucified
monkey rituals and opened fire.

If we do got some occult serial killer, cat's aiming lower each
time.

Killing these guys is beating up babies. No threat to anyone.
No real power. These were one degree over amateurs, not a Typhonian
Grotto or a second Hellfire Club. Oldest person here looks to have been
about twenty five and she's hanging from a ceiling fan. The wards they
had in place were nothing.

Bettina isn't talking to me. But she says, out loud, as if to no
one -

'They came in quick, clubbed two of the cats hard enough to
brain 'em, then stabbed another and slit that one's throat. Then they
hanged the girl.'

Hit gnosis and get psychometric readings. Men with some sort
of distortion on them. Shadowy like. Plays out like Bettina says.

'Stroller priests. These guys. The zoo. Those hippies. Racking
up a body count. We need to keep this quiet, lady. Don't need sorcerers
getting toey.'

Roll over one of the bodies. Blood pours out of the throat and
onto my boots. Teenager with a neck tattoo copped a strike to the face.
Close my eyes against that. Touch his corpse, hand on his chest like
comforting him.

'Lark?'

'Yeah.'

'You ever think maybe you got, like, depression or something?'

'What?'

Phone rings. Take it out but let her finish.

'I been doing this with you four years and I don't even feel emotions like a regular breathing woman. But you been in rooms like this for how long? Fifteen years?'

'Yeah.'

'Do you ever think that maybe it's ...'

'No, I don't.'

Answer the phone without looking.

'Yes?'

'Lark. It's Scarlet.'

I I I

The room and the scent of blood, grease and bodies fall away. Feel like it's some dark chamber now.

We haven't spoken in a long time.

Scarlet.

Distantly aware, somewhere, that my pulse has sped up. The shakes in my hands.

Jesus Christ. I'm *afraid.*

'Lark?'

...

'Yeah.'

'How are you?'

She expect me to actually answer that?

'I... I saw your report on what happened to you last year. I... I know you left a lot out.'

'You figure?'

Kinda surprised can even make that sound, if you want to know.

'Yeah, I do. We can talk about that another time, though. I know you're not going to want to talk about this. Don't hang up. But, let me talk about Elliot for a minute.'

...

'Are you there?'

...

'Lark, please.'

'I'm here.'

'We should meet. We should talk about this properly.'

No fucking way. Need some defences against you, Scarlet and a dinner date with you ain't how they stay strong.

'No, that's... I'm sorry. I shouldn't have asked that. It's just... the phone. Neither of us like it much.'

'Scarlet...' Feel in my voice the sharpness that gets used to let people know they're not important. That they're wasting my time. That lets me slip the coils of goddamn human goddamn beings.

Take it out of my speaking.

'Scarlet. Come on. You have to say something. We both know it's important.'

She goes silent for a while.

'Case File A221A. Go and look it up.'

A221A.

'Why?'

'Just... listen. *Listen*... My loyalties are... This isn't easy for me, Lark. But *listen*.'

'I goddamn *am*.'

'Things on the Executive Council are... they could be going better. Some mistakes are being made. You are not... I know what happened with Upstairs. I know you've got leeway.'

'How do you know?'

'I'm the Secretary of the Executive Council, Lark. I've known Velazquez almost as long as you. These aren't state secrets. We do normal human things. We do coffee. I went to her son's concert. I know for you people vanish if they're not in the life. I do normal human things now too, you be amazed how many Executive do. And normal people gossip.'

Sure.

Say nothing.

'Lark, I'm not taking your side on this. He's my *husband*. Do you understand that? But what he is and what you are... some things he's good at and some things you are. I need you to be good at what you're good at. But he's my *husband*.'

'A221A.'

'Yes.'

'Goodnight, Scarlet.'

'Lark, I.'

Hang up on her. Open my eyes. Did not *even* know that they were closed.

Bettina's staring at me with those black hole lamps of her. Dark as a warhorse.

'Could you hear her talk?'

She nods. Her eyes are calm. She knows how to act.

'She's manipulating me. There's a move she wants made.'

Bettina says nothing.

Nods.

I V

Then she holds up something.

She's found it in a body. While Scarlet spoke she scrounged in bodies and discretely fed. She doesn't want me to know that but there's blood on her breath and her dark hair.

A locket.

Carefully, correctly, open it up.

Wound round and round. A locket of hair. Dark and strong.

Jon's.

Someone knows about me. Someone is motherfucking *playing*.

V

Bettina takes me out for a drink and talks business.

Irish pub and we're drinking Car Bombs. Whisky, cream liquor and Guinness cocktails. These are well named. In the corner, a man plays the usual Irish favourites. *Let's Kill All English Bastards. Nazi Best Friend. My Daughter Is Starving And They Cut Off My Head. In Love With A Corpse. Turn Me Into A Flute.* Don't know the genre, you might say. Not here to dance.

'This is a trap.'

'You think I'm stupid?'

'No, Lark. But let's look at this head on. You're fucked in the head these days.'

'Piss off.'

'You piss off. This is an obvious sting.'

'Yeah. Course it is. They think the lure of Jon is one I won't ignore. And they're right.'

'So don't fucking take it.'

'Of course I'm going to take it.'

'Don't... fuck you, man. Are you stupid these days or something?'

'Bettina. Come on, lady. It's an obvious trap. They know I know. It's a real trap. They just want me to know they don't care if I take it. This is them flexing.'

Besides, if Jon isn't mine quickly, there's a goddess waiting to collect. Don't tell Bettina because she'll just fret at it.

Black wings rush in my head. It's out there. In the dark. Cruel.

Demons thoughts touch on mine, then. The Rabisu doesn't like the goddess. Don't like anything sniffing around me. Has plans for me. Don't like that thought but... not sure how to get out of it.

Knock on the bar. Hold up two fingers. Bartender lines us up. Throw my money on the bar.

'Listen, lady, you told me to be smarter. Not going in *rushed*. Yes. Yes of course I'm moving against these snaky fucks. If it was you they took? Same thing. Come in hard. But. *But*. Doing it smart.'

She looks into my eyes. Searching. Her eyes are dark as open graves and the sclera of her eyes is grey. Her long dark hair frames her face. Near the corners of her eyes, old scars that stand out against her copper skin. Scarred lip. Warrior face. Can't quite call her beautiful, not with a nose been broken and fixed a dozen times. But underneath that, *heart* you can warm your hands on.

'You're not quite playing it straight with me, are you?'

For once, don't have the heart to lie to her.

'Got an idea but it's... no. Not lying. But got an idea and it's not one you'd be pleased with.'

Bettina loves magic.

'Dark and spooky hoodoo?'

'Yeah.'

'*Smart* dark and spooky hoodoo?'

'If it works, it was smart. But sure. I bust this trap open... you fight a guy, fuck up his big power moves. What happens?'

'They get... like... it shakes them. '

'Cool.'

She nods, getting it.

V I

But first.

A221A.

Scarlet's getting me to move one way and that ain't like her. Been a while since she and me were that close but she was never a game player. At least with me. She just came at me straight.

She wants me to find something and she wants me to act on it. And she knows I won't play her.

See what we can see.

Library keeps records of every goddamn thing. All meetings recorded and transcribed and indexed. Once every ten years, auditors from the international headquarters come along and spend a month claiming important docs and records.

Rest it stored offsite. Not actually in the City but north across the bridge out, in a small town called Israel, is where the Library keeps those documents. We've been in the City for just about two hundred years. So, you know, every record, from power bills to what kind of cutlery was used at formal dinners to what the scrying division saw to employment records, add up.

So there's a warehouse where it's kept. Got a staff of document storage specialists.

Alone, nine in the morning. Hungover from those demented Irish cocktails and the sun is shining. Wayfarer shades and coffee from a local joint in a cardboard cup. Pay the cabdriver with Library money. Then onto the storage properties, following a map, walking easy.

Start on a dock, staring at choppy, murky water then start out walking in chasms between anonymous metal warehouses you could store planes in. Huge structures of pure function, rectangular and rusty. Now and again, carts full of dockers and teamsters drive by and men with full beards stare at me. Find the place. Wait a while.

Wait a while and a car pulls up. Out comes Libretto.

Libretto manages the offsite storage.

Sixty year old woman, in a black suit, aviator shades and long white hair in a tail down her back. Takes off those glasses and wolf blue eyes stare at me. All cheekbones and cold blood.

Libretto doesn't much like people who touch her documents. Libretto kind of thinks books and documents are best appreciated in the abstract, rather than having people, you know, *touch her stuff.* Word is she started out tracking down rare books. Then she got into the business of designing private athenaeums for the wealthy. Kinda people who could afford temperature controlled rooms and Lucite cases and lighting and all that, they come to Libretto. Travelled the world, building some spaces that a cat like me would, literally, kill for.

Before walking this way, kinda wanted to do that kinda thing myself.

Libretto is no magician but she knows she works for strange

people. She's a sacred guardian. Empowered and bonded.

'Mr. Lark. It's been a few years.'

She doesn't shake hands.

'Just Lark. How's things been?'

'Quiet. Quiet and uneventful. Which is a fine thing.'

'Not here to change that. Just need to look up a record.'

'Hmmm. You could have requested.'

Say nothing. Just let the sounds off the harbour wash over us.

'Alright.'

She leads me through some alleys of warehouses. Just wandering.This is necessary. Spells that keep the records safe a large and complex ones, reworked over decades and decades.

We walk the path, we walk a labyrinth.

Slowly, feel my body slip away and become unable to remember which way my feet take. Could fight it off but these are defences in place for good goddamn reason. Libretto is the only one who can walk this path and if when she dies or retires, there'll be no way through until she's replaced.

An ugly, dry industrial zone, overlaid with the magic of Inanna and Daedelus. Labyrinths are caveman sorcery, Neanderthal apotropaic. Primal symbol. Walk the maze, tread the winding path, leave the world a step behind you.

There are places like this all around you. If you've the eyes to see them and the taste for mystery. You've probably walked one but never knew.

Come at last to a great security door. No handle, no bolt.

Libretto stops to look at me as regular consciousness roils back into my skull.

Looks me up and down.

Turns her back and says words that cannot be heard by any but her. The door opens. We go in to darkness.

She switches on harsh overhead lights. They wake up slowly, flickering. Hum of electricity starting again.

Rows and rows and stacks and stacks of document boxes, filing cabinets, old computers and racks and arrays of big, big computers. Kinda thing I'd call a mainframe but fuck knows what they're really called. In front of me, rows and rows of mahogany card catalogues.

'Do you have a reference?'

Tell her.

'That's minutes of meetings. Please follow me.'

We walk up a gantry and my hip where Ludo smashed me complains as we go up the narrow stairs. Through grated metal, below I can see bound spirits patrolling the interior maze of shelves.

Libretto opens a series of boxes.

'Have at it.'

'Can't get any closer?'

'Your index number is incomplete. This is as close as I can get you.'

Thumb through for half an hour, painstakingly looking through meetings over the past five years.

It's not all sorcery and dead bodies, this work.

Libretto never takes her eyes off me as my hands carefully return files.

Then. A transcript.

MINUTES

MEETING CALLED BY. TIMEKEEPER. NOTE TAKER. AGENDA. DISCUSSION. CONCLUSION.

Elliot called it. Scarlet took notes.

Then... Bernadette turned up.

TEN

I

*He knows about her. He knows who she is. Elliot is getting in my business
and he's goddamn interfering and he knows he knows he knows.*

II

DATE: Six Months Ago.
S = Cordinatrix Scarlet
E = Senior adept Elliot Everett
B= Unknown adept, 'Bernadette.'

S: We call the meeting to order.

E: Thank you. Now, Ms...

B: Bernadette will be fine, Mr. Everett.

E: A bit of informality. I like it. Call me Elliot. My associate is Scarlet.

B: My understanding is you two are recently married.

E: We are. Coming up on our second anniversay. Is that a problem?

B: No, not at all. Congratulations.

E: Thank you. Thank you, that's kind of you to say.

B: Not at all.

E: Now, my role in the Library is partially... I suppose you'd call
    me Community Outreach. My prep for this meeting vis a vis
    your organisation says that you are looking to incorporate your

organisation, the, er, the Sothic Temple, into the Library.

B: Well. Not quite.

S: Excuse me?

B: Be quiet.

S: Excuse me?

B: No, I'm not here to incorporate. I'm here to take what's yours.

E: Scar?

B: Listen to me. Your organisation worked to cause the death of my father. My father was a great man. A great and terrible man. And at the moment of his ascension, one of your creatures stole his victory, a victory he had worked beyond the scope of your understanding, to achieve. And that means you took mine from me. I'd have become very much like... never mind. And you, you slag, when I had the devil himself on earth, ready to deal, you set that same creature on me.

E: If you mean the Librarian Custode Lark, he no longer works here. I can assure you.

B: You can assure nothing. So I am telling you now, it is swords between us.

S: Elliot, get out of here.

E: What?

B: Be. Quiet.

[UNCLEAR SOUNDS]

E: What?

B: You have choices. Establish me, immediately, as the head of the Library. Put your resources entirely at my disposal. None need know. Or, by God, the serpent will swallow you whole.

E: What is that?

S: [humming]

B: What is that? Grandmother magic? Granny magic! You absurd thing. I can smell him on you. Were you unfaithful to little husband? Oh, punishments are in store.

S: [scream]

E: Oh God, stop! Leave me alone! Take it away!

B: I have work to do. This meeting is at an end. You will pay me money and you will grant me access to books and documents that I require. Then, in time, you will introduce me to the elders of your order. Or I shall bring this serpent back. Am I understood?

E: [crying]

B: Yes?

E: [crying]

[UNCLEAR HISSING SOUND]

E: Yes.

B: And you will keep your creature Lark unaware of this arrangement.

E: Whatever you want. Just please... thank you.

B: You. Slag. Never forget what you saw here today.

S: Get to fuck, you

B: You have a daughter.

S: Shut up. How dare...

B: I dare anything. And you. Christ, stop your snivelling. What you saw was the shadow of the shadow of the reflection of what's coming.

S: You can't...

B: Her name is ...

S: Get her name from out of your mouth don't you dare

E: I can get you the money now. Just leave us

B: Good boy

[Commotion - Door opens. Third voice later identified as former Librarian Senior Custodian, Fellow Mully.]

M: Out, woman. By the Circle of Stars and the ...

B: Later for you. I'll go. But you're not forgotten either, Mully. My father hated you until he died.

M: Out. Or by God, you'll learn what your father learned of me.

TRANSCRIPTION ENDS

III

The graveyards in the City are few and far between. Ground is money and death is not. What use the dignity of our ancestors and a place for us all to meditate on mortality if you can't make a buck off it?

The one we're meeting in tonight is Municipal Calvary. Gated up and now, mainly for the great and the good. Here's where mayors and alderman and uncaught bankers and cats with parks named after them wind up. There's not many simple crosses or markers here. These are tombs. Statues of peaceful angels and great men in frockcoats, lapels held. Vast cruciform shape gathered under the sodium City skies. The occasional, but discrete, Magen David. Patriarchs and Matriarchs of generations.

This ain't no place for musicians and actors and working types. This isn't coarse celebrity. This is one final display of wealth, power, status, from beyond. Willow trees shift easily in autumn breezes and my mind shuts down. Memories of being hunted through a forest by a magician gone mad.

Scarlet used to love cemeteries after dark. We'd come out at midnight, drinking cheap vodka and she'd dance her swamp witch heart out to eerie swamp witch blues. Her in fishnets and shining mini skirts, dancing with her hands in her hair to Big Sexy Noise and Gun Club and Birthday Party. Feedback and black magic. It was her praxis. Bra and hot pants and bodypaint, red head covered in sweat like diamonds. We'd have each other in just this park, up against the cold concrete in the hot summer air, rat and bat for audience.

Good mojo. Strong.

Not here to remind her of that. Here because I never talked about it and can't figure it's the sort of thing she's talking about at fucking cocktail parties.

If she comes.

Put an unlit cigarette in my mouth. Take it out, put it back in the pack.

There's a black hole in my brain.

The rush of cruel black wings.

If she comes.

She's late.

Up against a tomb, kick my foot up behind me and tighten my grey peacoat. Adjust my hood. Unseasonable cold tonight.

Touch Kira's amulet under my shirt.

'Lark.'

She's coming down the curving pathway. Dressed in white. She's cut her hair very short and ... she's blonde now. White suit. White shoes. White hair. White overcoat.

Like a moonbeam in the night.

'I'm sorry I'm late. The kid wouldn't sleep.'

Don't say anything to that.

'Why put me after that file instead of telling me straight?'

She sighs. 'Elliot. We have a truth geas on each other. We're compelled to be honest around each other. But, and do not read into this, there's honest and there's *honest.*'

True enough. Nod.

'So you read the file?'

Nod.

'Come on. Let's sit.'

With two hands she takes me by the arm. It's not romantic and it's not sexual but it's intimate and it makes me feel trapped.

Sit on a park bench. She takes a moment to look around and sighs.

'It's bad, isn't it?'

Nod.

'I've read the file. Tell me about Bernadette, Lark.'

'What's in it for me?'

'What? Seriously?'

'You heard. What's my end?'

'Lark, she wants to kill you. Bernadette wants to *kill you*.'

'Sure.'

'Your end is staying alive.'

'Sure. But that's on me.'

She sighs again but different.

'Here's your end. Lark, Everett, Blossom, even Foulstone... they're *terrified* of Bernadette. Can't say I'm all that relaxed. She walked into the heart of our order and summoned up some devil snake thing that was... horrifying. Our wards were like trying to keep out a hog with a fence made of matchsticks.'

'Those folksy expressions of yours must be a hit with the City boys.'

'These the kinds of games you want to play with me tonight?'

'No.'

'Then shut up and listen. They're afraid. They didn't want you to question that prisoner because they're terrified, and listen, say it three times, terrified, by the notion of you angering Bernadette. Tipping her off. Anything. No one's seen someone of her strength.'

'Sure.'

'We don't have many ways to deal with someone like her. Could bring in assassin... '

'That's Jon. Dunno he's available.'

She frowns at that. Jon was her friend too, though she seems like to have forgot it. Move on, no need to bring pain.

'Scarlet. What do you want with me here? You wanted me to see for yourself that Bernadette has wound up the middle managers and made threats against the family. Fine. But you know... done met her already. Know who she is.'

She leans into me. Warm. Feels good. Feels right. My arm goes around her shoulders on automatic and might as well run up a white flag.

'I want you to do *what you do*. I want you to take her down and ignore what you're told. Elliot is intimidated. He still doesn't really understand what's going on here. He thinks... he just doesn't know. He can't appreciate any of it. All he wanted was to deal with a haunted family mansion. That's why he came to us in the first place. And he's suddenly standing in the presence of archetypal snake things.'

'Just...'

She looks up at me. Her lips go flat.

'Are you sure you want to talk about my family life, Lark?'

'No. Yes. No.'

She sits up straight and turns to look at me. Her green eyes go dark. She leans in closer.

'You read the transcript.'

Say nothing.

'What did Bernadette say to me?'

'*Granny magic.*'

'You know what that is.'

Sure. Folk magic. Kitchen witchery. Magic to find lost keys and cure small diseases. Crop magic. Water divination. It doesn't sound like much but them as don't live in the cities, Cunning Men and Wise Women and to chase away the local bogeys is for real. Might not shake the pillars of heaven but it's nothing to disdain.

She knows I know. She knows I know it was her only real praxis.

'She thought I was nothing, Lark. She treated me with contempt. And listen. *She was right to do it.* When we were together, there was Jon, who could beat up a goddamn house if he wanted to. You, with spirit allies and a mind that could find gnosis in a hurricane and a thousand different ways to use spells. And me. Doing tricks with salt. Making foaling season easier. If I stayed home, if I stayed out there on the bayous, it would be different. My magic would be something. But I didn't, and I wasn't.'

'Alright.'

She leans in closer still to me. Close enough to kiss me. But she doesn't.

Whole world is her eyes.

Never forget that image, moonlight swimming on her lips, no

matter what came after.

'I had *no power*, Lark. Not the way you do. In the Library, I though, have power. And you want to know the truth? I do love Elliot. I do. He's not you and it's not us and he shows you the worst sides of himself but I have a family with him and he's handsome and kind and you really don't see all of him. And he's part of my power in the Library.'

Say nothing.

Yes, Goddamnit, being married to Elliot and the money and connections he brings to the Library? That's part of what makes me an authority. Being senior? I get to *manifest my will*. That's my power.'

Something goes flatline inside me. Was there always this kind of ambition in Scarlet? Did I miss some essential part of her in ten years?

'Bernadette is threatening more than my life. My kid?... You can't know what that's like. But she's threatening my authority and that you can. Being able to ask you to help me? That's my power too.'

And it is. She knows I'm not saying no to her. And that ain't come from money. Stare at her a moment. She's too smart to play this innocent and too good with me to act smart. Just sigh and keep talking, like I already signed on.

'So how's she coming at you? You, personally? If it ain't just the family?'

She looks up at me, emerald eyes dark.

'I have a vision for the Library. I have plans. I know how I want us to be going forward and that's all under attack. Bernadette is scaring the people I need to do things. Messing up my timetables and that stuff. And Lark, listen. Listen. More than anything this: I need Elliot's money and that means staying married to him. I'll never leave him because if I do, the money goes and that's a resource I cannot lose.'

Say nothing for a long while. Then. Tell her true.

'I get you, baby.'

'In your head, Lark, in your head, you're looking for my angle. Fine. Here it is. *That's my angle*. Remember I was honest with you when your scorpion brain looked to sting. And remember one other thing.'

'What's that?'

'Remember who cleared the way for you to bring Jon home. Because...'

Her lips brush against mine. She's a blur of argent. She slides past my defences like a shiv.

'I want him home too.'

Pause for a long while.

'I will try.'

'Of course,' she says to me, her breath hot against my ear. From skull to lap... Kunadlini lightning. Spine serpent moving. 'I knew you would. I'm glad.'

Black wings beat somewhere. Cruel black wings.

I V

The Sothic Temple have Jon. Or know where he is.

The Sothic Temple are dangerous.

The Sothic Temple have baited a trap for me. They know I'll know it's a trap.

They just don't care.

They figure that we'll come anyways. Which means they're confident. Dangerously confident. We spring the trap, but that's their spring on us. They can't see anything we'll bring against them will beat them.

Can't expect much from the Library. Elliot and probably Foulstone just don't want to throw down. Scarlet's wanting me to make moves, though.

She wants thing to happen according to her desires. Just doesn't want the trail to lead to her.

Is this her now?

She's using me. But she knows that I'll get what I want out of it.

And her lips brushed mine.

God damn her.

She's taken me off Elliot's leash. But onto hers.

Bettina won't be pleased. But Scarlet's pointing her hound

where her hound wants to go.

Good enough for me. Good enough for now.

Fuck it. Time to get Jon and sort out these magician killers for good. Maybe tie off a wound.

V

Earlier, though.

The tallest building in the City is called 'The Jupiter'. Ninety nine storeys high. Two banks have their headquarters within. Law firms. Insurance companies. Whitest collars.

Never been inside before.

Closed down for the night but the security doesn't mean much to me and I ghost my way in. Curse the elevator until it forget which keys it needs to work and does what it's told.

Stare at my reflection in the mirrored cab. Camel hair overcoat. Gloves. A hood with fur inside on my head. My doctor's bag.

Rooftop access.

Cold wind hits me. Hence the clothes. Coat caught up in the breeze.

Hands on the balustrade and look over the City, made an otherworld by distance, by darkness. A thousand, thousand lanterns lit and making labyrinths of light. A mechanical answer to night.

Lay out my tools.

Onions and dates to entice it. Cedar, wool, flour. For it to eat. Incense, to show respect for it. Wool, Merino. 11 microns. Expensive. Paid for it myself.

Beautiful swatch of it.

Prepare myself.

One final thing.

Lighter fluid. Burn the wool.

I need power. I need strength. And I need it from something that has run from me.

I need the Rabisu. It hates me. It does. But it will come. It is always waiting for a way back in. Told you it wanted me. Now it has to invest in my protection. No one gets me but it.

And from somewhere distant. Somewhere dark. Somewhere soft and somewhere the rot has set in...

...*dark wings start to beat.*

VI

ARE YOU ALRIGHT

Karel's note is written in a shaky hand. He's nervous. He can feel it in me but he doesn't know what he's looking at.

It inside me. The Rabisu. Not possessing me but inside my head, ritually invoked. It roils and it claws. It is obedient but only just. Amused. One day it will come back. Can feel it. Staring. It finds the ruin it made in my skull... enticing.

It has supped well on what was given it and is curious about my intentions.

We're in the back of Aristide's hearse. Glance in the window. Face like strung out junkie.

Nod at him. He shakes his head at me, unbelieving.

YOU LOOK SICK

Say nothing.

Sasha isn't here. Don't trust her with this work. Figure she's been talking where she shouldn'ta been talking and can't see her use in a throwdown.

Sothic Temple has moved from the place me and Bettina scouted before. Or that was only ever just a satellite or something. Doesn't matter. The hair they left has lead us right here. Jon has spent a lot of time where we're going.

So fucking confident they'll take me they're inviting me to their sanctums. That hair they left me, the invitation into the trap, leading me. Sympathetic magic, like to like. It belongs to Jon and will lead me to him. He's unwarded himself to make it easier for me. Or someone else did it for him.

They know we're coming. They think they're ready.

Thinking about the action makes the Rabisu inside me writhe. It is suffering indignities but at least it will be free, soon. If it has allegiance to Bernadette, as it paid allegiance to her father, I won't know until it's too late. A risk is being taken.

Pull up a few blocks before the Temple.

'You know what to do?'

Karel nods. Pulls a hood over his face. Albino, even the lights of the car get to him . We drop him to the east of the Temple at a crossroads. He'll be using *szeptem*, Polish whisper magic. He'll be throwing curses down the wind at the Temple, keeping them off guard, heightening tensions in our ambushers. Bad luck weaponised.

A block or two closer. Pull in. Me, Bettina, Aristide. They kiss. Aristide looks at me once. Holding my gaze. He's expecting me to have her back. Hold that stare. Sometimes this *my woman* bullshit gets too much.

He'll be off somewhere skulking. He's not helping the raid. He's there for me in case shit goes badly wrong and what's inside me gets out of control. Can't handle it alone. Kongo packets in his pockets.

Bettina and me, we get to it.

V I I

Cults.

They're everywhere. You say that word and people think of compounds out in the bush, weird houses at the edge of town and, sure, that's real. That happens. But there's slim pickings out there. You want a fresh supply of new recruits and recruits with a bit of cash you can siphon… you want to be in a city. They sound cool. *Nixium. The Light Congregation. Sothic Temple.*

People in cults say they care about you and tell you God or whoever is looking out for you. Or it comes in the form of a marketing thing or offbeat seminars or a regular church but with a shine or… there's a hundred different ways to join a cult. Some cults are even straight up about what they are, be in sex, money or magic.

And some, not many, but some, know how to be slick.

Sothic Temple is calling itself *Sirius Solutions*.

Executive Solutions. That's what it says on the sign outside.

Tudor-Gothic building. More at home in a Frankenstein movie than in the City. Behind the gate, stairs lead up and around the four storeys. Long tall windows in rows and a peaked roof. The stones that make it are large and heavy and dark grey. Damn thing seems to loom. Or maybe squat. Can't quite decide. It's big but seems somehow... bulbous.

Would have been built in the 1910s. Find out later, by a mad French architect, killed his wife and kids here. No surprise, really. This is the kinda place that business would go down.

Gate is locked but Bettina's fists make quick work of that.

Lights on inside. Invitations.

Up those broad stairs to a door. Unlocked.

'You remember the word?'

My off-switch. Vital she remembers. 'Yes.'

What's inside me stops stirring and pays attention. Something it perceives as important in this place.

Storming the gates? Seems unwise. But straight up, there's no way to avoid the traps they so obviously prepared. Not without weeks of planning and Operations.

Nod at Bettina. She takes a step back. Sidekicks the door. Huge rush of noise and motion as the door goes flying off its hinge, taking doorframe with it.

In an atrium, waiting for us, six figures in ... not robes.

Wreathed in *shadows*.

And Jon.

ELEVEN

I

Jon is on a cane he slumps on. Etiolated. Shark vertebrae. Used to be mine a long time back.

His once dark brown skin looks grey. His hair, once so carefully cut and styled, hangs down to his shoulders and streaks of grey run through it. We're the same age and he looks to have thirty on me. On his face, scars from where the mask once rested. Under his eyes like tear tracks.

Eyes that stare at us with calm, clear hate.

How did it come to this?

'You. I remember you. We fought before you took the Teaching Darkness from me. You were good.'

That's for Bettina. She looks over him carefully.

'You look like you're a fucking dead man. And I know from that shit.'

He sneers at her. Never seen him do that before. His was a mouthful of whites he'd flash anyone. Never soft but he was, no doubt, the good cop on our team.

'Jon.'

He looks at me.

'What?'

'These people... they'll...'

'What?! What will they do?!'

Fury in him.

'You let the mask take me and helped keep it away from me.'

'Jon, you put the fucking thing on yourself. And you're free now. Did my part. You want it back now? Nothing to do with me.'

'Where is it?'

'Don't know where the mask is.' *Black hole in my brain.* 'Can barely remember how we got it off you. Things are... hazy.'

He says nothing to me but can tell he can relate to that. There's wounds enough to go around.

'Bernadette. She's fucking *diseased*, Jon. Dunno what her game is. Not for sure. But she's been looking for an alliance with some high dark powers for a real long time.'

'Lark. Stop.'

Say nothing.

'But Bernadette is going to fix me up. Help me. Where's the Library for me? It threw me aside and now the only one looking out for me is *her.*'

'The fuck am I doing here, then?'

He goes silent at that. The shadowy figures next to him are growing impatient. Not here for a reunion of old friends.

When Jon talks, it's the final tick of a dying clock. Final judgements.

'I choose her, over you. I choose what Bernadette can give me. A body. Health.'

This isn't how Jon talks. He's just reciting a script someone else wrote for him.

Shake my head.

'Don't believe you.'

'Lark. Oh yeah. Lark. I know, now. She hates you. You have to die here. Tonight. Be thankful it's me, man. I can make it quick.'

Something inside me withers like a flower in heatwave.

'That's how it is?'

He takes a moment. Nods his head.

'Yeah.' Almost a whisper.

'Jon. Does she know my name?'

'...no.'

Which maybe means his betrayal isn't *total*. Bernadette knows my real name? It's over.

'Do you remember it?'

Wiped it out long ago to all but those who wish me well.

He doesn't respond. He doesn't remember.

His good will is burned up like a cigarette and that it doesn't matter if he wanted to serve me up or held on to some... some... *vestigial* loyalty.

'You choose her?'

Says nothing to me. Eyes lower. He nods.

And something inside me gets carried away by desiccating winds.

He turns away.

'Kill them.'

The shadowy men move in.

Say the word. Bettina moves from me real quick like she was told. The sound finishes the ritual started up on The Jupiter.

And inside me, invoked into my body, the Rabisu *howls*.

I I

Can't rightly tell you what happened next. It's like remembering a black out.

Invocation is the act of allowing an entity into your physical body. Often gods, sometimes spirits. Normally, it is an act of worship. You allow a spiritual entity within you so others can interact with it. Give it an anchor to the physical world and it can be worshiped, act as an oracle.

Or in this case, kill a bunch of motherfuckers.

What's remembered is images through a keyhole. Childhood nightmares that stay with you, that you cannot shake. Fever recollections. Blackout drunk reminders. Strobe light illumination hallucination.

The men Jon has bought, they are all men, are bound about with spells to make them unreal. Perhaps they're actually astral bodies developed over long periods of time to become almost real. Who fucking cares?

Because the Rabisu fucking hates me, but we're linked. It killed me. Died at its shadowy claws. We're *linked*, like it or not. It's amphibious, half real now, half magical, half imaginary.

It twists me. Reshapes me.

Memory blocks pain but sometimes, can still feel the torsion in my wrists, spine, as it reformed me, made me fit for purpose.

Rabisu are ancient. One of the oldest demons our species encountered or created. Alone against disease and the defects our of grey meat brains, we shaped entities like it at the genesis of our civilisation to explain illness.

Hands turned, claws rip at shadowy men. Strings of darkness like mud, like molasses, like thick saliva, pulled away from their bodies. Spells prepared for hours, days, to render Lark to imbecility mean nothing to the Rabisu, an entirely different order of life than mere humanity. Arrows off a dragon's hide. Later, Bettina tells me they tried new tactics that made me bellow and scream like a lion drowning in petrol but Karel's bad luck whispers meant they could not easily change tactic.

Scraps of images of memories. Forcing shadow into my mouth, jaws extended and lubricated with darkness. *Rending,* fists balled to spread ribcages. The sick sensation of fingers crunching beneath mandibles gone wild. The vast sensation of wings forming at my back, a reticulated tail, strangling the life from some poor bastard.

And underneath it all... overlapping it all... the dark sense of triumph. The absolute and profound joy of *ruin.* How beautiful the mangled bodies of humanity are to the Rabisu. How much joy it takes in our pain and degradation.

Bettina has another word. My off-switch. She tells me she had to say it five times. The Rabisu was not keen on releasing my body.

Came to in a pool of shadows and five dead bodies. Their

essence fades, water on a hot white concrete.

'Shit.' Grab at some of it. Close an aching fist around it.

Stumble. Fall. Exhausted.

She helps me stand.

Look over the bodies. Not gouged and mangled like lions but their faces contorted in horror. Stripped of defences and bodies… they were not prepared for what they faced. They died ugly.

'Jon?'

'Went for him but he just vanished when I got him. Slid away.'

Keep two hands around the shadow.

'Not your fault, B. He might not even have been here in his body.'

'Sure. What do you want to do?'

This would be a real good time for a bit of therapeutic vandalism but… feel like someone goddamn stomped every inch of me. And have to perform the rites of banishment on the Rabisu properly. Bettina's word ended the invocation but the rite has to be more ceremonially closed.

Could have used a prisoner.

Not rightly ready to do much but get so drunk that this memory gets a scratchy as the rest of tonight.

Oh, Jon.

III

Sleep uneasily. Toss and turn on a couch. Wake up, dry mouthed and eyes straining. Allergen nightmares. Rabisu is gone from me but can feel it out there. It lingers over the memories of its kill, a cat keeping a rat alive for a long, long time. Feels my unease and purrs pleasure at me. It disdains me entirely.

Shadows.

Get up and walk naked to my desk, darkness heavy in the huge room. Switch on a lamp and open a book.

Shadows.

Ancient Egyptian souls were divided into pieces.

Jib, the heart.

Ren, the name.

Ba, the personality.

Ka, the animating force.

Ahk, the... intellect.

And Sheut. The shadow you make. Your visible soul.

The Rabisu tore their souls up like a cat with a mouse. Their bas and kas. Can feel *that*. If there is an afterlife, they will go to it hideously wounded. Their deaths were... appalling indignities. They were maimed in ways no human thing should be.

The demon thing understands my understanding. And breaks the connection with me, leaving me alone with the knowledge. It's amusement is the cruellest thing I have ever experienced. It's greatest pleasure is atrocity.

And I'm complicit in feedings its vile joys.

I V

Sometime last night in my illness, stashed the shadow stuff of the Sothists. There's a 17th century book *Saducismus Triumphatus, or Full and Plain Evidence concerning Witches and Apparitions*. Triumph of the Sadducees in English. Those priests who refused to believe Jesus was the boss.

I lifted this next spell from that book.

You see me making this stuff up, you don't see reading, reading, reading. It's a good, as happens. You should read it.

While I've got the blood of Bernadette's cultists under my fingers and their death screams fresh in my ears and the ragged ribbons of their shadow soul in my mouth... time to scry myself.

Take a bottle, called a Bellarmine, named after an Inquisitor. Stoneware, which meant I had to make it myself, which meant an evening at a pottery class taught by a man with a caftan which... we don't need to go in to. Then you've to fill it up with your wife's piss. Which meant for me, an embarrassing conversation with Katanya, who was the last woman who had the misfortune of sleeping with me. (Yeah, it's been a while.) She's a pro and understood and just came back with it, no questions asked. Owe her one.

Fill that up with pins, needles, your fingernails, wine, that stuff. Have to bury it to finish it and it'll protect you.

Poured the shadow in. The torn fragments of the Sothic sorcerers souls. Their blood. Their scream. Supposed to bury it but I'm underground here anyways. It's already buried.

Lift it up to the light.

Part of the essential human... soul. Captured.

Take it. Open the bottle. Breathe in. The shadow flows into my nose and mouth like opium.

Memories come through me. Surgeries. Klieg lights. Scalpels. Medical magic.

You'll find out what else I saw real soon. Don't want to repeat it.

Phone goes off.

'Yeah.'

'Meeting. Eight.'

'Fuck off.'

'Come in.'

Katanya hangs up.

Had the *fuck* enough of meetings.

V

Before Elliot tries his latest play against me, let me tell it straight - I tried to do the right thing.

Listened to Sasha. Listened to Bettina. Listened to Scarlet and Mully. They were right. *Do* have to play the game better. *Do* have to humor these money men. These Philistines, these goddamn ignorant sons of bitches. *Do* have to keep them off my back if nothing else.

But listen. Listen. There's only so far you can go. There's only so much you can take before good advice is just ghosts.

These boardrooms and these formalities and the judgement of

people whose opinions are as valuable as spittle… they test me. They bore me. The banality of it makes my bones ache and, in the end… just… not good at playing along.

You might think, *Jesus man, just cope.*

Can't. Won't.

No difference.

Watch this, though. This could have gone better.

Elliot. Tan suit and black shirt on. His idea of informal. Wedding ring polished. Slicked back hair freshly cut.

Scarlet with him. Black turtleneck. Grey pants. Broach and bracelet. She looks like a suburban mother at a fundraiser. Part of me hates her for it.

Sour part of me. Don't like it much but if you and me can't be honest with each other, why are we even here?

Elliot takes a deep breath. Blows it out again. Theatre.

'Lark.'

Say nothing.

'We have reports from last night. '

Say nothing.

Puts his face in his hands. Washes them off.

'You disobeyed a direct order. To leave the Temple alone.'

Let my eyes flick away and back. He's smart, he'll see it for impatience.

'Lark. I have to dismiss you. I might have to fire your juniors. Bettina's gone too. Scarlet is here because she's…'

'No.'

… see?

'Excuse me?'

'You bought Scarlet here to show her you've got power over me and so you knew she'd see me fall. Not fire a dipshit employee. But here's the thing - not going anywhere.'

'I have authority -'

Slam my hand on the table.

'You've got nothing. You're in the position you're in because you're useful but that's it. Do you know what I saw last night? What I did? What I *will do* for the Library? You want to push me, motherfucker?'

Keep my voice calm as can, but there's something in it that sounds cold as untouched knives. Keep going while it's on me. Lift up a hand and point to him.

'Time you got a look at what your people do. Time you saw something that your wife and your cronies protected you from all this time.'

'Lark...' Scarlet's legit worried what my play is.

She put her lips to my lips and thought that would keep me at bay. Keep my chain secured.

Point at Elliot. At his head. At his heart.

'Stop!'

Too late. *Too late for you.* Suddenly, the hate burns away from me. He's terrified. Trying to pull out of his chair. This is the sadist trip. This is me using power over a man who ... maybe doesn't deserve it.

Even so.

Gun finger.

Shoot it.

Let me deal with Elliot.

Memories flood into him.

Bernadette. His eyes go flat. Here's what I learned from the Bellarmine ritual.

She's in an operating theatre, masked and robed like a surgeon.

Six men laid out in front of her. Antique lamps overhead, the light enchanted and a searing the shadows off them. *Melting* the sheut into something malleable. She takes the scalpel, blessed and Worked, from some concoction that surely is not alcohol.

She carves the shadows from them and they scream. Watching through eyes as their lodge-brothers wail. Knowing they're giving up something essential. Vital. Shrieking and knowing, knowing, *knowing...* they're next and no matter what's promised, can it be worth the pain?

That's what she's doing. Mutilating souls for her own ends. Making humans into messy, massacred slaves.

Let it fade.

Give him a moment. Then.

'Elliot. That's who Bernadette is. You give way to her, she'll do worse. You can't feed the wolf and hope it gets full. She...' takes a second to find the word.

'She *despoiled* those men. She'll do worse if she can. You think I'm some low scum? You're right. Ain't like you. Never will be. But you need me because there's lower scum. Her plans aren't even started yet. She's been looking for an alliance with something terrible and she's been doing it for a long, long time. She's broken cover. *I think she has it.*'

His eyes are wild.

'Leave me the fuck alone, Lark. Do you understand? Do you fucking *understand?*'

He looks to Sc- he looks to his wife. She takes his hand.

'Baby, let's... just... Elliot, let Lark be. He's not wrong.'

She takes his head in her hands and stares into his face. Clearly, she's calmed him before. Granny magic. Like was said, don't disdain it.

He nods. It takes him a while but he nods. Kisses her on the forehead. Turns to me.

'Kill her if you can.'

Get up and walk out.

Turn to look back which, anyone knows anything, is never a smart move. Scarlet has her arm around him as he puts his face in his palms. Shaking. He's seen men wounded in ways he never knew they could be.

He's felt the *tremendum.* Maybe for the first time, the reality of his life is kicking in.

Elliot doesn't know it yet but... did him a favour. They threw him in then told him to ignore the shark fins cutting through the water.

His family is threatened and now he knows by who. Bernadette's a torturer, her own two hands wrist deep in pain. Now he knows that the world is filled with snakes and those snakes *bite.*

Scarlet looks up at me.

Smiles.

Someone's getting what they want at least.

VI

Need to talk some things over. Not Bettina. She'd be sensible and don't need sensible. Mully? No. Katanya keeps her distance. Only got one other friend.

TWELVE

I

i.

FROM his brimstone bed at break of day
  A walking the devil is gone,
To visit his snug little farm the earth,
  And see how his stock goes on.

ii.

Over the hill and over the dale,
  And he went over the plain,
And backward and forward he switched his long tail
  As a gentleman switches his cane.

iii.

And how then was the devil drest?
  Oh! he was in his Sunday's best:
His jacket was red and his breeches were blue,
  And there was a hole where the tail came through.

ib.

He saw a lawyer killing a viper
  On a dung hill hard by his own stable;
And the devil smiled, for it put him in mind

Of Cain and his brother Abel.

II

But the Devil doesn't come when called. Not by me at least, not now. Seems I overestimated my friendship with him. Figured he'd like that poem.

The Rabisu sneers.

III

Me and Bettina are going to an island. We are seeking out Bernadette's surgeries. The Bellarmine vision was clear.

This was a proper Sothic Temple project. *Something's* gonna shake loose here.

The runabout we hired is slow and the spray is chill against us. Winter will be here in two weeks and this oily water is cheerless and stings. The City sits on a bay. You can drive north but to the south, great docks. The mainland is an hour away over choppy, dirty water.

In the water, likes flecks of spittle on a madman's mouth, are islands. One is converted to rich type's private residence, splendid lonely mansions watching us with window eyes. One, a nature reserve. Another, a military base.

But we're heading to Black's Islet. On it, a Gothic lighthouse, disused for a century.

And an asylum.

When immigration got going seriously in about 1870, the City was briefly obsessed with the filth and disease newcomers were supposed to bring. Despite the fact cholera and typhus were already rampant. So any motherfucker so much as coughed spent a few months in the *Tarrant Sykhus* as they asylum's called. Not sure why it's in Swedish or Norwegian or whatever.

The mad, the ill and, eventually, the unwanted, they were

thrown into the vast house and left to recover from sickness or die. The mad were locked in cells to howl and dig the maggots from under their skin. Those who survived were sent by steam screw boats with no money and no way to contact friends and relatives, if they had them, if they were alive. The bodies soon stacked up.

WWII rolls around and it was shut down. Turned into a munitions dump. Eventually a Lord Mayor did a deal with fascists and sold the weapons and shells and rounds to blackshirt sympathisers who, literally on the same day as they took possession, declared war on the Country.

Ghost Hunters and bored teens and torture freaks are all who comes here and not many of those. Island's remote and they shut down all entry in the 60s when someone figured out diseases had stained the rocks and foundations of the Sykhus. Outbreaks of the likes of Scarlet Fever were linked to people who had been out this way.

Step off the ramp and onto the island. My hip aches in the cold.

Grey skies above, grey water below. Grey grass and bare rock.

Looming to the East, the lighthouse. Four storeys, a bare stone tower. Iron doors chained and rusted shut. To the west, a pathway of cobblestones, barely visible under creeping, sharp glass. We walk up the incline to the long since destroyed spiked iron fence. Beyond it, the asylum. Three storeys high. Grey again, as if camouflaged and patient as a mantis. A peaked roof in the centre, spreading out into three wings.

Got memories of madhouses, though not of this kind. My mother, twisted into sadism by her madness and the horror of visiting and the sour stink of madness.

Put that aside. Force that down.

Take a quick walk around. Looking. Rusted maintenance shed. Overgrown gardens.

Graveyard behind and old fence rusted through. Wooden gravestones, long since turned pulp and disintegrated by time, salt water air, raid.

This is Bernadette's hospital. This is where she took Jon.

This wasn't a place we were supposed to find. The Temple

overplayed their hand with that trap. They didn't know I could work *with* the Rabisu. They couldn't know this place could get made.

This is where she ripped men's souls from them and wrapped them all around with them like cloaks.

This is where committed horrendous crimes against the human soul.

The door is open.

The jaw is open.

'Let's get this done with.'

I V

You know what these places look like. Peeling wallpaper and strewn about furniture. Swastikas and racial slurs spray painted wildly on walls and cocks as well. Overwhelming stink of mildew. Leaked water puddles in hallways stinking of stagnancy and midges. Offices ransacked and beds overturned, used by the adventurous, desperate and sad for some sadcase rutting to brag to friends about. We're both in overcoats. We're not new to this. Our footprints are loud.

We walk together without much of a destination. Just scouting. Bettina turns a corner and murmurs. Look where she is. On the walls, a spray painted *serpent*, something might well be a sun in jaws, fangs piercing it.

Touch it in gnosis.

Yes. It has some juice. Warding.

Take a second to study it. It's like a mazing ward. Walk past it and we'll wander around her for hours till we make the choice to leave, then it'll let us go. Enchanted cat will just remember being annoyed, frustrated, lost.

Probably set off an alarm as well. Maybe to Bernadette, maybe to a Sothic cultist.

Deactivate the ward. Well, more accurately, get it to ignore us. Stare into the serpent's eyes, painted with carious slashes of red. Shoot null information into it, working with it, not against it.

We're rats, we're children, we're shadows, we're nothing for you to notice.
Draw stick figures of us on the walls in the grime. Rub us out with the
blade of my hand. Magic is done by *doing* magic. It is performative. The
actions matter less than the matter of action.

Sure, maybe you can do better art than the mass of stupid
shapes you see on some modern painting. But you *didn't* do it, did you?
That's art. That's magic.

The ward remains asleep.

We open up wards to see rows of gurneys overturned.
Necromantic information simmers here. Want to talk to a ghost, just
open your mouth and will it. Hundreds of spectres loom and whirl in
the ether. Scrawny victims of plague, sere, grey maniacs.

Generations of the mad and diseased felt it, this storm of spirits.
Graffiti on the walls is of skeletons dancing, shagging, screaming.
Mouths with rotten teeth. Someone's drawn a biohazard and it's leaked
like tears, melted. Broken and smashed hearts done in infection greens
and yellows.

Bettina purrs.

'Feeling... juiced up.'

'No doubt. You don't eat dead flesh cause you need enzymes or
some shit. You eat death. It's lingering.'

'Tell Aristide about this joint, he's gonna wanna move here.'

'Honeymoon at least.'

She pffts derision. 'He's gonna have to work harder, he wants to
lock this down.' Pats her rock hard stomach.

'He doesn't, he's a head fulla rocks.'

'Sweet talker, you.'

Move on. Staff rooms. Bodies of rats in here stink the joint up
and we leave it.

Then, finally. Bettina breathes in deep through her nose.

'This way.'

Leads us up a stairwell. Rotten wood under our feet. Feels like
walking on clinging mud. Pulps spills out under boot treads like pus
from infections.

Top of the stairs, some lunatic totem, a screaming man with a mouth bigger than his head. Smaller figures under it suck what you'd call his dick, but only if you were in hell.

Up to the second level and the graffiti lessens some. A grate is pulled across the hallway and locked. With new chains. They stand out against the grim rust of the gate.

Go out the hallway and into a private room. Looks like a guard's station. Must have been truncheons here once. Still a cage like helmet here. Rat piss stink.

Move through this station and onto the floor. This is where they kept the mad and the sick, all chained up to beds. They gurney are all knocked over, the beds soaked through. The mildew stink is overwhelming. But my shirt over my nose.

More dead rats on the floor. Half eaten. Skeletons of them, look brutalised. Written on a wall in what must surely be fingernail scratches: GOD PLEASE TURN AWAY. Someone's painted with a brush what seems to wolf head, jaws open, Christian cross coming up from its mouth. Someone's nailed a straightjacket, rotted through, to a wall. Smashed stethoscope on the ground. Children's underpants.

Sudden thought intrudes. That this is the kind of place Scarlet loved to explore. Force it the fuck out.

Then. Down one last corridor, a door marked THEATRE.

V

This is the room from the Bellarmine vision, sure as sure.

Bluish tinge to the tiles. Guernsey with dirty sheets on it. Lamp, anchored to the roof, some burnt out bulbs in it. Fresh and not so fresh blood on the ground. Rising above us, in lazy ovals, five rows of seats. This is a teaching place. Back in the day, you open a body up, demonstrate your skill, let the good students watch.

Know what kind of operations go on a hundred plus years ago in an insane asylum? Standard lobotomies twice a day. Sometimes they'd cut out brain tumours like kids with knives, hacking before they knew as they were doing. Experiments on glands and shit. Long spikes through the eye, carefully sliding up into the brainpan.

For women, shit was a lot worse. Pregnant, not pregnant, angry, homo, love your children too much, not enough, lighting in the brain and the guts taken out of you.

In rooms like this, people watched that torturous shit go down. And here's the thing. *They figured they were helping.*

As if to prove some goddamned point, there's a tray by the gurney. Antique surgical equipment. Radiating magical information. Whatever surgeons worked here recent, they wanted to resonance of antique butchery.

Rifle through the tools. Scissors, syringes made of metal, eared liked a dog. Knives, forceps, shit that looks like ice cream scoops and ice pick and *who knows?* Hand hovering over them, fever dreams of open brains and surgery before anaesthetic. Men and women ethered, waking up with their skulls opened and dirty fingers trailing through grey meat.

They're prepped somewhere else though. These victims. Can feel their *...unlucidity.*

Chalk from my jacket pocket. Carry it a lot.

Draw a circle around the gurney. Mark the Four Directions.

Bettina watches closely. She loves this stuff.

Step inside.

"Cast thy Eyes round about thee, and enter into the inside of Things, and with a silent distinguishing Thought, and earnest sedate Meditation, and Contemplation, behold the wonderful Operations of the serene silent magick Powers of the Coelestials, and also of the Terrestials..."

Null thought zone. Narrowing the field of gnosis and shuffling through time like cards.

Need to see.

Watch. Just the last few months.

Men in full Egyptian ritual magic panoply in this room.

It's not like tv. More that you get memories of being here, watched it, even though you weren't.

Yeah, there's that fucking child murdering motherfucker Elliot made me let go. What was his name?

Black hole in my brain.

William. Right? Anyways. In comes a tramp, tied up, too tired and sick to resist. Start up the mystic surgery. It goes wrong more than once. Took them a while to get it right. Sometimes Bernadette watches from that ring of seats.

They take the soul, the essential patterns of information that make up human identity. Take it out. Try to... *invert?* it.

They do it a lot. More than a dozen people died in this room the last month.

Watch them get better and...

They got to a certain...

'Bettina. I can... see...'

Information goes wrong. Gets loose. Lossy. Fuzzed. An old VHS tape rewound too much.

Something hazy. Something. The... feel the serene silence wrap myself in to do this work get compromised. At least one went wrong. Turned into something bad. They had to strangle a woman to death on the table.

There's shadowy figures watching. Like silhouettes. Magicians, warded, protected. Overseeing. Get closer to them. Start to chant to myself, asking spirits and gods for more power. To break those wards and *see* who was here.

The shadowy forms start to waver and then... as if they saw me, they turn to stare.

Shit. Shit! I've made a mistake. Too much power, too much magic, in a place of suffering and death. It's like it... broadcasts from this room, breaking out of the circle. Into the psychosphere of the hospital. Think of it like feedback whining. Whining. Loud. Waking.

Things.

Up.

Shit.

'Bettina, get ready.'

They figured someone like me would come. Someone who could see.

'Something's fucking coming.'

Downstairs. Ghosts. Woken up. Woken up confused and angry. Scenting blood in the ether.

They're sharks and I'm the chum.

V I

Ancient Egypt was afraid of spiritual monsters and they were afraid of the spirits of the dead. Mummification? That shit's a technology used to deal with an afterlife that's hard on people don't die *correct*. A ghost was a dude with problems, man.

Ruined tombs, unfaithful inheritors. Or *wooden gravestones, long since turned pulp and disintegrated by time, salt water air, raid.*

'Bettina. Step into the circle.'

'No.'

'The fuck, woman? Army of -'

Howling. Surging. Screaming. Shrieking. They're coming.

'I know.'

Moving quickly. There's a form of modern magic called Zar, got roots in Ancient Egyptian magic but it needs tool and equipment. Also, be honest, don't know enough to use it.

Run through ghost protection technique in my head. Too slow! Thinking too slow! *Black hole!*

Stop. Take a breath.

Yantra. Indian magic. Yantra means machine. Sorcerous diagram with strict values attached.

Get to drawing it sharpish.

'Bettina, get in.'

Drawing fast as can. Throw the gurney out the circle.

Draw a triangle within. Each point, a swastika. Don't have to explain that ain't Nazi shit, do I?

Howling gets louder. Roil of ghosts coming. Quick. Fuck fuck.

'Get in.'

Shit shit there's some Devanagari text that...

No time. No time! *No time!*

Pocket knife. Stick the blade into palm. Pain is a way to enter into gnosis and the panic rising up in me is making that hard.

'Bettina. Now!'

She's ignoring me. Maybe there's something riding her. Something distracting her. Reach out to grab her, pull her in. But she don't want to move and, best day of my life, couldn't overpower her on her worst.

Doors fly open. Two dozen ghosts. Hazy, fucked up, barely real. The echoes of once was human life. Lobotomised and wounded and abused. Sufferers of theories that were tested on victimisable flesh.

Lured to me. To possess me and take out what they suffered on me. They get into my body, Bettina's too, well, we won't enjoy the rest of our afternoon.

But they will.

Bettina though. Scream at her to get in the *goddamn fucking circle!*

Ghosts surge around her. Can't do anything. Yelping, biting, clawing. Some grab her. Lose sight of her.

Oh Christ oh no.

Stab my hand hard.

They hit the protective circle *hard*. Huge waves of pain crashing against my body. Can't help her. *I can't help my friend.* Listen to my voice as it screams mantras and chants and formulations against the dead.

Inside. Falling to ash.

Bettina.

Oh no.

I

can't

without

you

The ghosts shriek.

They whirl of them, the stir and mixtures and howling of them gets frenzied, a mist gone mad. They stop their attacks on my protection.

But it ain't nothing from I've done chasing them off. Just trying to get through this. Scope the scene.

Through the fog, Bettina grabs at ghosts. They're as flesh in her hands. She breathes them in like tobacco, like PCP smoke. She snatches them with fists and licks it up like ... spun sugar.

Ghosts figure out what's happening. Scream in horror. *What?*

Takes a second to figure it.

They're trying to run but they're compelled to be here. Too much pain here, too many memories for them to leave. They *can't* high tail it. But they're in a cage with a wolf who eats their kind. The panic of the dead is a pitiful fuckin' thing.

Bettina's black eye is wild and lambent with power.

Could try to break the spells, free the ghosts. But one time, took Bettina's eye.

Sorry ghosts, but she's owed a feast. Watch as she gluts herself, smacking lips as the last one goes down.

Sorry.

'You told me you did this once. Ate spirits.'

She's telling it true. Ate a sick tulpa in the form of a fly. Didn't make me as strong as this made her.

I'm so tired. The black hole in my brain... it responsible for me fucking up the rite back there? Who knows.

'How is this even happening?'

She shrugs. 'Been dead a while now. My partner is you. My boyfriend is a death houngan. There's strength in me, Lark. I'm ... not a queen of... necromancy, like. But ain't a dabbler. Not no more. Aristide is gonna fucking *freak the geek* out.'

Sure he is. Cos his girlfriend ain't no zombie no more. She's something... more. He's gonna dig this cos I got a feeling he's turning his fetish into a relationship and his relationship into a weapon.

And she's a weapon now.

'Oh. Yeah.'

She smiles at me again.

'It was Foulstone set this up. Recognised him from the ghost's memories. That's your shadowy figures. Fat boy's a traitor.'

THIRTEEN

I

Day or two later. Going through reports. A werewolf cult dead. Bernadette's not finished. Three suicides should look into. Cleopatra style, locking themselves in with snakes. Investigate like it's nothing big but just waiting to make my next move.

Foulstone's files.

Already know he's gifted with ghosts. Like, *real* gifted. Should have been a hint.

He's actually Rhodesian. Moved to England with his family as a kid. Dad gambled all that sweet imperial money away. Killed himself when the boy was just ten. Mum remarries to some wideboy. Wideboy has himself a court magician. Foulstone learns from court magician. Realises he has a gift for necromancy after torturing his old man's ghost.

Scarlet's taken a bit of a risk to breach security getting me these notes.

Ghosts are handy for crimes. Used to consult with gangsters myself when first left the Library. People talking after their dead alone. So with that skill under the belt, Foulstone began to make money for himself.

Didn't get ideas above his station. Stayed as advisor. Studied. Got stronger. Mastered the Endiku ghosts that became his trademark. And that bought him to the attention of a London Libray chapterhouse.

Thing is though... this is reading between lines now... Foulstone learned how to politic in a world where a wrong word, a hurt feeling, a regulation fuck up that ain't even your fault, leaves you with a cut throat. Ten years, he sat up high.

So why'd he come to the City and fuck up my action when first run into the Devil?

Foulstone had a bad habit of cornering young adepts. Young women adepts. 'I can help you out here, love. Come to my sanctum.'

He gets caught out. Half a dozen good prospects, women and girls the Library could have *used*, left the order or their practice entirely. Just because of him.

Stupid fuck.

Cat like that? He has dirt. He's owed favours. He gets transferred here and by then, he's great with the dirty tricks. If there's dirt on Elliot, he has it. Dirt on Velasquez, he has it. Explains why he's back Upstairs in the first place.

And then, apparently, sold us out to Bernadette.

Can't move against him openly. Not with all the shit going on. Can't accuse him. Well, we could. But he'll find a way to weasel and worm it.

No.

Now, there's no real rat squad in the Library. No Internal Affairs, like. Or if there is, it's people like me, headkickers and sheriffs. Or trusted seniors like Mully.

Could go to Mully.

But no. Hell with him. He coulda had my back. Didn't.

Have to do this myself.

Drum my fingers on desk.

Which gives me the idea.

I I

My shadow hand.

Never had a familiar. Not like in the old days they did.

No black cat or toad all a suckling on my nipples. Seen 'em, though.

Most of the time, figure familiars for a trap. You put some of your ability to do magic into something else and the world, being the pointless, stupid place it is, you can get your staunch magic ally all hit by a car or poisoned by some bastard or the local kids'll shove a firecracker up its arse.

Which isn't exactly what you want out of being a sorcerer.

Not me, anyways.

But the tulpa-thing, a shadow puppet made from my hand, comes close to being a familiar.

Shirtless and surrounded by candles, throwing shapes over my sanctum, summon it. It's held in place in a shade shape, a star that was made special for it. Middle finger like a dinosaur head, walking unsteady on four fingers.

Need to hold it there because, well, little shadow's getting a promotion.

Pick it up with the care of a shy child with a baby bird. It's nervous around me but is aware of my authority over it. Does its best to hide... not quite fear and hard to say it's nervous but that's how it seems.

Open my mouth and it crawls it. My breath and spit cover it and it drinks deep from both. Bonding. Tasting me. We know each other. It sups on the particles of food in teeth, the moisture in my breath.

Crawls out. In the inky shade stuff that makes up its body, write my real name. Binding us more closely together. It gets taken, there's a risk someone will learn my name from it but not much of one. And besides, it'll fade away like fog if needs be.

Touch the sclera of my eyes. Moisture again. Let it sup, finger head lapping. Let it crawl on my face like a spider and it noses my ears. Can see and hear through it now.

Our deal is for it to be fed in return for service. Pat it like a pet. Tell it that tonight, it'll eat my dreams. Which is more than it sounds. Means the link between us will go both ways. Something wants to come at me that way while it's eating, leave me vulnerable.

Take Foulstone's photo. Show it to the familiar. Whisper to it my history with the fucker. Let my hate leech in, which mars it, no doubt but if you're sentimental about that, you'll never be a magician. Tell it what needs to be done.

'Follow. Learn. Watch.'

It shakily bows. Pluck out some of my hair, feed it to the little shadow hand. Eats well.

Blow out the candles in ritual order. Darkness takes us. Which means no shadow. The operation is ended. Break magical consciousness and go pour myself a triple of Talisker. Turn around and it's gone to do its work.

I I I

Realise something. Foulstone hasn't spoken to me since he got back. Take a brief moment to indulge myself in some paranoia. Maybe he's not real. Maybe he's a spell in my head, a curse, makes me hallucinate someone I fucking hate. Maybe... no.

Sometimes being a magician is just thinking like a schizophrenic but finding your way out of the maze of symbolism and secret meaning. Trick to being a good magician is to know how to use that thinking.

Turns out, the paranoid is justified.

But we'll get to that.

Here's the problem. Foulstone is probably as paranoid and cautious as me.

Now it's known he come up through crime, rather than any kinda more formal tradition... well, that's insight can be used.

His first priority will be to outlast any motherfucker coming at him. To survive. Fine. From there? He'll be looking out for himself, looking to get his fat hands on whatever he values.

Just sic the familiar shadow on him, he'll make it, make me. Don't need that.

Trick is... ok. Pay attention. Here's what some people would call the occult tradecraft. Good word that. Worked with some spooks a while ago. Coffee and Valier were their names. Picked it up from them.

Tradecraft is just that. Techniques of the game. Got someone needs surveillance but who's protected against it? No one's capable of watching out for eyes 24/7. So he'll ... automate the process. He doesn't seem to practice any serious discipline except necromancy. Ghosts will be bound to him. Like machines, won't get tired, won't get bored.

Ghost got *feelings* though. Emotions.

You figure Foulstone's good to his servants? Think he makes friends with 'em, works with 'em? Or you figure him for the kinda man to starve his dogs to make them meaner?

Tell my familiar to make *friends* with the ghosts. It's a good natured thing. Shy, nervous. *Kind* might be going too far.

Instructions given. Nothing to do now. Wait.

If they kill it, I'll know.

And then, I'll try again.

I V

'Wake the fuck up.'

Aristide doesn't get up before 3 in the afternoon. One of the best things about him. A man keeping sensible hours. One of the worst? He's sloppy and he's only disciplined when it comes to fucking up people he figures owe him money.

He gets up, goes for the machete keeps by his bed. Holding that for him.

'Lark, the fuck are you doing, man?' That rich East African accent. Not gonna lie, dig it. But not enough to buy him shit from me.

'Bettina. You been *changing* her. Just saw her go to town on ghosts and figure that's you.'

He pushes the dirty dreadlocks outta his face. Strung with Catholic medallions, bird skulls, finger bones. His room is small and dark. Got a pair of Bettina's underpants next to him as he sleeps. Hoodoo veves drawn on his walls. Candles unlit, most now just piles of wax. CDs for the stereo next to his bed. Spent frangers on the carpet. Empty bottles of some Ugandan banana wine. Posters of black women in hotpants. Dark and hot in here.

'I ain't done shit to B, man.'

Say nothing.

He shakes his head. Waking himself up. Shot of adrenaline is already levelling off.

'And if I did, what's it to you? She's my bitc-'

'None of that, fucker. Keep it holy.'

'You're funny, Lark. You think she never heard the word *bitch* before?'

Bring the machete down against the cheap wooden frame of his bed. He jumps. Dunno what Aristide thinks but almost guarantee he never thought of me as someone to worry about in a punch up.

In a way, he's right. Not here to *hit* him.

'Not about words. About the way you *talk* about her. To me.'

'Fucking... alright then. I won't call her no mean names. Fucking hell, Lark. How do you...'

Know what's coming. *How does a guy like you survive down here?* Not the first prick who thought seeing me read a book meant I was weak sister.

'Shhh. Tell me what you did to her.'

'Did not do *shit.*'

Sigh. Leashed to me, *meme-wasps.* Every humiliation and doubt and pain and shame and embarrassment. Taken, turned into weapons.

Point at him. They pour into him. His back arches and he gasps. Doesn't... doesn't hurt like a strike or a burn. But by God, all of it, pin pointed, unexpected. Raw, hateful emotion. Every sting of shame, failure, humiliation, pouring through him.

'Make it stop! *Sa Dechennen!*'

Snap my fingers. Call it off. Little bit of theatre never helps.

'Here's the thing Aristide. Dunno you, but Bettina likes you. Good enough for me. You join the Library? Fine. Cash money for you, we get a man handy in a fight. But Bettina? She's not a fucking project.'

'Fuck you. This is not your business, Lark. You think I do not see you taking her out? Doing things with her? My *woman!*'

'Secure that noise. You know that isn't how it is. Don't even pretend. You're fucking caught out, man. Don't try to make this -'

'Baron Krim-'

He cries out an evocation to his patron but ready for that shit. Wasps strike again. This time, the memory of the Old Man's muscle, Ludo, working my hip until I screamed. My pain in Aristide's body. That cop... what was his name? From Crossroads, tasering me.

He passes out from the pain. It's a lot, concentrated.

Find me half a bottle of his banana wine. Pour some into jam jars he uses as tumblers. Wait for him to come too. Shit tastes like banana juice. Not as interesting as you might hope for. Grab a chair from his kitchenette. Sit down beside his bed.

A minute goes by and his eyelids waver and he comes back. Hand him his drink.

'Just talk. Talk and we can end this shit.'

'Fuck, Lark. You could have...'

Looking up at me, that dies.

'You have the eyes of a Gregory *mweusei.*'

'Fuck is that?'

'A doll. You look like something that only *looks* alive, Lark. You have nothing but ashes where you should have a soul, man. I bet your semen is *cold*. Do you shoot frozen pearls then, Lark?'

Hand him his drink.

'...sure.'

Lift up the machete.

'This is a good knife, Aristide. You've Worked with it. It's for... punishing people, yeah?'

'A man is only good as his reputation.'

'What's my reputation.'

Slowly, he reaches for his drink. Sips deep, watching me careful.

'Got my smokes in that drawer.'

'Sure.'

He moves slow. No tricks. He knows pulling a gun or a knife is a bad move for him right now.

He lights up. Doesn't offer me one.

'No one likes you, Lark, is your rep. You're not a man with charm. Unlike myself.' He smiles, teeth filed and white against his African skin. 'But if there's one thing everyone says that is not *he's not a lot of fun*, it's that you don't fuck around.'

Sure. Whatever.

'Then tell me what you did to Bettina and you won't have to learn that shit first hand.'

He looks up at me. My face is still as a corpse. Meme wasps fly invisibly around my head like a pain halo. Aristide breathes out slow, smoke obscuring his eyes.

'Sure. But we must go somewhere.'

V

'She is like a goddess to me, Lark.' He grins again and I have to remind myself that he may very well have to fucking die tonight.

'Not a lwa. Not like that. A thing to worship. An *ideal*.'

We're at the park where Bettina died now. Some low pimp took her out and buried her two feet under. He's long gone. For a long time, she had to return here to rest on the reg. Still does when she's hurt bad.

But it passed me over she's gone stronger, for longer, without it. Bad me.

Aristide is in full voodoo regalia. He's passed over the Hollywood and is in a long headscarf and what seems a skirt he calls an iro.

'When I meet her, I want her. Not just for,' he grabs the outline of his dick. 'Although that's a part of it. Big part. But Lark, you know my story.'

Indeed. Caught up in a war in Africa and all the brutality that means. Escaped to Haiti and the vodou gangsters there.

'The death saints love me. And in time, you know, I love them back. And a woman who goes down into the water, the cold, cold waters? And comes back? She is *made* for me. I feel that she is perfection, you understand? Perfection.'

He kneels, puts his hand in the patch of dirt. Grass all around but here. Size of a coffin, a barren scorch. Death information leaks from it.

'One time we were, and I must say this for your baby ears, one time we were *together* and I realised I am praying to her. Whispering my worship into her. She is a thing of sorcery, Lark. Not just a woman. It gives her a kind of power. After we are done, I see it works. I make this...'

He starts to dig into his robes.

'This is why I dress proper. Respect to her.'

He kneels next to her grave. Starts digging with a hand.

'So I start to make it more... serious. Respectful. Proper. I learn some things from you, hey?'

Say nothing.

'My love, she gets strong. Stronger. And so do I.'

Say nothing.

'There is no harm. And she gets new... abilities. You say she eats ghosts? News to me. But a thing to be looked forward to. Celebrate! It's a fine thing. A strong thing.'

Maybe. Maybe.

'Does she know?'

He finds what he wants in the grave. A corn doll, dressed up to look like Bettina.

'Eh?'

'Does she know what you are doing?'

'Ah, you know Bettina. She is a thing of bones and muscle. This sort of thing it bores her, hey?'

No. No it *doesn't*.

So now a choice.

Could take him out here. Kill him. Leave him in ruins. Rip the aura off him, leave him prey to any kind of etheric fucker that goes looking for a victim. Plant a suicide curse into his nervous system.

Bettina won't thank me for that.

Rat him out to her? Tell her the man she loves is using her? She thank me for *that*? No one likes a rat but then again, my loyalty is to her, not Aristide, who's whispering sexy shit to a doll of her.

Tricky, tricky, tricky.

Aristide reburies the gris gris and wipes his hands on his clothes, stands up.

'Watch you want to do? You know this is good for everyone. You gonna spoil her being happy over a teeny lie? Are you her friend?'

Sure I am. And her *master*. Bought her back to her half life. Me. Gives me authority over her.

That's…

Hits me.

That's part of why Aristide is doing that. He wants her all. To himself. He wants that authority.

I am suspicious and I am low and I do not give the benefit of the doubt. But what if he loves her true?

What if this is something he wants to do for her but just doesn't want to come straight at me with? What if he thinks I'm a slaver?

Click my zippo open, closed.

No.

He lied to me. Bettina loves magic.

Scarlet's advice rings inside my skull. *Have to do better with people.*

Ask Bettina. Isn't that what… isn't that how people do?

Aristide looks at me. He seems cool but the tension is there. He doesn't know which way I'll jump. I do. I'm taking this fuck out. Just a matter of how.

'Keeping looking out for her.'

'Oh, Lark. You know I will.'

V I

A day at the office. Discrete check in on Foulstone. Dunno how discrete it is but basically… send Katanya into his office to steal some shit for me.

She's in faded jeans, slim blazer. New tattoo on her hands. Roses and thorns.

'That looks good.'

She's unimpressed with flattery and just mutters she and her wife got matches. We have lunch together. She's gone vegetarian, she tells me. Before ordering a steak.

'My wife is vegan and she made me go vegetarian.'

'You're doing great.'

'And you're keeping your goddamn mouth shut if it ever comes up.'

'Snitch on you? Never.'

'How's my office?'

'Can't give it back to you. Figure that you wouldn't want that anyway.'

'I'm kidding, Lark.'

'You is. But only just.'

'Look, let's just...'

'Just... stop.'

'What? Lark...'

'Listen. Please. Trying to do better by people. Shit doesn't come natural to me. People... people bore me. What I dig, not many other people do and so... assume I bore them back. Even in the Library... always the weird kid. Now, that's ok. Fine with that. But Bettina tells it... have to do better.'

Wave my hand at the two of us.

'This is me trying. Normal shit. Co workers eating together. '

She puts down her knife and fork.

Looks at me.

'You listening to her advice?'

'Looks like, lady.'

She purrs a little. 'That's a fine woman.'

'I know. So listen. Can't give you back the office. Don't want to, on top of that. But. You want, you can move in. We can share. Not there much anyway. And if they say that's against some rules or protocol, fuck 'em.'

She stares at me.

'This isn't you looking for a shag is it? Cos that's over.'

'You know this isn't me looking to get a leg over.'

'I do.'

Say nothing.

'Thanks, Lark. I'd like that.'

'But there's a cost.'

'Pfft.'

'Need access to Foulstone's office. And his office is protected.'

She takes out her phone and taps away on it as I put cold beer into myself. Five minutes later she hands it over to me.

'This is Foulstone's laptop. We have remote access.'

'Shit. Cool. This is a good spell, lady.'

'It's not a spell. Foulstone's even worse with tech than you are. I'm thinking of redecorating our office, by the way.'

V I I

Foulstone works Reclamations. He finds rare books and gets 'em for the Library. That's his main duty. Not as easy as it sounds. Liaise with book seller, dealers, private collectors. Locate books. Some of them don't want to sell. Some books are dangerous. Sometimes they're not books but scrolls, frescos, tapestries. *Text* is what we want. Interview writers. Bookbinders, editors. Everyone.

Secure, catalogue, store. Then hand it over to the curators, who are weird even by my standards. Years and years guarding actual blasphemous and potent tomes leaves them all pale, pop-eyed and intense.

Kinda dig them, actually.

Get his notes on the books, right there in his computer. He's sloppy. Can tell the work isn't passion for him. Just a gig. All the right entries are there. ISBN when you can get it. Size, condition, title, author, subject. But the notes are minimal. Bare. Most times, reclaimers babble like maniacs in excitement.

His journal entries are boring. Just times and dates of meetings. Minimum effort.

His diary though... see, now that's useful.

Because tomorrow, he's got a meeting with... C&V is all that's written. C&V. Does that ring...

No... No way.

Touch it. Feel it. Real names flood into mind.

Agents Valier and Coffee. Feds.

Feds I know.

There ain't no such thing as coincidence.

FOURTEEN

I

Bettina and me are on the subway. We're watching a blind man tap tap tap his way down the carriage. Grizzled. Long hair and beard. Ratty overcoat. Dark glasses.

He's not human. Something is riding him. There's people like this all over the City. All over yours, too. Ever see someone in the crowd and something in you reacts wrong? You're probably right to. When that feeling comes for you, the ice in your belly, the fear jolts in your fingers, listen to it.

'Aristide is doing shit to you. Magic. He's not telling you.'

She turns to look at me.

'You maybe wanna throw me a detail?'

'Homeboy is turning you into a goddess.'

'*Turning?*'

Say nothing.

'This got to do with the ghosts I done ate?'

'Yeah. That's... you're gonna get stronger. Because of him.'

'Why is this bad, man?'

A child starts to cry and her father gives the blind man paper into his tin cup. Walks on. Child starts to shriek hysterically as blind leans in, smiling wrong.

'Just go!' hisses daddy, throws in a fifty. Blind man smiles, showing off messy, ragged teeth. Watch him force his hands onto poor old dad's. That kid will remember his father's panic all his life.

'It's bad because he didn't tell you. It's bad because he can't know where it ends. Theurgy. That's magic of gods. Most of us do it but most of us know about respect and limits. Aristide... dunno. Voudou lwa ain't quite like other gods.'

She goes silent.

'So what will happen to me?'

Sigh. Shrug.

'No way to know for sure. But you won't be... you'll change. You can't be a human and a god. Humans can touch, even dead humans, can touch the divine realm. But we can't *stay*. Tam Lin gets kicked out of faerieland. Endymion can't be with Selene whole. Acteon. Orion. You just... can't.'

She nods. She loves myths.

'Like Wick.' The girl turned Archon.

'Yeah. She couldn't come back.'

'Why?'

Blind man comes to us. Looks at Bettina. Moves off. Tap. Tap. Tap.

'Why what?'

'Why has my man got this in his head?'

'Dunno. The action is clear. He gets a goddess. But why? Obviously, he's got a thing for death and... you, well.'

'No. Why he ain't come at me straight with this?'

'Bettina, you know this ain't my riff. Motivation.'

'No.' She sighs.

Train stops. We get out. Slide tickets through the slot and push turnstiles. Ticket box slams shut. 8 at night now.

'How you know this?'

'Got suspicious. Forced it outta him.'

'So this a snitch?'

'You and me, lady, there's no snitching. Coming correct.'

'Yeah.'

Fists knock together. We walk up to the cold night air. Autumn is well on us.

'Let's go get the low down on that limey maggot and I'll figure out what to do about all a this.'

'Sure.'

I I

Valier and Coffee.

They started out careers as spooks, doing G-work on the low down. Both of them from anti-terrorism backgrounds but they ended up in Religious Crimes or something. Came across them when they were tracking down a scroll came outta Iraq in the 90s. With something bad written on it. Valier's a tall blonde woman and Coffee's an amiable black guy who could lose a few pounds.

Same office as they used to work in. Had to light out of here once. Stupid fucks tried to arrest me. Fingered me for being involved in smuggling that scroll.

We get through security and into the protected elevator. Shit's easy for a magician.

Just a fancy open office inside. White desk dividers. Cubicles. Some big plasma screens on the walls.

Nice conference room, all glass, in the middle of the floor. Even late, there's people working. Drones who stare at us. Not important.

Me and Bettina walk quick to Coffee's desk.

He glances up. Sees us coming and eyes go wide. He's on the phone.

'Have to call you back, baby. No, I'm sorry. No. I have to go!'

He stands up. He's the kinda cat always seems rumpled. Moustache needs a trim.

Not a lot of warmth in those eyes.

'Lark.'

No hand.

'Don't suppose you've got your authorised visitor badges.'

Bettina laughs. Me?

Say nothing.

Coffee goes on. 'As usual, Lark, your personal charm has quite disarmed me.'

Neither of us say anything.

'I'll get my partner.'

Texts.

'I don't suppose this is a social call, is it?'

Cock my head at him. Let him know he's wasting time. He gives me a kind of 'aw shucks' grin.

'And... how are you, Camilla, is it?'

'Bettina. I'm cool.'

'Excellent. Come on and step inside the Echo Chamber. Can I get you a coffee?'

'No thanks,' says Bettina.

'Tea?'

'Nope.'

'Have you eaten? We just ordered about ten minutes ago. I can get them to add more. Chinese.'

'We're cool, man.'

'Seriously, it's no trouble.'

Walk past him to the glass room. He can get his thrills playing wind up later.

'You're not a fun man, Lark.'

Coffee opens the door and we sit at a conference table. He wanders away. Comes back with a cardboard box of Chinese food and a cup.

'Green tea. Trying to cut down on coffee. My wife says it makes me jittery. I don't see it myself but then again, I don't have to live with me. Do you guys find that? Caffeine giving you the shakes?'

Say nothing.

He sighs. Forgot he's a talker. Starts to eat like we weren't there. Perhaps there's something be learned from his everyone's pal style of talking but his fucking... *bonhomie*... gets on my tits. Bettina backs my play and stays frosty.

Not long after that, Valier enters behind us. She looks tireder but dressed smarter than Coffee. Sharp suit, flatters her. Badge on her wasp waist. Bit of grey at her temples, which suits her. Calm. Calculated. She crosses her arms. Leans against the glass wall. She's not a big woman but she's the kind radiates capability.

'Lark. Bettina. I can only assume this is business. You can understand we're not all that happy to see you.'

'Foulstone.'

'What's that supposed to mean to me?'

Sigh. Like she's just said something lame. Get up. Bettina stands too.

'Alright. Fuck it. We'll move on him without you.'

'Wait, wait, Lark.' Coffee.

'No need for the dramatics. Sit down. Please. But you have to understand we can't just blurt out what you need to know. The informant/agent relationship is...'

'Informant?' Bettina does not like that.

'Well, it's just a word.'

'Find another.'

'Foulstone.' Enough of this shit. 'We know you're in contact with him. He works for the same organisation as us.'

Valier hasn't moved. 'Please sit down. We can talk. But spare me the autistic sociopath bit.'

Sit. So does she.

They're waiting for me to say my piece.

'Foulstone. He's *fucked*. You might think you know what you have with him, Valier, but you do not.'

'Define... fucked.' Her voice is crisp. Like she's letting me know she thought over the curse.

Shit. Talking to civilians. How to... move ahead?

'Just tell 'em.' Bettina knows how this'll sound.

'He summons ghosts. Hurts 'em. And I think he's involved in some real dodgy shit with some real, real bad cats. Need to know what you know about him.'

Valier and Coffee meet each other's eyes.

'Come with me.'

III

You want it to be a high tech room. Like in the movies. Elevator shafts down to the 20th sub-basement.

It ain't.

But we're inside a cage at least, in a cramped section down in at least one basement. Valier tells me it's a Faraday Cage which isn't anything I could tell you about, but... recognise warding when it's seen. Heavy lights hang from the ceiling. Coffee switches on the illumination and it's stark, our shadows sudden and immanent.

The whole room smells of mildew and we are cramped.

Valier talks to us.

'After we met you and worked that case with the scroll, we started to take all this... occult... a lot more seriously. We've seen some shit, Lark.'

'Sure.'

'And as we started to move on it, we learned more and more. And whatever resources you have, you're probably unlikely to have access to things like the Six Eyes Agreement or ECHELON sigint or Global Telecom Interception.'

'Dunno what any of that shit is.'

'Our organisation has access to a lot of information and more importantly, a lot of analysis of that information. The Country is signed up to half a dozen programs that our division has access to. We can cross-reference across a hundred different disciplines. And we learned some shit.'

Say nothing.

'You know about something called the Sothic Temple?'

There's no such goddamn thing as coincidence. The world works in ways that are not ours.

'Yes.'

She stops. Sighs. Thinking how much to tell me and how to make sense of it.

'Look. I can't explain it all to you right now but we saw a sudden spike in occult crimes. Real ones, you know what I'm talking about.'

'Sure.'

'So we did background checks on all the murderers and all of them had ties to the Temple. We started investigating. We tried to do what we usually do. We got one of ours to the inside. Same as we'd do with any kind of cell we needed to keep an eye on. We set up an informer. We had bad luck turning an asset, though, they were very loyal to the organisation. Whatever the Temple promised them was something we couldn't compete with. Normally, people turn for money, or for ideology or revenge but we just couldn't work it that way.'

'They're hoping for a reward and not in any afterlife.'

'Yeah. So we tried it different. We took one of our agents, trained him up. Had him make contact. Took a year, which was quick, all things considered but he was initiated into the cult.'

Coffee swivels in his chair. 'We're assuming you have a strong stomach.'

Nod. Bettina crosses her arms.

He brings up a video on the computer.

Man in cell. The walls are like crash mats. Floors too. Toilet is padded and a basin with taps wrapped. What a padded cell actually looks like.

On the floor, in like a ... poncho of clear plastic, with his hands held in built in restraints, his hands slipped into sleeves that don't let his hand emerge, what they now call *suicide prevention gear*, but used to be straight jacket, is a blind man.

Blind because he's got no fucking eyes. Just black shrivelled remains. Scars on his face. He's babbling.

'That's Middle Egyptian. It hasn't been spoken in 3000 years. We had linguists look at it. He's talking about a snake god called -'

'Apophis.'

'Yeah. We found him with his eyes under his fingernails and his... he'd set fire to his genitals.'

'Christ,' murmurs Bettina.

'You should let him die.'

She turns on me at that. 'Or we could help him!'

Shrug. No you can't. Then a sudden chill goes through me. Sudden thought, unbidden, unwanted. Suddenly realise... out in the forest last year... this is *what Bernadette would have had her magician do to me*. Insane, self-mutilating.

'Never mind. Go on.'

'Those linguists gave us a report on what he was saying.'

'Lady, you got a point, time to get to it.'

She takes her time.

'Coffee. Show him.'

He does.

I V

IMAGE

Seal of the Religious Crime Department

TEXT - IF YOU ARE WATCHING THIS YOU HAVE S-CLEARANCE. IF YOU DO NOT HAVE S-CLEARANCE, WATCHING THIS BRIEF IS A FEDERAL CRIME. END TRANSMISSION AND REPORT TO A SUPERVISOR.

IMAGE

Circular Wipe counting down 3, 2, 1

IMAGE

A man, Caucasian, balding, spectacles, appears seated behind a desk. A desk plate reads DIRECTOR OF RESEARCH ALAN SPAULDING.

SPAULDING:

I'm Alan Spaulding Vice Director R&D and this briefing is for agents with S-Clearance on Case OMEGA SUMMER.

I've been seconded to the Case on orders of Director Gibney and am recording this report on his order, er, 1123 - ADE.

My usual work is in deep space telemetry. I track celestial object that may potential present existential threats to earth.

IMAGE

A rock in the depths of space. Fat, curved in the middle, pitted with blisters.

VOICE OVER (SPAULDING):

This is 99942 Apophis. It was discovered 2004 a Kitt Peak Observatory. It is 350 metres long. Bigger than the Empire State Building. And it weighs four trillion tonnes.

IMAGE

Closer in on the rock.

VOICE OVER (SPAULDING):

On first discovery twenty years ago, there were concerns 99942 Apophis would enter a 'gravitational keyhole'. If it hit this patch of space, it would very likely strike Earth with considerable devastation. It is not hyperbole to discuss it as an extinction event.

IMAGE

GRAPHIC OF LINES OF DIRECTION OF THE ASTEROID AND LINES SHOWING VECTORS TOWARDS EARTH AND THE MOON

VOICE OVER (SPAULDING):

However, five years ago, on the [EXACT DATE] 99942 Apophis changed course, seemingly without motive. How it did this remains... completely mysterious.

IMAGE
Back to Spaulding

SPAULDING:
It's coming. It's going to hit us.

CUT
A blonde woman with a short haircut.

VALIER:
 I am Agent Valier, lead on Case OMEGA SUMMER. We have reason to
believe this sudden change in direction is the work of... occultists in the
City. Please cross reference with my report labelled NC 8892 9.
We have worldwide reports of visions and prophecies regarding the date.
Again, please see the report but notice the outbreak in Mali, Uganda
and Papua New Guinea, where rebel groups around the world began
spontaneous use of serpent symbolism in their iconography.

The closest we have to a beginning of this phenomenon is [EXACT
DATE] in the City. Extensive research have discovered this woman has
been involved with an least seven of our cases.

IMAGE
A woman with medium length brown hair, wearing sunglasses, taken
from a long range. She stands among bodies in what seems to be a
prison compound.

VOICE OVER (VALIER):
We do not have a verbal identification for this woman although she has
been identified as a considerable occult worker. Currently, she leads the
Sothic Temple, a small lodge with members in Europe, North America
and South America and Egypt. This Temple works in what these
organisation call the Ancient Egyptian "current" or tradition.
She has proven considerably elusive. However, we have a high level

operative, Agent TORC, working to infiltrate her organisation. We understand this tactic has failed in the past but due to Agent TORC's specific credentials, we felt the attempt was worth making one final time.

IMAGE
Back to Spaulding

SPAULDING:
We have two years until the asteroid makes contact with earth unless it changes again.

IMAGE
Back to Valier

VALIER:
It is our belief that the Temple worships the asteroid as they might their God, the 'chaos serpent' Apophis, of Ancient Egyptian mythology. We shall continue to monitor the situation and update Central on our findings.

END

V

The exact date the asteroid Apophis changed direction to earth?
Same day we killed the Old Man.
At least in part, this is my fault.
Somewhere, the Rabisu is laughing.
Laughing.

V I

Bettina talks first, as I'm reeling. Bernadette's looking to end the fucking world and maybe she can.

'Foulstone's this Agent Torc motherfucker, right?'

Coffee nods. 'You're more than just a pair of fists, aren't you?'

He looks her up and down and smiles. Less him perving but that paternal shit don't fly with her either.

'Yep.'

Then she grabs him by the lapels, drags him off his feet. Quick like a bear trap.

'The fuck, man? The world is gonna end!?'

'I don't fucking know! Yes? Maybe?'

Put a hand on her shoulder. She don't even look at me. Grab the arm she's holding the 120Kg Coffee up with.

'It might not mean what they think it means.'

She looks at me.

'There's different ways to end the world, Bettina. That's not just a rock. It's a spirit, too. A god. Reckon Apophis is just the.... A symptom, a cause, a rite. Apophis is coming but not out of space to blow us up like dinosaurs or eat us up. But no less apocalyptic for all that.'

'Fuck does that even mean, man?!'

She's not happy.

'Put him down.'

She drops him. Valier eases back. She was looking for an in on Bettina from the rear. Good luck, lady.

Coffee straightens himself up.

'Yeah. What do you mean?' he asks.

Take a second or two to think it through. They stare at me hard.

'Apophis is a vast *idea*. Something that stays with us, with humans, forever. *The end of all this.*'

'I dig it.'

'Apophis is the primordial chaos that will end day and night. He gets his way, we all go into darkness. But we all know there's no big snake gonna eat the sun. Apophis is a primal *thought* humans have. When the world ends, it's not literal. It's a metaphor for the end of all we know.'

'I'm not sure I follow there, Lark,' says Coffee.

'The scroll case we worked together. That ended with a girl becoming spirit and now she's suffused with everything in the City. Living or not. She's in us, the stones of buildings and the leaves on trees and the rails of the subway. But something like Apophis will spread over the fucking world, man. Read the news. Apophis will end the world in our heads. Laws, customs. Morality. That woman, her name is Bernadette. She's steering alla this and she's not looking to make a heaven on earth.'

'How do we deal with this?'

'You don't. We will. You can go in, Waco the Temple if you want. Won't stop Apophis coming. Way you help me, is you tell me about Foulstone.'

Two agents aren't ready to talk.

'Don't be fucking stupid. This isn't the time to worry about vetting me and giving me security clearance or whatever boring arse spook shit you have to do. Tell me.'

They don't want to. But they know they have to.

Valier talks.

'It's not that simple.'

'Lady, it is.'

'We could...'

'Got a fucking rock from space coming at earth and you know who's behind it. That more important than ...'

'You're asking us to believe too much!'

Yeah. Ok. Alright. That's fair. Valier's history, remembering it right, and no promises I am, is pure politics. She came to work for these cats because she wanted to run for office or some damn thing. She's not natural for the hoodoo.

Some people spend their lives looking for the divine, the miraculous. Some people run away from that shit like scalded motherfuckers, afraid there's more to live than meat.

Hmmm.

Valier's retreating into *rules*.

Got me a choice. Can put the voodoo to her. Charm her. Ensnare her. Or.

Play it her way.

Need to know things. Need to... compromise.

'Alright. We'll do it your way. Debrief me. Sign me up. Whatever you need.'

She sighs.

Sign some papers.

FIFTEEN

I

'Foulstone is working for us. He read your reports on the incident with the scroll and he found us that way. Told us you and the Library had been compromised by the Temple, who were serious bad news. Knew we were investigating and wanted help in extracting himself from the Temple.'

Coffee pours us some goddamn Irish cream into our coffee. We're back in the glass room. He yawns.

'Sorry. Late night for me.'

Say nothing.

'Anyways. We checked him out. Learned what we could. He's like some sort of hotshot fixer, right?'

No. No he's not. He's charmed them himself.

Shrug.

'But what's happening with the Temple? He says it's too far beyond him. That *even his conscience has limits.* He wanted help getting out so he came to us.'

This story is flimsy as fuck. These agents are... why are they falling for such a bullshit weaksister stor -

Shit.

This is all a trap.

Foulstone wants me here and he wants me to listen to what they have to say.

He's got access to all my old files. Fucker isn't suddenly moved to pity by working with bad people. He's manipulated these two to make me think the better of him. He knew I'd come to Valier and Coffee eventually... me being here in me being *manipulated*.

'So we formally recruited him as an asset. We pay him and he gives us information.'

'What information?'

'It's only been two months. These things take time.' Valier steps in.

'Are you telling me a man you pay for and who approached you, who has evidence regarding a cult that seem to have the power to, you know, end the fucking world, has *nothing* for you?'

'It's not that simple.'

Yeah it is.

Fuck. Fuck!

Then why let me see the Apophis tape? What does he... no. What does *she* want? Why does Bernadette want me to know this?

Don't know. Don't know.

Fear shoots into my fingers. Bernadette has Foulstone. She couldn't flip Scarlet and Elliot's bullshit so she just recruited Foulstone? Has to be that, right?

Fuck. Fuck!

Don't know.

'Can you call a meeting with Foulstone?'

'He contacts us.'

That is not how that relationship should work. Do not work for intelligence agencies but by God, do know that if we had someone on the hook, came to us, wanted help from us, no way *we* dance to *their* tune.

Hit gnosis. Hard.

'You alright?' Coffee asks but it's like he's underwater.

'What's he doing?' Valier's voice is panicked.

Bettina strikes Coffee hard, grabbing him by the throat. She kicks Valier in the belly, winding her. Thing about a blood choke, a carotid strangle, is that it's quicker than you think. Her fist has the heavy man in a clutch could snap a bone, she wanted. His black skin gets blue real quick, his eyes bug and it's just seconds until he passes out.

Valier goes for a gun she forgot to strap on. She's just in her office, no one straps there. Give her this, she's trained and tough.

But Bettina is Bettina. She grabs the agent by her arm and puts her in a hammer lock, arm behind her back.

'Move and I'll snap it, slapper. You got any doubt?'

A faint increase of pressure. Valier's tough but she sobs once with pain. Anyone would.

'Alright. Alright.' Bettina eases the lock. But not by much.

In gnosis a long time. Staring down at Coffee. Losing myself. Staring. Falling backwards behind my own face. Looking into ideaspace, the astral, the half-world. Whatever you want to call it.

There are spirits, waiting for just this. *This is a trap too.*

In the astral, can see the charms on Valier and Coffee both, lurid mists they breathe in and out. But wrapped around their throats... reptilian tentacular things. Who have one instruction. Attack whoever can see them.

They launch at me.

But you know... Bernadette ain't the only one can plan ahead.

The amulet Kira made for me sparks up like white phosphorous. The lizard things lash at me with limbs that are thin and wild. Terrible speed.

But the death saint the amulet is sacred too is old and the death saint is powerful and has tasted my blood.

The eregores Foulstone left behind with these two are potent but... ain't new to this.

They burn. They shriek and the sound of it rattle me, almost out of gnosis.

Which would not be good.

Keep the state, though. Low rez zen even in the face of this bullshit.

The spirits burn. They burn and shriek and die.

Still in gnosis. Look into Valier's eyes.

'Foulstone comes here again? Shoot him. He's playing you.'

She nods.

Bettina lets her go.

Release gnosis.

'We have to move on Foulstone. He'll have felt that. Now.'

11

Don't go into work. Fuck 'em.

Go back to my basement. Clean it. Tidy it. Getting the mind right. Take that pack of smokes bought a few days ago. Think about having one but ... ever since the doctor told me about the black holes... just haven't felt it.

Do the same to the sanctum. Go out and buy a duster, even. Stupid image, me with some goddamn feather thing going at it but that's all part of it. To give something up. In this case, a little dignity. Spend some time setting things up.

Fasting. No coffee, no food. No sleep. Meditation.

Ten hours of it, on and off. Meditate all the damn time but even so... that's a strong drink.

Sun goes down. Turn on the burner on the stove. Hold hand over it until the hairs on the back of my palm singe down. Rummage in my fridge. Psilocybin mushrooms. Normally, don't take the drug trip to enter serious altered states of mind. Can hit gnosis anytime I want, really. But this will help. Neck half a dozen and spend half an hour working to keep those down.

Ritual preparation. Foulstone will know his spirits got fucked up. He'll suspect me. Who else could he. Which means he'll be ready for me to move on him.

Which is gonna happen, yeah. But he's used to me working empty-handed magic.

What I can think up on the sly, on the quick. Proper ritual magic? Not something I spend all that time on. Not the full throttle.

Thinking all this and the whole room goes... long. Mushrooms kicking in. Head to the sanctum.

Candles burning inside.

Strip off naked. Wash my face, my dick, under my arms, my hands, my feet. Into a robe. Midnight blue silk. Slippers of the same shade. Play music that helps relax me.

Dvorak, Symphony in ... no. Not that. Mully put me onto it. He uses it. Still not ready to deal with the old man sticking it to me.

Don't know classical music but what I do, comes from him.

Use this kind of music when I need to feel dramatic and different. When I need to feel formal. When I need to feel like a *sorcerer*, not just some chump knows some tricks. Not dirtbag weirdo Lark who can barely talk.

Faure's *Pavane in F sharp minor*.

As the psychedelics kick in, feel myself almost floating. Bodiless. The music moves and my body moves with it, so it seems. Let it happen. Let it roil over me like mist in morning.

Cast my circle and secure the Watchtowers. Carefully snuff some candles until only a few behind me make my shadow loom upon the wall. There is another world close to us. A shadowy world. A black city. John Dee found his great treasure, the shew stone in a shadow. Dark places are more than just somewhere the light is not. Shadows, to a magician, to me, are hole in the world where things come in and go out.

Extend my consciousness through the shadow and into my puppet familiar, the shade of my hand.

It startles.

A primitive thing. Seeing through its eyes, feeling through its limbs. Sharing its emotions. It is all reception, really. It has no consciousness to speak of. Fear, curiosity, hunger are the closest it comes to higher states.

It feels my mind within it and greets me in the manner a dog might greet a new master. Tacit excitement but wariness. Take a moment to comfort it.

Then...

Empower it.

A day of fasting, prayer, meditation. It strengthens. It gives whatever force motivates magic ... power.

Where are we?

Foulstone.

I I I

We walk in his shadow. Finger feet scurrying to keep pace with him.

Walking with him. Tracking him. He won't see us because we're not worth noticing. Just a little piece of nothing in the world. Around him as he walks, the familiar can see old ghosts at a linger. They wrap around him, twirling between his legs, over his wrist, around his neck, like serpents.

Slaves.

They scream. If we had the ears to hear, it would unnerve us both, the howls of the dead.

The familiar has little sense of time. Borrow it.

Foulstone is dressed in a cheap two piece, better than the usual track suit he wears. He goes to a bar where he leers at the barmaid who is clearly not into it. He meets with someone other fuck up north under the bridge and buys some under the counter pornography. Let's not look too close at that.

Eats at a cheap pasta place, gorging himself on plates of cheap carbonara and sickly sweet wine. Looks directly as his waitresses' tits all night. Reads a tabloid with stories on immigrants swamping the Country and how a pop singer has been voted best arse and that shit.

Then, when he's had five glasses of wine... the familiar climbs up his leg. Pours itself into his ear.

This is why the day was spent preparing. Bypass his ghosts.

Bypass his defences which, ghosts aside, are surprisingly shit.

They're prepped somewhere else though. Full operations were done on the asylum but got to figure Foulstone for knowing where the basics are done.

Whisper to him. 'Go to the Sothic Temple.'

Whisper it over and over.

'Go to the Sothic Temple.'

Say it over and over until it sounds like nonsense to me. Which is what's needed. No longer a command in my language. A string of barbaric syllables. A breakdown with the concious mind.

Which makes it sorcery.

He hails a taxi.

Says the address.

I've got you.

I V

She picks up on the second ring.

'Sup?'

'Come to my joint. Please.'

'Sure.'

In the background, Aristide yells 'Is that him?!'

She hangs up.

V

Bettina knocks on Scarlet's door.

A maid opens it.

A fucking *maid.*

It's five in the morning and she's in housecoat and slippers. She and Bettina rapid fire some Spanish at each other before my girl just pushes past her.

This is a penthouse apartment. One whole wall is just window overlooking the City. Sun starts to bruise the sky. Buildings spilled beneath us, lit up. It's like Tir NaNog down there. Rows of lights in the dark picking out streets and towers.

Sunken lounge, boundaried by a vast white leather lounge. Huge TV. In the distance, and it is distant, a kitchen. Everything is white, achingly modern. A dining table decorated with some exotic flowers never even seen before. Original Rothko on the wall. Some bullshit rectangles. Learn to paint, motherfucker.

'The fuck are you doing here!? This is my house!'

There's a spiral staircase of what seems glass leading up to… fuck knows. Probably bedrooms. But on it, looking down in silk pyjama pants and holding an actual gun, is Elliot. He works out.

'Put down the heater and pull on some clothes, Elliot. We need to talk. Actual emergency situation.'

'This is my *house!*'

'Probably why I'm here looking for you.'

Bettina goes to stand next to that dining table. Probably looking for something to peg at this stupid fuck.

A child starts crying.

Scarlet's child.

Oh fuck. Don't want anything to do with that. With *it*. The kid is proof of something that, back of my head, will never be true. That's she's past me. That she'll *always* be past me. She could come back to me, she could throw the kid away, but here's something she has that I can never, *would* never, be a part of.

Then she comes down the stairs, pushing past Elliot.

'Put it down, darling.'

She's in a silk robe and it clings to her but not noticing *that*. Kid in her arms. Not yet two foot tall. How old is that? Judging by the hair, it's a girl.

Her mother's red hair.

Scarlet comes all the way down and nods at Bettina.

'Oh my God, Scarlet, she's so beautiful.'

My ex-girlfriend smiles like she's just found money.

'Do you want to hold her?'

'Sure.'

Not every day you see an undead cage fighter hold your ex-girlfriend's kid. Kinda thing that would give you pause if you had a single correctly-wired *goddamn motherfucking* emotion. Shut that noise down.

Almost twenty years of diligent, rigorous occult practice and at least it's good for something. Go smooth insides.

Bettina coos at the baby, infant, what the fuck ever it is.

Try not to think it. The baby that could have. *Try not to think it.* Been mine. *God fucking damn me.* The house is great and Scarlet looks beautiful even startled from bed. But there's not a part of me that ever wanted this happy family bullshit.

The kid looks at me. She's got Scarlet's blue eyes.

'Lark. Lark!' Scarlet snaps at me.

Jesus. Staring back at it. It's not mine, by the way, in case that's how your mind inclines.

Elliot comes over and with a kind of contempt, takes his daughter from Bettina. The kid is still staring at me.

Scarlet walks past me and sits at the dining table. We all follow. I sit, Bettina doesn't.

'I'd invite you into the office but honestly, it's not cool that you're here, man.'

All business.

'Your goddamn right.'

Scarlet puts her hand on him. 'Darling, please. Could you ask Zoe to bring us some coffee?'

He gives his usual attempts at staring me down but too busy staring at his kid. He finally notices.

'Of course, dear.'

Darling. Dear. Fuck me.

Elliot know's he been dismissed. Sit my arse down at the lounge room table, big as a car. Bettina stands over me.

'What's her name?' she asks.

'You don't know my daughter's name?'

'Nope.'

'Jesus. Lark, do *you* know her name?'

 Say nothing.

'Do you ever think... no. Never mind. Her name is Dakota.'

 Feel myself blinking. 'No it's not.'

'Of course it's fucking not, idiot.'

'Out with it.'

'Her first name is Luanne, which is a family name.'

'Your aunt.'

'Yes. But we call her Jet, her middle name.'

'Jet.'

'Yes.'

'Like a plane.'

'Don't be a dick about my child, Lark.'

'Wasn't -'

'Fucking hell, you look terrible.'

'Heroic dose of mushrooms.'

For a moment she looks away. Eyes flickering. Remembering. Scarlet always had a taste for the pipe. Guess there's none of that in rich lady land. She gathers herself. Watch her force away good memories.

'What do you want, guys? You coming here to my house damn well better be important. I'll be fighting about this for weeks and you have no idea how boring that's going to be.'

Boring. You have to know by now that, petty as it is, that goddamn cheers me right up.

'Foulstone's a traitor. He's working for the Sothic Temple. Or with them.'

 She goes still.

'Lark.'

'This isn't personal, baby. This is for real. He got flipped or he joined up on purpose. It's for real.'

'Don't call me that. Not here.'

 She's right.

'Yeah. Yeah ok. Sorry. But this isn't personal. This is for real.'

She looks up at Bettina.

'You're a sensible woman. Is this…?'

'He's for real, lady,' my girl says back.

'Elliot!'

He comes in, maid behind him with a tray. He's found a t-shirt, thank fuck. Yacht club sigil on it. *These fucking people.* Maid takes the kid and goes. As she walks it upstairs, it will not stop *looking* at me.

Tell it to the both of them. Everything. Tell the fucking truth for once. Valier, Coffee. Even the familiar eregore. The traps laid. The videos.

But.

When it comes time for Apophis, the meteorite, Elliot stands up.

'Are you telling me the fate of the world rests on you? Jesus Christ, I always knew you were off in your own little world but this is… preposterous. Absurd! Fucking hell, Scarlet, what's wrong with this guy?'

She's staring at me. Intent.

Asks me, 'It's not the meteorite that's going to hurt us, is it?'

'No. A bad spirit will come to earth.'

Elliot is pacing back and forth.

'You've gone fucking mad, Lark. You've fucking lost it. Get the fuck out of here.'

He stops. Screams again.

'Are you listening!? *Get the fuck out of my house!*'

Bettina steps in.

'Cool your boots, man.'

'How dare you!?'

She takes him by the arm. Chill of death fills him. He tries to pull away.

'Get your hands of-'

Bettina squeezes with fists could crush diamonds from coal. Leads him away. He yells at her some more which bothers her about as much as a yapping dog might. Then it's me and Scarlet. She sits. Across the huge room from us, Bettina is nodding and nodding as he waves a finger in his face. Fuck, this cat is dumb.

Look at Scarlet in those eyes that have seen so much of me.

'Scarlet. I'm gonna move on Foulstone. Elliot's not going to believe he's a traitor. Foulstone's a manipulator. He's gonna seem clean. He's gonna have Elliot wound up. He'll probably have Blossom in his corner, too.'

'Blossom?'

'Yeah. And so Elliot's gonna get in the way. Which means I will body him if he tries. Because I'm going after Bernadette and I'm starting with Foulstone.'

She sighs.

'Lark, I'll come at you straight, I'm not sure we're ready to throw down with Bernadette. And... my kid.'

Open the zippo, close it. Look up at you.

'I'm here because I know this puts you and the kid in the firing line. Leave town a month. Tell,' thumb over my shoulder in direction of her husband, '*him* he'll still be boss when he gets back.'

'Will he?'

With that, something clicks inside me. *I'll come at you straight.* That's my way of speaking. She's trying to flatter me.

She's working this. She wants this to happen. Hold her gaze. Look carefully, deliberately, to Elliot. She follows my gaze. She wants me to give her an excuse to ditch Elliot.

She whispers to me, 'Lark, is this Apophis thing. This is real?'

'Yes.'

She looks at me again. She doesn't smile. Her eyes aren't warm. Realise *she knows I know.* Elliot's always been the money. Elliot's the house and the kid and her base of power in the Library.

But she doesn't want him calling the shots anymore.

'Whatever happens, you back my play?'

Tilt my head. *You even have to ask?*

Scarlet leans in and touches my hand.

God damn her. *Will my sentence ever end?*

Then she gets up. Walks over to Elliot. Murmurs something to

Bettina who comes over to me.

Low, she says to me 'This motherfucker makes a whole lotta ruckus. One long audition to star in a next level beating'.

First time in a long time... smile for real.

'Watch this.'

Minute later, Scarlet comes over. Elliot storms off back up his stupid glass-looking staircase.

'We'll go. Probably stay in the Perth chapter house.'

Nod.

'What do you need from me?'

What do you know? A second smile.

SIXTEEN

I

We're in one of those mini-buses. Bettina's driving. Scarlet and Elliot are in the wind. No one's got my leash in their fist now. This is where my familiar followed Foulstone. No traps laid for us now. This is their home.

Karel's bought a gun. Take that shit off him. Thought we'd covered that.

'Bring a gun, you're a thug with a gun. You're a magician. We use magic. This weapons disarms you.'

He nods.

Katanya hands him something. Blasting rod. A wand. She's in black with her short hair slicked back. On her face in henna, warding sigils. A sun in a triangle in a circle for the forehead. Eyes drawn under her eyes.

Sasha is with us. Wearing a katatagae amulet. She's repurposed geomantic magic into ward against metal. Knives, bullets. She's nervous as hell.

Karel holds up a knife. *Yeah, fine.*

Katanya's bought some of her crew. Some faces known to me. Ziegler, a former soldier who lost his legs in a war, came to us for help when no one else could. On those eerie curved prosthetics. Mary Sour, the Iraqi witch. She's in full niqab with bangles and trinkets at her wrists. Behind her veil, her eyes are electric. Two or three others never seen before. Get to know 'em if they do alright tonight.

'Look, we're cleared for full raid,' says Katanya in team leader mode. 'That means, we're cleared for anything. You see a motherfucker, put him down, ask questions later. Everyone, show your wards.'

Hold up our wrists. In waterproof ink, on our wrists, drawn the alchemical symbol for phosphorous. Lightburst chemical. Group warding.

Me? Check the wine that we'll need real soon.

'They're using some kind of shadow magic so don't be afraid to call on that. *Lux protegas me* is a good charm. Use it.'

She's doing good. Feel like we're in the Marines.

'We're looking for a dude named Todd.' She holds up her phone, an image of some anonymous looking white dude with a moustache. 'You've all got his photo. Take him if you can but not at risk to yourself.'

Now comes the hard part.

'There's a guy in there. Polynesian dude. He used to be a stone badass. Like, for real. But word is he's been cursed or he's sick. He's former Library. Do. Not. Engage. You see him, you call for Lark. Ziegler!'

'What?'

'No cowboy shit. This guy is for real.'

'Sure, sure.'

Reminds me of Anton. Poor little bastard.

'Other than that, we're trained. We're ready. Work together, stay with your partner at all times. Don't fuck up.'

Sasha is trying not to throw up.

Lean in to her. 'Stay by the van.'

'What?' Her voice is taut.

'This isn't your bag, the throwdown trip. Don't force it.'

'Really?'

Nod. She goes to hug me. Pull away. Smiles at me anyways and tells Katanya she'll be hanging back.

Which is why she dies.

I I

A new temple.

They've set it up in the old meat-packing zone. Old L-trains used to come here, decrepit and unused, looming overhead, casting shadows. There's a dock near us, the cold wind coming off the bay, getting into our jackets like pickpockets who don't need the light touch. Used to be that livestock would get off the boats here, trundled into abattoirs and slaughtered. This is where they recruit and this is where they sort out who gets to have their soul mutilated for the cause.

Mully remembers this area from when he was a kid. Talked about it with him. Told me about the stink of the joint, the cries of the animals, the miasma of suffering. A long time ago, that conversation. When me and Jon were kids, the mood would take him and he'd walk us through the City, showing us secrets hid in plain sight.

They tried to gentrify the place in the 80s but it just never happened. One hundred years of pain soaked into the walls and the bricks and the gutters. Sex clubs and flogging shops for perverts who like pain are the only places make a profit here. Sex workers of every blender of gender walk streets here and the cops can't be fucked policing.

Kind of a perfect place, you wanted to be able to work in silence and in the medium of pain.

Long, low white building, sunk into the earth. Barred windows set in the front face us.

A wooden bridge goes into the third floor and the bulk of the former slaughterhouse goes down three storeys.

Feels like a reversed building. An upside down place. Staring down past my feet at a building going down into the earth. No wonder they use it for an Operation like this.

Step up to the bridge. It creaks under my weight. The door thirty feet away is iron and tall and dark. And locked. Bettina steps up near me. She prepares herself for her work. Start my own.

Hit gnosis and stare. Protections and wards and all the rest.

Was a time I had more options. Made a god for myself, the Omegamantis and the Ultrascorpions were my eregores. Dig scorpions, me. Was a time could rely on Jon's mantic martial arts. Was, was, was. Not now.

Now there's a black hole in my brain and the Rabisu is watching and somewhere out there, the Devil is waiting.

But it was the Rabisu gave me the idea for this. Aristide too, that rat fuck.

These cats are on the Egypt trip. Let's work with them. Take that wine I had in the van.

'Sekhmet! Lioness of Might! Goddess of Wrath and War!'

Bettina glances at me. Feels it starting. Her eye gets a golden sheen.

'Drinker of beer, wine, blood. Bless this undertaking against the enemy of the sun, Apep Apophis!'

Screw top wine. Cabernet Sauvignon. No taste for wine. Liquor man, me. But the goddess drinks it so I drink it. Not much of a sacrifice but you do as you must. Neck it, stopping only for hurried breaths.

Bettina swells with power.

Sekhmet invocation. Warrior goddess, drunk on the blood of humanity. Fierce hatchet woman of the Gods of Egypt. Bettina's filling up with divine information. Her teeth seem longer, fingers curving up like cat claws.

Takes me about two minutes to finish the wine. Belly is full of it, sick roundness in me. *Don't fucking vomit don't you dare.*

'Mistress of Dread! Look upon our work with favour!'

Bettina stares at me, intense. Lion spirit inside her. Nod permission.

'Christ Lark, it's like eating lightning!'

God-ridden starts to race across the bridge. Speed and power of the spirits inside her. She charges and the doors smash open. The wards light up but she just ignores 'em.

The team follows her as I struggle with guts full of fucked up booze. Smash the bottle on the ground while it works its will with me. Only thing I can think to do as the rest of the crew march rapid, obeying orders to ignore me.

III

Not the most subtle plan but there's no time. Inside, can hear dim yells as Bettina goes to work. Monster priestess for a while yet. Sekhmet is a war goddess and a solar goddess. Good fit for B.

Bottom floor. Time to work.

Dim lights and white cements rooms. Bettina's hit one dude in those white robes they wear so much his head looks like goddamn pulped fruit. Turn eyes away.

Follow on alone. Don't have long before being drunk. Even now, wearing stumble boots. Hand pressed against the wall to help me stay upright.

Foulstone. If Foulstone is here, have to be ready for those fucked up ghosts. Down some stair and stop to fight off vomit. Sounds of fighting.

Me and the team follow her, looking to get to the killing floor, where they'll be.

Shit.

This place is amazing. A warehouse sized room. Every inch turned into a new Temple.

How much money do they have?

This is a long way from the amateur hour bullshit seen before. They've bought in pillars and painted Egyptian style art over them. All electric blues and golds and umber. They've underlit everything and immediately, we're in the deep past.

This is fine stagecraft. This is good magic.

On the walls, tail starting where you walk in, oozing along the roof, the great Serpent itself, Apophis is painted. It stretches along and great jaws open at the far end of the temple, surrounding and highlighting an altar.

On the roof... this was an old slaughterhouse. Meat hooks hang and swing and they are... in use. This is a human sacrifice cult. What's up there, you can guess and... don't want to dwell on it.

A sudden burst of light distracts me. Someone's activated a spell and a shriek greets it, a shadowy man stripped of his spell. Around me, fights breaking out, the ether thick with bound spirits, shrieking spells and shade.

Walk along, ignoring the battle. See, there's a spell at work here. Just for me.

Calling to me.

Bettina, fists laced with blood, glances up at me. Falls into line with me.

Feel something splash my face from above.

Blood. From the hooks.

There. The altar. Walk up five cement stairs all painted gold and black. Jaguar fur rug covering them. At the summit, a throne. There. Taped to it… that strikes me as almost funny. So out of place here, sticky tape, securing an envelope with my name on it.

Jon's handwriting.

'Thanks, Lark. We've been waiting on this. Now I can do my job. PS Foulstone says hi.'

The stomach goes out of me.

Can't help it. Vomit up the wine.

Whatever the fuck is happening, too late. They had this scouted. *They figured on us coming!* Bettina snatches the note from my hand and wipes the red spew off it. She pats my back as the back of my hand wipes the sour from my lips.

We clear out, in a rush, moving back up to the surface and what sins await me.

I V

She's dead. Sasha's dead.

A rain of blood is crusted to my face and Sasha, my student, is dead. The second in a week.

Her neck snapped. At least she didn't suffer too bad, spinal cord severed close to the skull. Tell myself that so as not to think about her suffocating as her lungs stopped working.

Seen Jon hit people with moves like this before. He's sick now, a lot of his strength gone but he's still got the moves, the techniques, the knowledge and the will to use it. Fa jin strike. 'Explosive power.' That's the jargon for it. One inch punch trip. Master's business.

Sasha came out of hell and Mully saved her and I tried to train her.

She died from my help.

Look down at her. Fucking *horrible* red mark against her neck, lurid and raw. That's what gives away it's Jon. Seen that wound before.

A girlhood of abuse and horror. Trying to make something of her life. Just dead now.

All for nothing.

Just dead.

Oh, Jon. This isn't what you were meant to be.

How to tell Mully? He loved this girl and raised her up out of the black horror that took her.

The bus we rode in is gone.

Jon must have taken it.

But where did he go?

Ignore the soft growl Bettina makes in her throat at the smell of dead woman's flesh.

'Lark. Call a cab. We have to get back to the Library now.'

Reach down to Sasha to close her eyes. Their wide and ghoulish and drying out. Soon, flies will come to lay their eggs there and... no. Not...

Touch her and Jon's will flashes in front of me.

'No, not the Library. He wasn't thinking about the *Library*. Let's go.'

Bettina looks at me.

'Let's fucking *go!*'

My face is covered in blood and Sasha's dead.

V

We move through traffic like a shark through schools of fish.

We're heading uptown. Where the cafes have umbrellas on stands out the front and the bookshops are good and the markets sell fresh vegetables.

Where he's lived for forty years.

Mully. My master.

We pull in and ...

Oh no, oh fuck, oh no

The front door to his apartment is open. Look carefully and it's been smashed in.

The place is trashed. Mully has a thousand protections but Jon's been here a hundred times. He must have been full on assaulted by thought-forms and guardians but he's aware of passcodes are charms to keep them off. And Bernadette must have warded him.

I ain't the only one who can use sacrifices to power my magic. Bernadette let us hit her crew. Sacrificed them to give power to Jon. Power enough to come here, the baddest magician in the city's Sanctum.

Move upstairs, checking bedroom, bedroom, bathroom, sanctum. That's locked. Try to hit gnosis to open it but the panic that's opening up my stomach like a purse fights it.

Then Bettina calls my name.

Rush down the stairs ignoring the pain in my hip.

Out the back. That little garden of his.

The white wrought iron table and chairs were we talked and he taught me so much. The vines on the back wall.

And Mully's body. Struck from behind.

Dead.

SEVENTEEN

I

Burying my mother wasn't anything to me. She died, my dad told me, she was cremated at the mental hospital. Dad never even bothered to pick up her ashes.

He was dead soon after.

His funeral was on a Thursday afternoon and there was me and Jon, not even in black, the Social Worker from the orphanage who drove us. And a man and a woman from his work. The man didn't even look at us. The woman told us he dad was a good guy and then drove off together. Never even knew their names.

Mully's funeral ain't like that.

This is the Jubilation of Mystery. Library specialised ritual. Heavily influenced by things like the Gnostic Mass and Silver Star formality.

Mully was a believer, though what denomination he never got into, if that even meant anything anymore. But we're in a Church anyway. Christ overlooks us all, pinned up there to the wall, smugly knowing that no imitation of him will even be good enough.

The celebrant is an old priest, friend of Mully's from long, long ago. He's so old his voice sounds like a breeze through reeds. But he speaks warm and he speaks true about my old master.

The place is *packed*.

Before we went in, stood aside and eavesdropped men and

women from dozens of Orders and from all around the world. Locals talking about the killings. Some talking about the rash of bad omens from around the world. Some even talking about Mully.

A murder of crows, an unkindness of ravens, freaks and sorcerers draped in black, eerie rings on fingers and tattooed temples. My people, supposedly. Don't want to be near any of them now. Sasha is dead and Mully is dead and who knows, among this collection of mad people, that maybe those deaths are my fault?

More speakers come. Some foxy old granny who speaks about him in tones that are maybe a bit too erotic for a funeral. Never knew Mully to have a girlfriend but guess he was young once too. Some demented Luciferian and one in a goat mask praises his scholarship and the books he wrote. Velasquez makes a speech and breaks down halfway through telling a story about how Mully fought off a possessing entity in the 70s that had been killing women. The last speaker is a middle aged man in a suit.

He tells everyone that he's not in the life, but that Mully rescued him from what he alludes clearly was more cult abuse. Him, his sister and some friends. And how even though that was thirty years ago, Mully still wrote to them, checked this citizen was ok, remembered his kid's birthdays even.

He was just that kind of man, says the citizen. That breaks people up. Because... he was.

Telegrams. One from Scarlet that twists with her heartbreak she wasn't here. Some of this older students, some in their 60s even, from all around the world. *Jesus, how old were you, man?* Two of them even name check me, his last apprentice and his pride in me. As if that can mean anything to me now.

But that's not true. Sasha was his last apprentice. Dead on the ground, neck snapped.

And my last words with Mully were not kind.

Finished, the coffin is taken and the congregation moves outside. Sunglasses on for a cool, bright Autumn afternoon. Bettina stands by me the whole time. Talking to the faces that I can't even recognise right now, though some have been with me fifteen years. Every single one of them talk to me like they're putting out matches with their fingers.

Some of them are weeping. Some heartbroken. All sad. Except for me.

Except for me.

Mully's body dead on the ground. It opened me up to let in too much ice.

But ice burns too.

Jon.

How could you do this?

How dare you?

A murder is inside me. Growing.

II

Kira, my mechanic and blacksmith friend, who made for me my periapt, spent some time inside. All her family have. For her, it was a short stretch, a year. Assault. Some cat tried to tell her she didn't know shit about cars, in her own shop, so she broke his arm with a wrench.

No justice in the world.

After the funeral, Bettina wants to hit a bar or something.

'Lark. These are... these are people who will want to talk with you. Mully was... everyone loved and him and everyone knows you worked with him.'

Among those crow-coated occultists... couldn't stand to be with them for a second. One more sympathetic handshake and my shins would vomit out of me.

'Lady, no. Not this time.'

We stare at each other behind our dark glasses.

She nods. Drives me to Kira's joint.

Her brothers are there but no time for playing.

'Leave.'

With some mojo behind it, they decide it's union break and put aside their tools. Kira pulls herself out from under a car and gives me a speculation look.

I like Kira.

Sit down at her card table again. Take out my phone and show her a symbol.

'Need this tattooed on me.'

She frowns.

'How'd you know I did that?'

'My job is to know things about people. Inside, you got real good at ink.'

'Wasn't a pro or anything. We did it with biro ink and paper clips and shit. You're looking for an actual tattoo...'

'No. Want something rough. Something that will hurt.'

Take out cash. A few hundreds and lay them on a card table.

'You'll be paid.'

She doesn't touch money.

Wipes her greasy fingers on her overalls and drums her fingers.

'Seems to me like you need this done with a savage quickness, Lark. I'd be a fool if I didn't bargain for all your worth, man.'

This is not the fucking time.

Got a thousand ways to hurt people. Plant a meme in her head, make her hurt herself. Grab some of her hair, her skin cells, sympathetic voodoo her, throw that shit in a fire, pound it with a hammer. Curse her so that pain falls on her in a hundred different ways. Let loose a spirit of fire. Just need time and the will and there's a twisted up part of me that wants to do it. That wants to scream it all into... someone.

But it's not Kira.

Put my face in my hands. Something comes over me. Want to just say nothing. Want to just stare at her and say nothing. People hate that. People make mistakes every time you withdraw oxygen from those flames.

Something comes over me and it gets given away.

So tired.

'Lark?'

She sounds so far away.

'Lark?'

Look up. There's a look on her face. Don't know what it means.

'Forget it, Lark. Just... give me the money and we'll sort you out.'

Don't know why she changed her mind. Don't know how to read the twist in her lips or the softness in her eyes. She raps her knuckles on the table twice.

'This won't be fun. Let's get to it.'

She takes the money.

I I I

She's right. It ain't fun. Kira takes a sewing needle, ties it to a pencil, snaps open some biro pens and gets to work on me.

There are occult tattooists. Plenty of them. Don't want to show them the design. Who else has Bernadette leaned on? Don't want to wait for them, don't want to barge in and demand. Don't need bad blood with even one more solitary motherfucker. Not now.

But there is a need for this to be sorcerous. To be a tattooist tattooing in a sacred space.

Kira's turned down the lights and entered gnosis and is out of her overalls and in a simple grey dress. She looks strange in it, dressed up with her hair slicked back.

But that's the point.

Kira stabs that goddamned needle into me and into me. Sadistic pointillism across the back of my hand. Maybe, in time, regret having something that's easy to remember so visible but that's for another day.

Right now, just lose myself in the pain of it. Listening to Kira hum to herself some eerie melody means something to her.

One of the oldest solar symbols is the actually hieroglyphic. Circle with a dot in it. Remove the dot, add a snake tail to the circle, that's uraeus, symbol of their royalty who's the sun. No, need to fight against that current.

Don't want a fire with fire.

Bone script, ancient Chinese writing had the same symbol, dot in circle and for that, so does modern astronomy. Ancient and modern symbolism together. Has its appeal but, to be honest, want to break totally with Egypt. There's a lot of cruciform imagery with the sun but used that shit when dealing with the devil and don't want to...

Different mindset then. Different... this is just different. Use different tactics. 'From symbol to symbol leaps the mind of the genius.'

Symbols change the way your mind sits in your skull, they magnify, refract, inform.

No crosses. Not this time.

The Sun of May? Might be an ancient Incan symbol, face in a sunburst. No.

Verginia Sun, old Greek symbol. Talked about it before. Too... kingly for a scumbag like me.

Christ, everyone looks up at the sun. Everyone since caveman times. There's no point in running through every solar symbol.

And that's why the *Black Sun* goes on me instead.

Jon has wrapped himself in his Sheut, his shadow soul. They all did, Sothic fucks. But me? Don't get into some light *vs* dark bullshit.

Need to hit them where they live.

The Black Sun.

It has a... traduced... history. But for now... alchemy.

The dissolution of the body. The Original Sin. Some traditions claim it was made from black fire. The Original Sin is the defiance of authority.

Can relate.

Kira finishes and the white fire of pure alcohol breaks the spell.

She wraps my hand in sandwich wrap.

We banish together.

On my leaving she puts her hand on my shoulder and turns me to face her.

'You're on some dark road shit, yeah?'

Nod.

A long length of silence.

She doesn't know what to say.

Whatever was in her face is gone and she's still again.

'It's better to feel things, Lark.'

Want to laugh at that.

'Thank you, Kira.'

She wraps it.

Leave.

I V

One final Working before whatever needs to be done.

Time's running out with the goddess, too. Bendis lurks on my field of vision, waiting.

Take that final hair of Jon's from before.

Summon up my shadowy familiar.

Naked on the cement floor of my house. Back in my sanctum. Candles lit.

Back of my left hand feels like cats have been at me. The heat tells me infection is trying hard to get in.

Good.

The pain will assist in what's coming. And what's a wound compared to a black hole in the brain? Make allies of the biota feasting on the pus. Fever spirits.

Bettina phones me but put that on ignore. There's nothing but tonight.

I feel a murder inside me.

The shadow familiar appears in front of me. Its nervous movements, its shyness... they charm me.

Take it in my hands.

'Nemesis.'

The divine force of justice. Which even gods and heroes must fear. Ceaseless, restless punishment for those who defy the natural order.

Like patricides.

'Strengthen me.'

The shadowy creature feels the force of it come into my sanctum.

'Strengthen me in my righteous endeavours.'

The puppet tries to run but my fists close around it and squeeze.

It has no bones to snap. It has no flesh to crush. It dies and liquefies. That tattoo in my hand pulses with agony that cannot be abated. Even deep in gnosis my cries are clear to me. Take a moment to compose.

The shadow stuff of my eregore familiar splash away and evaporate.

Deliquescence. The Black Sun.

A sacrifice.

I am ready.

I am dedicate.

I feel a murder inside me.

V

Five in the morning and my power is on me. My cause is just and my sacrifices accepted.

All that good shit.

Walk, without aim. Without purpose. Walk until shins splint and feet hurt.

Car comes past me, slows down. Rolls Royce Silver Shadow.

Got to figure that for the Devil but he can wait. Had his chance.

Not looking for Jon. Letting the City show itself to me, it feels like it. Enchanting without desire. Trick of the trade.

Late night buses streak past me, leaving smears, blurs of light in my vision. So deep in gnosis that it feels like morphine and nothing's important enough to fret over. Building waver like heat mirages.

Come at last to another one of the wretched flop houses Jon

stays in.

The City doesn't have suburbs. They're all over the bay. But on the East side are these terrace houses, remind me of London. Not cold enough in summer, reverse as well, they're where you take your big family if your job is shit. Slab of flat red bricks going up and down a street, identical in architecture, unique in squalor.

Magic halts me outside one with a smashed in window and graffiti on the front wall.

Plus Jon's chop written on the wall in white.

Martial artists will know it and not set up dojos and shit near here without asking permission. To everyone else, just Chinese-looking symbol.

Door's open.

Mully's dead. Sasha's dead.

No lights. Flick on the switch. Flares up and burns out with a too loud crack.

Should have bought Bettina.

No. Him and me time.

Me and Jon. Together since boys.

Me and him.

Oh, Jon.

Up rickety stairs, complaining at their work. Threadbare ancient carpet.

A light on upstairs.

On the landing. Music. Soft music.

Hah.

Disco.

Jon loves disco.

I Feel Love, Donna Summer.

Not the soundtrack you anticipate to murder your oldest friend.

It's so good, it's so good, it's so goood.

Walk down the corridor.

Jon.

Jon the Hollow.

Who I am here to murder.

But he is not done and he wraps himself in his shadow and prepare for murder of his own. When you've killed your father, your brother don't seem to matter much.

Open the door. He's on his bed, his head in his hands. Almost like a man grieving. He looks up at me. First time I seen him wasn't a fight in years. There's scars on his face where the mask had him. Never noticed that before.

I feel love I feel love I feel love

EIGHTEEN

I

Stand up fight? Jon kills me with his first shot.

Not wins. Kills me.

How do you win a fight like that? *You motherfucking cheat.*

Tattoo is feverish with infection. Which is what's needed.

Pain. Shame. Sickness. Rage. Pain.

Grief.

These are things that happen to other people. Spent my life one step away from it all. Three people mattered and this one killed another.

'You come to kill me, Lark?'

Turn my hands over like *what can I do?*

'I wish I didn't have to kill Mully. Or the girl. But they were in the life. They knew the risks.'

'That girl was Sasha.'

'Oh, shit. Mully's... that girl we took off the Satanists...'

'Yeah.'

He'd seen the marks they'd left on her.

'I'm sorry, Lark. But all this is locked in.'

Jon is coming towards me fast, and he looks like a man of smoked glass. Cold and sure as light through ebon ice. His mask-wasted body doesn't need strength, supported as it is within the butchery he's made of his soul.

Step by step along a filthy threadbare carpet between sticky walls under a water stained roof, brothers look to murder one another. Original sin. Powerful hoodoo.

The Black Sun pinned and sliced into the back of my hand catches black fire and sin burns with an anti-luminosity and the two of us turn photonegative.

He pushes against it, walking up the ratty hallway like a man breasting tide. He screams. The mask, Bernadette, they've slashed at his soul to turn him into a patricide. It's tender, so I go for it.

This is a crime against Jon. Don't forget this. Don't forget what I have unleashed here and do not forgive it. These wounds struck on him are perverse and deep and intimate as love. Black white flash on flash off, my magic raw and cruel, radiating malice into the man who killed my master.

The power is too much to simply channel. It comes in waves, the Nemesis information flowing through me, bringing all the cruelty of justice.

And Jon

Keeps walking

To me

His will is inhuman. Five steps from me.

Four.

Black

Three

White

Two

Fuck!

'Rabisu!'

It hears.

It laughs.

And that's the final edge needed.

Jon aims a strike at me but falls to his knees.

The shadow boils off him, mist at dawn.

And the dark spirit who once was bound by the Old Man is inside me again, without the restraint of sorcery.

At last. He's mine. I should kill him. I should murder him as he sleeps.

My hand on his throat.

I let him go.

I I

It cannot *control* me. But it goes through my memories at length, amused by my mother's elaborate and sadistic madness. My beating at Ludo's hands. Sex with Scarlet, the warmth of her mouth the skill of her fingers, the fire in her eyes. Sex with Katanya, her surprising shyness, her determination. Jessamyn, the madwoman scientist-magician who meddled with death intrigues it. Bernadette...

They say Post Traumatic Stress Disorder is where you cannot help but to relive some wounding experience. Feels like that now.

Memories so strong they collapse me to my knees.

The Rabisu is inside me. It killed me and now it rides me.

Shit's a two way street, though. It's vulnerable to me as well.

Not now. though.

I call on it and it laughs and laughs and the strength of it pulses from the black hole in my brain to the black sun tattooed on me. The lights in the ratty corridor we battle shatter. The paint on the walls starts to peel. And Jon, finally, finally...

falls.

I stagger against the wall. Exhausted. But no rest.

If Mully is to have justice, the best *goddamn fucking thing is just to kill him now, kill him now, this is Jon he's the most dangerous kill him now!*

The black spirit inside me laughs at that panicked though. *God, it's so heavy, so vast.*

And I begin to suspect it came, not to answer me for its own amusement, but rather because it has some plan for me. I think that, and it laughs to hear it.

Drag Jon into his cot, the threadbare thing he sleeps in. Put bindings on him. He'll go nowhere.

Go out for coffee, food. For us both.

Bettina calls me on the way back.

'You alright?'

'Sure. Hey, you free?'

'We got another cult murder here. Some sort of... puppeteers?'

'Never heard of them. Puppet sorcery? Voodoo?'

'No. Like, magic with dolls.'

'Look it up later. Right now, we've got something. Can't talk about it on open lines.'

'Also, we have that Todd guy, head of the Temple. He was taken in the raid. We figured out who he was.'

'Not entirely fucking wasted then. Come round.'

'Sure. I'm in the car with Aristide. Won't be long.'

So that didn't end in break up, which... kinda figured it might.

Stop. Buy a pack of smokes. Don't want them, I realise. What? Then get us food. He may need something. Donuts and coffee. He'd whinge but fuck him. He can eat what he's given. Man's inside reading a newspaper. War is back and murders are in style and heroes are raping from one end of the world to another. Jobs are down and people are sick and the skies are sicker.

When I'm back, Jon's legs are stretched out in front of him on the bed, back to wall. Waiting for his judgement.

I I I

The Rabisu purrs.

Jon can't even look at me.

'Look at me.'

Nothing.

Throw him the food. Put the coffee down next to him. He tries a swipe at me but he's bound in chains he can't even see or feel.

Once, his skin was brown and gold and his hair was thick and black. Now he looks almost like Bettina when she ain't fed, but he isn't even dead, so there's no goddamn excuse. Ribs through skin and face like a skull.

'You killed friends, Jon. You killed -'

'I know what I did.'

'You killed - '

'I said I know!'

Say nothing. Wait. Sip my coffee.

'What do you want from me, Lark? How's this conversation go?'

To kill you. To get my revenge for Mully and Sasha, who both deserved better. To punish you for putting on the fucking mask in the first place. To punish you for leaving me in the first place. To send Bernadette a message that when she turns mine against me, she will be annihilated.

'Not quite sure yet.'

'Make up your mind. People know where I am.'

'That's probably true. But check it. You hit me hard, sure. Sasha and Mully. But.

We took the entire Sothic crew. Bettina just reported we even got your Lodge master. Todd what's his face. Bernadette ain't breaking cover for you. Bettina's coming. My man Aristide's coming. We'll throw down together. Let her try to save you. Seems her style, yeah?'

'She'd kill all three of you, Lark.'

His voice is thin and sick, halfway to whisper. But firm. He believes that sure as sure.

'Could be.'

'No, she will.' Says like he talks about the sky being blue.

'She... She's a hundred years old, Lark. I've seen the proof.'

Say nothing.

'I chose her for a reason. Something is coming and it's going to change everything. The world is fucked, Lark. Beyond repair. And you? You don't care. Books and an obsession with a woman who doesn't love you, you won't help fix it. You don't care about anything. '

'And the Sothic Temple cares, yeah? Murderers and torturers.'

'Bernadette cares, yes. She's more than you know and what's coming is more than you can know.'

'Apophis. The primal chaos.'

'Yes! We'll make everything better, you'll see. Bernadette will be the Secret Queen of the world. She remade me. She healed me when the Teaching Darkness was taken from me. I owe her. I'd like to say you can come with me but she hates you. You should kill yourself now. Quick and clean. Pills. That sounds like a threat but it's not. That's good advice. Because she *will* make the world anew and then...'

'Sure.'

'It is sure. Jesus Christ, you never cared about anything your entire life. But she does and she's planned this for a long time.'

'Thought she wanted the Devil.'

'She did. But that was always... the Apophis plan was always the main one.'

There's a knock behind us.

Bettina.

'Hey.'

She comes over, stands behind me. Stares at Jon.

Jon says, 'Hey, look. It's your consolation prize.'

Just straight up ask it.

'You kill Mully just to fuck with me?'

He shrugs. 'Yep. It was easy, too.'

Bettina doesn't take the bait at this casual cruelty. Isn't like Jon at all.

'Lark?'

Look at her. There's a guillotine in her gaze and she clenches her fists.

'Yeah.'

'You have to kill him.'

Say nothing.

Jon tenses but he's not killing old men or girls now. He knows it's over if Bettina says it's over.

'Lark. You know he has to go. I know what this cat meant to you. I do. But I ain't telling you what you don't know. He's lost. Whatever he was, the mask and Bernadette wiped that away.'

That hole inside me, the one that blows with cold winds, the door Mully's death opened, widens just a little more.

'Yeah.'

Whisper it. Lips say it before the mind can even think it.

Death sentence is passed. Jon has to die.

'Lark…?'

Jon's voice is… frightened. Never once heard him *frightened*.

Bettina puts her hand on my shoulder. Look into her black eye and see what only people like us recognise as a kindness, because she says 'I'll do it.'

Tell her, 'I have to watch.'

She nods at that. She understands.

'Lark, please, don't do this. I want to see what's coming. I'll be healed.'

'Nothing is coming, Jon. Not for you. You rolled the dice on someone wasn't me and in the end, it just got you dead in bed.'

'Lar-'

He stops.

The Rabisu stirs in my head. Have to banish it soon as we're finished here.

'Lark.'

It's Jon's voice from Jon's tongue but it's not Jon's saying it.

Bettina goes as still as a corpse. She hears it too.

Bernadette is speaking through Jon.

'Lark and his creature. How lovely, the gang's all here.'

Slam the backs of my hands together, fingers intertwined. Mahakala Mudra, invoking the Fearsome Protector. Jon's body flinches from it.

'Lady, behind me.'

Bettina does. She knows this is for keeps and knows this ain't as simple as a kick to the head.

'Do you know, Lark, I never expected you to come out of those woods. You walked into that trap so *easily*. I've known a thousand little chancers like you but not many who were as addicted to knowing things. But I didn't expect you to take so freely to my father's pet. I see it behind your eyes, chained and seething. How pathetic. Both of you.'

The Rabisu stirs in fury at the mention of the Old Man. It hated its captor as it hated me.

'As it was father's creature, so Jon is mine.'

'Can't figure on Jon liking to hear himself described that way.'

'Jon is named and mastered. You should have done the same ten years ago. Made him a slave. Even in his weakness, he has competencies I find useful. This slapper as well. The dead are useful things in hands such as ours.'

Jon's chin lifts at Bettina.

Bettina half smiles at that. *Her, a creature? No dice.*

'And today, you should have killed Jon the second you laid eyes on him. Instead, you have bought me a creature made slave to my blood long, long since.'

Jon's hands lift up and he makes a ritual gesture. Bettina steps ahead of me and goes to strike him but by then... it's too late for me.

I V

The Rabisu shrieks inside me. This is not it's dark purr of satisfaction in atrocity or its wicked delight in suffering.

Panic. Fear. Horror.

A demon thing is screaming in my head. Drop to my knees, which fucking hurts. The black hole in my brain lights up and oh Christ the pain in my head is... can barely see. Ten, twenty red wine hangovers slam into me at once. The crippling headache of a blow. Vomit.

But what's happening to the Rabisu is worse.

It's tearing out of me, scratching as it goes.

A demon like this is a bad thought given life. Given form. In the world, it's a vast dark form of wings and jaws but in my head, just every cruel and vicious and spiteful thing given life.

Rushes of memories of cruelty. Fights with Scarlet. A fit of temper that had me kill some bounty hunter called Crazylegs.

Unworthy thoughts about Mully, my last before his murder.

Taking Bettina's eye.

Washing over me. Vicious as torture. Start to spew up from the...

Taking Bettina's eye!

...no, it's not vomit.

The Rabisu pushes itself out of my mouth. That vast darkness is gone. It's ragged. Wounded.

Bernadette's torn it in two.

And it goes rushing into Jon. Through his nose, his tear ducts, mouth and ears down into his pants and up his arse and down his cock.

Bettina is a pro. She punches to kill but Jon's hand deflects it. Taken off guard, he rallies and counter strikes, hitting her thigh with a move that's been known to break thigh bones. He's too weak for that but, Jesus, *still*. She stumbles.

He rises up. Bernadette breaks my spell like ripping paper.

Three gazes through one set of eyes.

He'll go mad now, Jon. The mask, Bernadette, the frothing, thrashing of a monstrous crippled spirit, all have staked out territory in his head and that's too damn much.

The Rabisu lingers in me but its bisection is done. This gives me some time to try some desperate Work.

'Infernal powers take this-' but Jon leaps from the bed, stomps me and my collar bone feels like its smashed. Bettina strikes him and

this is too much.

The pain pulls me under.

NINETEEN

I

Wake up in hospital.

Bettina's shaking off a nurse who's trying to get her to admit herself.

She's fucked up, though. Her glass eye is gone and around the socket, the shards of it are embedded. Fingers all messed up. Must have been a hell of a throwdown.

'He got away.'

Nod.

She stays by me in a chair. Doctor comes in and tell me about the clavicle injury. Sling, ice.

Rest. Sure. They want to keep me in for a few hours. Sure.

Bettina's pissed all the way off. Arms folded in her chair.

'This mood for me?'

'Yeah. No. Just everything.'

Nod.

'Go see Aristide.'

She shakes her head no.

'What do we do now?'

Shrug, which hurts right now.

'Maybe talk to prisoners from the raid?'

'Can I kick the everloving shit out of a bunch of them?'

'Looks like.'

'That'd cheer me up.'

She did.

I I

Spend the next day at home, on my couch. Watch some television but that shit nearly kills me and the news is like a butcher's shop. Read. LeLoyer's *History Of Ghosts And Demonology*. Regardie's measured prose and some Sandra Cicero as a chaser. Some Palamas and Bertiaux to try and lift the mood. And on the stereo, J.B Nelson sings about stealing the money from dead men's eyes.

If there's one good goddamn side effect of what happened, the Rabisu fragment inside me is quiet and the black hole throbs like the old cigarette burns my mother left on my back. But no more than that.

My phone rings. Hidden number.

Scarlet.

'You alright?'

'Yeah. Fine. Hiding out still. I read Bettina's report. Man, you've got to tell her to put in more detail.'

Say nothing.

'Are *you* alright?'

'Beat up and sore as hell, but yeah.'

'I'm glad. I was worried.'

Want to say nothing, make her work a little, but Bettina's advice about going along to get along is still good.

'Thanks.'

A long silence. In the background, a kid is laughing. Jet.

'Where's Foulstone?' she asks.

'Jesus. Dunno. Forgot all about him.'

'He's a...' she lowers her voice 'He's a ratfuck.'

'Why, Scarlet. Such language. What are you wearing?'

Can feel that long cool stare she gives me when she doesn't want to respond to cheek she likes.

'I'm working remotely and-'

'Working remotely. Great way to think about organising an occult order.'

'...I'm working remotely and I wanted to know if you feel you'll be fit for duty soon.'

'Find me a doctor who'll give me pills and sure.'

'Done. We've had a meeting and...'

Say nothing.

'No. Not over the phone. Tonight. Dreamspace.'

'Sure.'

...

...

'I'm glad you're ok, Lark.'

There's only so much a man can take. Hang up.

III

Ancients knew dreams you had in sacred sites were the real deal. Touching onto the other world. Like that monk I talked of before. They took it seriously. We should too. Spend a third of your life in that world.

On good terms with the moon goddess right now. For a bit longer, anyways. Head down to the cemetery where me and Scarlet hung out. Call Katanya, ask her to guard me. She meets me outside the gate.

It's a pretty nice night all things considered. First week of autumn.

She turns up. Looking beat up herself. And pale. Ignoring the sling my arm's in.

'What's all this about?'

'Meeting with upstairs. They want to do it in dreams.'

'No one asked me.' Wasp voice.

'Makes you feel better, thinking it's to tear strips off me.'

'Fine, great. Whatever.'

Say nothing.

'Fuck it. I'm over it. I'm over *you*.'

'Gonna talk to me or stick pins in my eyes all night?'

She sighs. We walk in among the headstones.

'Ah, it ain't all you. Sasha. Mully too. Sad, pissed off. But it's Sasha that's under my skin. She was... she was a nice kid who fought her way out from under some truly vile shit and that's her reward?'

What's to say to that? We walk a bit more.

'As ever, Lark, your warmth is a great comfort to us all in time of sorrow.'

Stop.

'Lady, you ain't alone in anger. You might recall you weren't the only person who lost her. Or Mully. Feels like there's a hole in me where cold winds blow through. But talking about it won't change how you feel. Sharing won't help you. But stick with me and maybe we can share our feelings with the fucks who put us here. *That's* healing.'

'That's not exactly healthy, Lark.'

'Fuck that. Fuck is happiness? Next to getting some justice?'

We walk a bit more. Moon's up. See it through the haze that hangs over the City night.

'Don't think that's how I can play it.'

'Don't then. Not giving a *lesson*. It's just one way of getting by.'

'Getting better?'

'Getting by. '

Find an impressive statue of angels and skeletons, properly pompous.

Lay down on the grass.

'You see me struggling, screaming, whatever?'

'Don't wake you up no matter what?'

'Fuck no. Shake me like a bastard. Means something got me. Sharks in the waters I'm going.'

I V

Normally, a hit of weed or something helps with this but the painkillers Scarlet had couriers bring over are good enough. Slip away on a stranger's grave, mind prepared. And the second sleep gets me, dreams start.

The logic of dreams hold sway. We're on a suspension bridge that's over a vinegar coloured sea far below. There's no other person but me and some pillars of flame that shoot out of the bridge's white stone road from what seem fountains distributed all random. No handrails, no nothing. Just a long spar from horizon to horizon. Peer over the edge and even though the sea is miles away, there's vast schools of fish below us that are clearly visible.

Probably other dreamers.

A shark or two as well.

Things live in dreams. No one's ever closer to mystery than here.

'Lark.'

Scarlet's voice from one of those flames burning. They all leap up to about my height. Figure for a session in order.

'This is a meeting with seven Sanctum heads.'

'Are you the head of the Sanctum now? What about your hus-'

She steps out of the fire, dressed up like a French Duchess, wig huge, skirts wide. Her hair is red diamond. The logic of dreams.

'This isn't about that. All you need to know is that this is a sacred quorum. This is a formal convocation of Titled Members.'

Means the Library is going to *do* something. Something big. Across the entire order.

'We could have done this by teleconference or something but some of your criticisms of the way the Library has acted this last few years have been heard. Nor was yours the only voice. We are an order of sorcerers, we shall act as such.'

Don't recognise the speaker's voice in the fire.

'Lark. We've been looking at your work. We've been reading your, or rather this Bettina and Katanya's reports.'

'Not to be distracting from the proceedings but you simply *must* report more frequently.'

'Not now, Basil. The reports on the Apophis entity would be concerning enough. The grandness of this working, this mad astrology... but with the death of Mully...'

'He was a popular man.' A German accent. No idea. But Basil's from the New Zealand chapter.

'He was a powerful man,' that's Vimbo, from before. The African elder. She goes on.

'That's what's made this decision for us. This Bernadette has struck at the man who was perhaps the most potent living sorcerer. We are no longer calling this a local problem. We are diverting considerable resources.'

Say nothing.

'Wait, wait, wait. This man is possessed!'

Voices rise up. Wait for them to calm.

'It's wounded bad. It ain't listening. And reckon it'll be needed before the end. Tell me more about these resources. This operation.'

'We will start a program against the Apophis rite. And we are making you, Lark... *you* are the one to lead it.'

Say nothing.

Scarlet's voice. 'Lark. This is a promotion. We want you to take up the mantle of Sacred Executor.'

'Cool.'

'Lark,' she warns.

'There hasn't been a Sacred Executor since the 1960s, Lark,' continues Vimbo. 'Until now. You will be inducted at your earliest convenience.'

I go real still. Suddenly it all clarifies for me. Sacred Executor.

This is... a deal.

Part of me though... opens my mouth and says... fucking this.

'What's in it for me?'

Silence.

'This is an honour.' The German.

Say nothing.

'An honour, I say!'

'You say so, man. What's in the honour for me?'

Vimbo talks then.

'Lark. This is not... '

Say nothing.

They talk over each other, all eager to give me some GBH of the ear.

Say nothing.

Bettina's right. *Should* go along to get along.

But not always.

Time stretches out but this is just a dream and it passes as it's told to pass.

Just let it all wash over until what I want to hear is heard.

'Alright then. What *do* you want?'

Elliot out? Figure his wife has him out already. Foulstone? He's already wanted. Bernadette? That's what they're offering me anyway.

Fuck. Don't know what I want. At all. About anything. Just took the shot when the prey turned up.

But...

I do know.

'It's Bettina. Her eye...'

V

Katanya watches me wake. Throws her hand down, helps me up.

'So what's all that about?'

'Good news is, you're getting promoted back to your old gig. You're senior Custode.'

She stares at me a long moment.

First time seeing her *really* smile.

V I

Bettina and me hit the bars. Katanya joins us. They tell me to bring Karel so he comes too. He's lost two friends in a week himself. We are... celebrating?

'Kid needs something.'

Sure. Why no Aristide? Don't ask.

Bettina and Katanya are the talkers but Karel, tongueless, reveals how much you can make two women laugh with just your hands.

Whisky flows and the memory of the four glasses held up against the warm yellow light of the bar will stay with me until the end.

There's a black hole in my brain but it hasn't taken that.

Maybe it will leave me something.

Be good if it left that. Tiny moments, snatched against the dark. A moment of warmth even for someone like me. Maybe I deserve it. maybe I don't. But I have that memory and the wounded monster inside me ain't taken it yet.

In the end, that's all any of us have. Perhaps they're enough.

They are for me.

TWENTY

I

The Sacred Executor is the one who makes the will of the Library manifest. Agent number one. You know they used to think Jesus was the greatest of magicians? It's not up to me to compare myself to Christ but, you know... here we are...

Wish it came with extra... dunno how to say it... *powers* or some shit like Jesus had, but that's not how this works. What it does give me is what's needed - authority. Only people who can yay or nay me now is upstairs and upstairs need quorum.

That means full access to resources and co-operation with every Chapter House in the world.

First thing is to write me up a list of proscribed books from every House we have. *Suckers.* Some of those they been trying to keep from me a long while. Another time, might have gotten what someone else might call excited for that but for me, it's like knowing you got china white on the way when all you've had for a while is black tar.

Something to look forward to if Jon and Bernadette don't ghost me.

Second is a good office. Proper office. Seven bookcases filled up with what's good. Big Tasmanian blackwood desk. Venetian blinds made from agar wood. Computer looks like it come out of a movie. Someone's filled up three crystal decanters with Irish, Scottish, Japanese whiskey. Hell, behind a wood panel, even a bar fridge/freezer for ice.

Essential part of magic is fighting the ego but, goddamn, *be hard in a joint like this.*

Then comes initiation.

II

Formal affair.

In charcoal robes, belted at the waist. Hems are stitched with runes. Hoods. Suit on underneath. Single breasted.

Won't go into it. Lasts a long time. Three figures in robes take me through it all. Formal circles cast, prayers offered. Even a sacrifice of rare bird feathers, burnt and sacred words spelled out in the smoke.

An altar, book opened on it. Old book. Write my name in with a hundred year old fountain pen, costs about as much as a one bedroom unit. Name above mine? Mully.

Glance up it. 1953, woman called Vesna, who talked to me once about her time dealing with Fascist magic. 1943, someone called Angela, her handwriting the shaky kind tells you whoever wrote it wasn't great. 1924, someone called Prince Duke.

Stretching back. Maybe some weird cat with a heavy job to do will wonder who Lark was in a century. If there's what you'd recognise as a world. Apophis comes and we'll be in ruin, killing each other for crumbs.

Chrism drizzled on my forehead. Oaths of loyalty made with a rod of office in my hand. Sombre. Serious. Velasquez holds the *Bibliotheke* out and my palm touches it like you touch a live wire.

Give me a ring to show my authority. Middle finger left hand. Flash signet. Not my thing but a few days wearing it won't kill. Not just authority though. Remind me of my duty. The trust placed in me.

Once, and not so long ago really, this woulda meant a hell of a lot to me.

Would have had Scarlet and Jon in there with me. Mully too. Gone, dead, betrayer.

Then again.

Bettina watches too. Bettina loves magic. Loves the robes.

Figure she's enough. She flashes me a grin. Which is pretty good.

Say my final oaths and we banish together, the hot electric hum of sorcery fading from the room like a song fading out. Hands shaken and good luck offered. One of them warns me to take this serious who the fuck listens to people like that?

'Can I keep the robes?' Bettina asks Velasquez.

'No.'

She steals some later and uses them for a bathrobe.

Show her my office. She finds, behind a panel, there's even a pretty good bathroom.

'This is the big chair, hey?'

At the huge black swivelling throne of a thing they gave me, nod. She pours some whisky for us both. Both of us sigh. We don't get much in the way of the good booze.

Bettina just looks at me careful once we finish breathing that fire down our throats. Raises up her glass and we clink them together. Best congratulations in my life.

'Big time player,' she tells me.

'High roller.'

'What's next?'

'We left the Temple raid kinda in a hurry and then... well... got a bit distracted. Still not sure if we got out before a trap got pulled.'

Distracted. With Mully's funeral and all.

'You remember prisoners?'

'Surely. Was gonna talk about that in a piece.'

We drink some more.

'How it play out with Aristide?'

'Dunno yet.'

She wants to talk about it, she'll talk about it. Bit later, she does.

'He's... can't figure out if what's he's doing is cool or not.'

'Ask me, no matter how it benefits, he shoulda come at you straight.'

'Yeah. But he says if I knew what was going down, I mighta said *no*. He ain't the kinda man likes hearing that word.'

'Bettina, come on, man.'

'I hear it. I do.'

Shrug at her. 'Tell him not to make a move like that again.'

'You think he'll listen?'

Long patch of silence we walk down together. Think we both know where it's gonna end.

'No.'

I I I

'Todd, right?'

He's nervous. He should be.

Still in my new office. Wound about with so many spells, could be in here with a shark, it wouldn't come at me. He can attack me like his money is in my chest and he couldn't hurt me worth a damn.

Decide we're gonna be good cops for this. Keep up that empathy thing.

Behind my desk with combed hair, shaved face. White shirt on, even a tie. Gotta look like just a citizen. Bettina behind me, in shade. He can see her, she's not invisible, but she's so still he flinches when he first sees her, like the movie just had a fright.

'Yes, Todd Roberts.'

Lean forward, shake his hand.

'Hey man. My name's Lark. My job is to... Well, I'm here to deescalate the situation between your order and mine.'

Keep the bass outta my voice.

He just nods, wary as hell.

'So we just need you to talk to us here. You want something to eat? We can get sandwiches.'

He shakes his head.

'Plus we want to set up a meeting with Bernadette. If we can.'

His jaw starts working weird and his eyes go wild but he don't say a thing. Then he doesn't stop and his eyes roll back and he gets to frothing.

Shit. That were quick.

'Lark,' Bernadette hisses at me.

Know what she's getting at. Seen it before. Bernadette likes her kill switches. Figure that someone not in the cult says her name, it kicks in.

Bettina leaps across the desk, grabs him by the throat, tries to pry his jaw open. Jaw's just about the strongest muscle there is. Even for *her* strength, not all that easy. She gets there and a gout of blood shoots out between his teeth.

Motherfucker's been chewing off his own tongue. Must have been biting at it like a beast. Tongue's tough, man. She holds his jaws apart like a vet might hold a dog. Sounds he make are hard to hear. Get on the phone and call up?... who? Ain't no doctors on staff.

Rip that tie off my neck and stuff it in his mouth. Prevent him biting down, staunch the bleed. That's the risk, that he loses blood enough to... his hands pull at it as it hang down his mouth like a hound's tongue all lolling. Bettina wraps arms around his wrists to control him.

That's what lets him kill himself.

Sound of his shoulder blades dislocating is no fucking good but not as bad as the one where he strikes his forehead on the desk. Bettina still holding him almost comical, behind him like a wrestling hold. He hits himself again. She moves on instinct, hauling him back to control him better.

Which is all he needs to spit out the tie and bite down again.

He dies soon after, in the kinda pain don't bare too much contemplation. Too much fucking blood. My office, all new and bright, is a butcher's shop at closing time.

'Well, that went tits up,' says Bettina.

She takes a photo.

'Maybe show this off to some cats. That's the second time she had this suicide pill bullshit. Let 'em know what they can expect.'

Which is true. Bernadette set up some magician to come at me, programmed his death right into him. She's *cold*. She has to know that a desperate suicide is a black, bad one. She just does not give a solitary goddamn.

Bettina walks out of the office and comes back in a bit with a chisel. Drags him to the bathroom. She strips down to bra and pants and cracks open his skull. Play some music loud to cover up the sounds. Half an hour later, she's fed well. Stands up, face covered in blood and other things. Call someone up about the body.

'Anything useful?'

'Take a while to sort it out and mainly he was... it was a bad death. He didn't want to go. He was so scared, Lark. He was so fucking scared and it hurt so much and he wanted to stop but he couldn't. He was...'

'Geased. Compelled.'

She slips on her trousers, boots.

'But he trying to figure out a lie to keep us out of that new temple we raided. Something in there he worked hard on for her.'

'You right to keep working?'

'Sure.'

Call up the cleaning crew. Poor bastards.

I V

The Temple basement is dark.

We have flashlights.

Above us, the hooks jangle in breezes we can't feel. The bodies of the Templars who died here have been removed. Hit the gnosis and study the altar, the long image of Apophis drawn across the walls.

They're luring it here with atrocity? Serial killer shit. Feel diseased, hot, and my mouth is goddamn dry.

On the altar, a list of names. One column - most of the cults and prominent magicians in the City. Some citizens. Animals as well. Second - which divinity they should be sacrificed to. The monster snake, enemy of gods, would recognise only those specific, Egyptian, divine energies.

The reason some got bought here to this torture chamber was for some dead Osiris, buried. Reason why the neopagans got their guts out was a sacrifice to Anubis. Specific kills in specific ways.

Starting to clear up.

That's why the lions that started this whole thing off.

Lions are Egyptian symbols of divine wrath. War goddess Sekhmet only was convinced to leave mankind alone from her warpath was convincing her wine was blood. Savage information projected into the dark of night, the space between worlds, to bring Apophis closer.

You're probably thinking *that asteroid was always coming. For millions of years. How'd they summon it?* That's magic. Cause and effect aren't so simple to it. If you get told the magic went back in time? That's not true. They were always gonna invoke the primal serpent is more like it.

There's patterns under the skin of the universe. Magic's a good way of seeing them. Manipulating them.

Bernadette's arranging time and space for this Operation.

The altar is thick with old blood and pain and, tell you straight, don't want to look at it in gnosis. It bruises the world and I am so done with pain. Weary of people getting hurt for sick, sad ambitions.

'Hey lady?'

'Yeah.'

'Smash shit out of this, would you?'

She ate half a man not an hour ago. She smashes it in showers of shards.

Sometimes you manipulate the secret processes of the universe.

Sometimes you just work it so you get lucky.

Under altar, a manhole. Bettina nods at me. Shines her torch down it.

'Cool.'

She climbs down.

Follow her.

V

Secret passage, which is groovy.

Cold down here. Roaches running from the beams of light but not goddamn quick enough for me. Stop and do us up a quick sigil to repel the little fucks. Resent having to do it as it means moving a hand from away from my nose and mouth.

Kinda fragrant down here, you know?

This is what Todd died for. This secret way to somewhere... it breaks lucky, somewhere I get answers. I can make Bernadette, Library will come with the big guns, the old books, the *old* books. And the numbers.

Just got to find her.

Bettina just straight up kicks the rats, which are big as cats. Flies down here too, which is not as you'd call a welcome surprise. Find out later they're called drain flies. *Fucking hell.*

We walk an old straight track and the way is cold. There's an old English term, Lyke-Gate. Lych Gate. House where you store the dead before walking them into the graveyard. Feels like we're walking through it. Death information heavy in the air. Like we're walking in an invisible river, corpse-currents washing all around us.

Weakens me, strengthens Bettina. Guess that in that feeling, she finally decides to talk to me about something that's on her chest.

'So,' says Bettina.

Wait.

'I think I'm a kill Aristide.'

'Kill?'

'Yeah.'

She stops. Stares at me. Not the ideal place for this kinda talk but she wants it. Not gonna stop her.

'Been thinking about my dad.'

Her dad and her uncle dropped her into blood battles when she was a kid. She killed other children before she finished school. Her dad and her uncles made stacks off her and then walked out of her life. Then her old boyfriend shot her dead.

You should know that about her.

'Sure.'

'He...'

Trails off. Looks around. Stomps a rat.

'It's not just that he threw me in to that world, you know?'

'Sure.'

'It's that he took me away from any other way to be. When I was really little, I liked horses, you know? Sounds stupid, I know. Never even saw one for real and maybe you think it's lame for a little girl to like horses. But I did.'

'Horses are good.'

'Yeah! But how I'm a learn all the stuff to look after them... how they gonna let me ride them knowing all the people I put the hurt on?'

She's not talking literal.

'They took that away from me. Think a horse want me around? They made me a pair of fists and that's all.'

'Not now I'm not. You took me outta the grave. You didn't... I'm glad for the two of us but you didn't *make* me what I am, which is more than a fighter. You helped but this isn't about you.'

'Yeah.'

'And that dude in your office. Compelled. That's what you said.'

'Sure.'

'So when I thought about Aristide... working to change me. Without knowing. Without asking. Without caring what the *fuck I thought about it?*'

She strikes the walls. Concrete explodes in a clouds and grey shards.

'I kinda get angry at him. I kinda lose my stack.'

No anger in her voice but her eyes are hot stars.

Part of me wants to defend Aristide. But that's the part that used her too. That looks to excuse myself from it. She forgave me but that's not good enough.

And it ain't about me.

'You think I should kill him?' She looks are her fist under a leather fingerless glove.

'You actually looking for advice?'

'No.'

'Then you do what you wanna do and I'll back your play.'

'Cool.'

Three minutes later, we come to a door. Grated. She bends the bars back and we go through. Stairs lead up to a manhole and we open it. Into a basement.

'So what bought that on now, lady?'

She looks back at me. 'I think about killing every dude on earth every goddamn day.'

V I

Not long after that, we find a ladder. Up the top, another manhole. Locked and pretty heavily warded. Specifically, warded against *me*.

'Someone anticipated me getting in here. Not break that ward empty handed.'

To my eyes, in gnosis, it's a black heart, slowly pumping. Fucked up thing, the blood inside it cold.

Bettina's got feelings right now. So she just punches the living shit out of it and we're through. Climb up the sewer ladder careful. Wait for Bettina to give the all clear and haul myself in.

Feels like an abandoned church in here.

Vaulted ceiling. Frescos. Is that the word? Patterns on the ceiling, anyway. Elaborate circles and a vast eye within.

Dozens of cardboard boxes down here. Stacked up high. Stink of mould is heavy here and it's covered most of the place like leprosy. There's an old billiards table, felt rotted through, cues all black with the plague of black.

There's a huge set of drawers, five feet tall, like where architects and engineers store plans. Bettina knocks the lock off for me and open it up.

Mummified bodies.

Weird mummified bodies.

Skeletons, long as a hand. Some with wings, some with four arms. Something with desiccated webbed hands. Five headed serpents. One with what seems like antlers or maybe branches sprouting from an oversized head. What seems a monkey with a vertical mouth. A puppy with baby hands for paws. Capering imps and lupin armatures with deep sea fish tentacles.

Drawing of what they must have looked like in life, drawn in a cranky, jagged hand.

Drawers below, more documents. Most in Greek or Latin or Arabic. Recognise some words. Gnostic terminology. Aeons, monad, things like that.

Gnostic. Like the scroll turned Wick. A bad sensation comes on me.

The last drawer, photographs. Faded, sepia. People in Edwardian clothes, Victorian even. Recognise a few faces. Spiritualist and theosophists. Hell there's even some of those... think they're called silver pictures. Hoods and robes. No historian but maybe 1800s. One photo has a dude in stockings, if that helps you.

And under a hat, a face I know. I think.

Yeah.

The Old Man. Bernadette's father. Sadistic sorcerer boss.

Show it to Bettina. She nods. One time she told me dead women don't have much to fear like that was a sad thing. Envy that some myself, right now.

Up the stairs and out of the basement. The wood shrieks as we come.

It's the Old Man's house.

We were here on the search for the scroll a few years back. Not the kinda place you forget.

Ancient old building, two hundred years at least. It was shit then, it's worse now. Whole place is so poorly kept it feels like the core of it melted. Like there's black milk, hot and sour, underneath every hard surface.

Long, narrow staircase with rickets going up. Old wallpaper rolled up in strips dangle from walls.

There's rooms at the top. Locked. Warded. Guarded.

Look, this... this next part happened over a few days, ok. It didn't quite happen the way I'm telling it now but... just stay with me.

Real truth was this Operation took proper preparation. Didn't get through the house in one go but easier to tell it like we did.

We also stole a lot of stuff from the basement and had is stashed in Israel island. Libretto didn't warm much to me after that, which I thought was somewhat... uncharitable.

Eventually, we calmed the house down enough, we figured we could go upstairs. And we did.

Did not goddamn expect what we found.

VII

Rooms like this used to be called Solariums. Big room that fills up with sunlight. That's its purpose. Sun rooms. We look out over the old town of the City, the hobbled together townhouses of dark bricks and long twisting lanes.

In here, on four pedestals, are four jars.

Clearly meant to look like canopic jars. You know them. Store viscera from mummified bodies. Find 'em, where else, but in Ancient Egyptian tombs.

One two jars, in hieroglyphs - image of Apophis.

Other two jars, in hieroglyphs - images of Sekhmet.

Got to see inside them. The magic leaks off it like radiation off a nuclear rod.

Call in Katanya. She's been looking for Foulstone but this is more important. Together we draw elaborate mystic patterns in this room. Protections, wards, blessings, prayers to spirits and gods and allies from places beyond.

Hell, even invoke Wick, the spirit of the City. Figure she's got enough attributes of a God by now.

We paint ourselves in runes, calligraphs, occult syllabary and the sutras of the Thai abugida. Fuckin'... *all out* is what I am telling you.

This is the Old Man. He's deader than Elvis and he still scares me. The whole three day Operation, feel like there's someone right behind me, razor in fist.

Then, together, me and Katanya with Bettina bouncing the whole thing...

... we open up the first Jar.

Didn't scream.

Wanted to.

TWENTY-ONE

I

The four jars contain four fragments of the Old Man's soul.

Be wrong to tell you they cut it in four or whatever. Soul isn't a ghost inside you that jailbreaks when you die. It's energy and information and ... shit, you know what a soul is, no need to be technical.

Like got told a while earlier, the Egyptians saw the soul as divided into parts.

This is a bad metaphor because the soul isn't cloth or paper but... it's been torn apart. The Old Man died and coming back... it *can* happen. Anyone ever had mouth-to-mouth knows that. But not the way *he* died.

Someone's reached into the other side and bought parts of him back and divided them. Hideous Operation.

Wrong to say they're screaming themselves. Not even really sentient, sapient, whatever you say. But they're suffering and capable of experiencing that. Watch them black bad souls for a while, like fish in a boiling tank.

They're weakening.

Draining, slowly. That information is breaking down and going somewhere else.

Hits me like a shock of embarrassment you can't forget no matter how you want to, no matter how old you live. But with more *force.*

Bernadette's sacrificing her father's soul to Apophis and to Sekhmet.

She's sacrificing, in torment, her own father's soul.

II

Hard to care about him. Sure. Old Man was a bad cat. But seems there's no ground floor for Bernadette. Nothing she'll say no to.

Then again, could be revenge. Can't exactly see him as a fine example of fatherhood, you know?

Sekhmet. War goddess. Lion goddess.

Have to think on that.

But that's not important. Not right now.

Right now, this shit has to stop. This kind of malice, this kind of power... it'd get the attention of *anything*, including the primal serpent.

Bettina and me are downstairs, in the kitchen, sitting by the Old Man's table, drinking tequila. Telling her about it. She loves to hear the technical stuff.

'This is a key to Bernadette's plans. She's been killing in that old Temple. Killing sorcerers and magicians. Making sacrifices where she can. That's what that information in the tunnel was. Sending it into this room. Killing the soul. Powerful sacrifice.'

We're at my new joint.

Bettina's found lemons and salt. We both like a ritual. She wets the glasses with a bottle of water she bought, shit from the taps here is brown. Puts it in a saucer of salt. Mine are the limes, cutting then into slices.

'We cut off the information though, right? The flow of it.'

'Sure.'

'So what now?'

'Sooner or later *she'll* be back here. We been sneaking in and covering our tracks. But she'll be back to check. Lych-gate? That tunnel's a passage for necromantic information, feeding death straight up here to fuel her Work.'

'So why not take her out?'

'I don't think we can, lady. I figure she's just too damn much for us. But I'll put in the call.'

'Take a while. What about if we fuck up those jars upstairs?'

We throw back our shots and set it up again. This is how Americans drink tequila but we like the rite.

'Ending this now won't stop the Apophis Working but it'll slow it down. Ease it off. Give us some time.'

'Ain't that what we want?' She salts 'em back up.

'Sure. But also… we stop it now, we shut down this particular Operation, well, she could just set it up again. Reach back into whatever death is and grab pops back and do it all again. But in the wind, on the run. Hidden.'

Slug back the fifth shot of the night.

'Kill the soul.'

'What?'

'Listen man, it's easy. You need his soul for anything?'

'No.'

'Then just kill it. Banish it. Fucking… stomp it. Wipe it out. *Annihilate* the fucker.'

Go silent a long way.

Kill a soul.

Sounds criminal just to think on it. *Blasphemous*, like. Kind of thing magicians should not do.

Then again, these days, ain't just a magician.

Sacred Executor.

Kind of cat to make decisions like this. Kind of the hard part of the gig. It ain't all fancy offices and enough money to buy the top shelf booze.

'Alright. Working idea, kill the soul. But listen. Top death mojo guy is Aristide. Figure maybe you don't want your partner talking to the boyfriend you're halfway set to murdering.'

She shrugs.

'Do it, don't do it. Fuck do I care? Not about me and him fighting. You know you gotta cut real sick in this gig and maybe you got duties that are *bigger* than you.'

Sixth shot.

'Let me get to ten of these. Then we'll go pay a visit to your boyfriend.'

'Let me go first. Gonna tear off a piece one last time. Then maybe get him thinking about your problems.'

Pour her another drink, open another bottle.

'Thanks.'

'*De acuerdo*, man. This is some good booze.'

'Nothing is too good for the workers.'

I I I

How do you kill a soul?

Booze and pills, that's a good answer. Love gone wrong. Probably won't work on a cruel man shredded in ways that insult the profoundest part of the human.

William Burroughs describes destroying baboon souls with nukes. *No job too dirty for a fucking scientist.*

Might be a tough requisition, a goddamn neutron bomb.

Christians don't think the soul ever ends. The Second Death is eternal. *And fear not them which kill the body, but are not able to kill the soul: but rather fear him which is able to destroy both soul and body in hell.* Some Muslim scholars think you go to hell, get punished, then... dissolve. Jehovah's Witnesses too. Popular in modern religion for people who don't like to think God's a cruel bastard who sets you on fire for a laugh.

They call it Annihilationism. Good term. *Annihilationism.* Some people think the soul sleeps forever, unaware. *Soul sleep.*

Make a note of that.

Buddhism says there's no soul, no unchanging thing inside of you. But that's caught up in self/not self. Some Hindus believe there's nothing on the other side at all. Those are too far outside experience for me to use.

Can't go there.

Annihilationism, then.

Writing this down in notebooks at my joint.

Phone tells me it has a message.

Bettina.

HIS PLACE NOW HE TRYING IT ON GRAPEFRUIT

I V

Scrambled rush in cabs over to Aristide's basement apartment. Door's locked but fuck that. Sense of panic inside me. Jon showed me how to get through a door long since. Could use magic but honestly, no time.

And here's the thing about Aristide. He smokes enough dope to kill a cow. He's got locks and locks but never uses them.

Want to get through a door? Don't shoulder barge it. You'll fuck yourself up. Plant yourself and kick it near the lock and take your time. The door swings towards you, you've got no chance. But this is an old basement. It goes in.

Plant myself, breath deep, kick, kick, kick, kick and suddenly, it opens. My hip groans. Won't it ever heal?

Aristide's face looks through the crack and he drags me in.

'Fuck are you doing?'

Push past him.

Bettina's on a couch, one of his shirts pulled over her. Turn back and Aristide's only in his little pants. They been on the job.

But Bettina's eyes are dark in a way that ain't about light.

Look around.

There, on the wall, painted is a syncretic nightmare.

Aristide's drawn some melding of Erzulie Red Eyes, the sexy, spoiled Lwa. But her face is melded somehow with Bettinas. Over all, a veve of Mamma Brigitte, the death lord's wife. Beneath it, altar of candles, black cock's feathers, pack of condoms. Offerings.

'Lark,' says Bettina, but it's the painting that talks. Or perhaps it's the other way around.

Aristide strikes me, a good left cross. It's only because he's off his face from dope and rum that it doesn't take the jaw off me but still, it takes me down. He's on me. He's bigger than me, heavier, stronger by a long way and he starts strangling. One of his dreads falls into my mouth and another brushes my exposed eye.

Funny what details your brain focuses on, time like this.

Panic starts going off in my brain.

Black hole in my brain.

That thought, that refrain, brings me back from the edge. Air shutting down quickly. The agony at my throat.

He's stripping Bettina of all she's got. She'll be a husk for his bizarre new goddess. Stripped of everything he doesn't want from her.

Made a deal with the Library to replace Bettina's eye. If they could. Not so easy.

But here's Aristide, staring into my face. Fleck of his spit as he screams into my reddening face.

Stab him in the eye with my finger. Hard as can.

It bursts and he screams and lets me go.

He's still got another for me.

Aristide drags himself off me, two hands holding the wound in his skull. Fight off coughing and move quick. Grab a bottle of the rum they been drinking and... you try to smash a bottle like they do in the movies, you end up with a fist full of broke glass and blood.

Throw the bottle full at Aristide and it strikes his skull.

Don't break. Try again and so it does.

Grab a shard. Slices my hand on the edges. Blood is fine. Useful even. Hurts though.

With a sharp edge, marr the painting. Smear it with the blood from my fingers. Knock down the altar.

Then Aristide is back on me. Hits me in the back and my head slams against the wall. Bell rung and lights go wild in my head. Pain does me in. This isn't my thing, this throwdown bullshit. Go into a ball and wait for what happens.

Nothing.

Then there's a sound of bone on flesh.

Bettina takes him apart.

First strike see her making? Smashes his jaw. Second is an elbow to his back. Spine goes and the legs go out of him. She raises her foot and brings it down. Back of his ribs splinter like the concrete she struck in the tunnel.

She pulls him over.

'Wait.'

She's calm as can be. Looks up at me as if this is nothing at all.

'Take his eye.'

She does. There's screams.

Throws it to me. Is splashes into my outstretched hand and, friend, that's a physical sensation you don't easily forget. Put it in the fridge for later.

'Lady?'

'Yeah?'

'Get dressed.'

She looks down at herself. She's still just wearing one of his black dress shirts. She starts ripping it off and so...look away.

She stops and takes her time as her ex-boyfriend screams. Slipping on underpants and bra, humming to herself as my back is turned. Don't listen as she finishes the job.

It doesn't take all that long.

But even in the City, this kinda shit doesn't go unnoticed. Bettina gets all the way dressed then looks down at Aristide's body. Kneels down beside it.

Kisses his forehead.

Drives a fist through his ribs. Takes the heart from him.

Sirens in the distance.

She runs her tongue over the red thing. As if it turned her on. Squeezes blood into her mouth. Bites it deep.

Cop cars pull up outside.

Take her hand.

We fade into the Black City.

We come back a while later. Get the eye. Destroy the rest of the painting. Make sure that Bettina's soul is in her body. Banish and banish and banish.

V

Later, cleaned, dressed, we go back to the Library and my favour's called in.

Give up the ritual room and lay Bettina down.

Karel and Katanya watch, Karel handing me such tools as are needed, drumming his hands on the floor to give me a beat. Katanya murmuring prayers and incantations out of books we marked up together.

The eye is ruined for any natural purpose.

But this ain't that.

There's a lot of occult resonance with the eye. Evil Eye, Odin's sacrifice, Polyphemus, Balor. Evil Eyes, protecting Eyes, Third Eyes But in the end, there's only one clear choice.

The dark god Set took the eye from the sky god Horus. They have a whole battle in which semen is the weapon of choice, which was left out of *my* childhood books on mythology. Anyways, Set takes out Horus' eye but the cow goddess Hathor fixes him.

That's not the choice.

Ra, the sun god. He had an eye symbol too and Ra? Ra the sun god fought Apophis beneath the world to free the sun. The Eye of Ra is linked with fire, with flame, with power. And the Eye of Ra could take the form of goddesses.

It is a *dangerous* symbol.

And check *this*.

The Eye of Ra and the Eye of Apophis were *opposing* powers. All that could damage Apophis was the Eye of Ra, all that could damage the Eye of Ra was the gaze of Apophis. *It is the flame of the following of Osiris guarding from the powers of his enemies.*

Bettina's fist tightens as her glass eye is removed and Aristide's fresh one slides into her socket with a sound you don't wanna hear. She says nothing as the needle and ink tattoos a serpent, an uraeus, from tear duct, curling under her eye.

Offer up the Working to Ra, to Seth and on a whim. Sekhmet.

Bettina sits up slowly. All three of us kiss her eye lid.

She opens it up. One dark brown eye. One black.

She smiles.

'I can see. Through the eye.'

We banish with laughter and, got to tell you, easiest banishment in my career.

V I

Later, we go to Lionel's restaurant. Fanciest place I know. Lionel's an obeah man, alchemist, chef, who has a hoodoo on half the high rollers in the City thanks to the hexed five star food he sells them. We're eating all lobster and like that, rolling high class.

Bettina talks first.

'You saved me. I was thinking with my dick.'

'Everyone's done that.'

'No, man, no. But I think maybe also he mojoed me.'

'We're over this. You and me. Who saved who. Makes no never mind.'

'True. So what was he trying to do to me?'

'Hollow you out. Put his goddess inside you. Your dead body and his crazy homebrew god inside it.'

'Felt like that. Like the... hard to say. But yeah. Like who I was, was less important than what he thought he could turn me in to.'

'Sure.'

She fingers the eye.

'Don't touch it. Tattoo's fresh.'

'Shit yeah, I don't wanna get no infection. In my dead body.'

'Point. But let it be anyway. We're at a nice joint.'

'So anything I need to know about this?'

'In time, you might be able to use it as an... anchor, for spells.'

She grins.

'Me doing magic?'

'More like it's a magical tool that you carry everywhere. Linked to the... hate saying this but think energies of the god Osiris. Like that's its *theme*. We'll have to do some work but you got you a goddamn gun in that face of yours.'

'Fucking groovy.'

'Fucking groovy indeed. Any.. side effects?'

She pokes it again, moving it in the socked. 'No. Not yet. But there will be. Can feel it.'

'Come at me straight up with it when it happens.'

She just nods. But can see the split second hesitation.

'Won't take it from you. And if I do, we'll figure something out.'

She nods again.

We'll see.

'So what now?'

'Now you tell me what's in your head on Aristide and that.'

She calls over the waiter, after another bottle of hundred buck wine. Can't blame her.

'Lark. You're my partner. We're together. On your back, you on mine. Figure you won't get all pissed off by this but you still a dude. And Lark? Aristide was just another dude, figured he'd get what he wanted, pussy, fun, then put a hurt on a woman just for fun.'

Nod.

'I don't feel shit about wasting that motherfucker.'

Cool.

IV

Annihilationism.

Been thinking.

To kill the soul.

The work of God. God alone.

Back in the room with the Old Man's souls, walking around, pondering.

Got some ideas and a plastic bag in hand.

Bernadette's been here but our elaborate wards and disguises and stealth has held.

Can a magician invoke God?

No.

There's henosis, a kind of theurgy, or divine Working. The idea there is to become *one* with a divine force. The Gnostics believe in that sort of deal. The Old Man himself seemed on the Gnostic trip.

 Closest thing to a God in the world, proper, from *outside* the human mind... is Wick.

Street rat turned Archon.

Talked about her before. How one magician is too small for her. But she *did* give me something. A warning. About this. This room, this plan.

Plastic bag in my fist is filled with spray paint.

Gnostics. They believed humans were body, soul and *breath* or the spirit. The highest divine spark, trapped here in a fallen world of matter. Could ask Wick, if she can even be spoke to, to strip the Old Man of his spirit. She's a creature of high grade divine power now.

Here's my thinking: Tag up this place to try and talk to Wick, the spells we have up here will be broke. Here. In the Old Man's house. This will tip off Bernadette but that'll happen not matter what.

 No. No, that's asking too much of Wick. She's pissed at me as I didn't give up the freak. She felt his connection to Apophis and wanted a taste.

Just don't see any other move to play.

Summon Wick, which might not work, tip Bernadette off to me knowing her big move?

Leave it be and the Old Man fuels this whole Working.

Could just burn the whole place down. It wouldn't stop what she's doing. Not forever. Could steal the jars but she'll just come get them and no way to know if we could even end the Working.

Can't see a winning move. Moves to delay, moves to fuck up her action. Not *win*.

Sit down, back against the wall of the room with the jars in it. Toss one of the paint cans from hand to hand.

Bernadette's better than me. Meaner. Sure, we took out the Sothic Temple but no way she doesn't have more crew. Her will is strong with a soul that'd burn your hand to touch. She'll recruit.

Smashing it up, right now, would buy some time. But if stopping this and stopping it now is the winning move, keep her from bringing the spirit serpent here? A delay just ain't good enough.

Can't see a winning move.

Just can't.

There's a black hole in my brain and can't see my way to beating her.

Black hole in my brain.

No matter what happens - probably gonna lose.

...

So.

Why not lose all the way? Play it out that way.

Me? Right now, I'm losing. What would the Old Man do? What would Bernadette do? What's she *done*?

Sekhmet.

TWENTY-TWO

I

'Why her?

'The goddess of murder and the goddess of doctors. They called her *mauler, mistress of dread, mistress of slaughter.* Vicious judge of the citizens of Egypt, guardian of borders and yet, a terrible judge of humanity. Sekhmet.'

We're at a formal meeting. Velasquez chairs it. Scarlet and Elliot videoconferencing in. In front of me, big stack of books had bought to my office. Blossom's there as well.

Keep going. 'She's come up a few times. Got an idea but want to run it past you all.'

Elliot shrugs. Brave man over an internet link.

'We took out the Sothic Temple.' We. 'She's weak. Can't you just hunt her down? You know she'll go back to her father's house. Wait outside and just... take her out.'

Ignore that.

Velasquez says nothing. She's told the meeting that Bernadette is numerologically a 4, which means her auspicious stone is moonstone and her colours are white and pink. She knows her business, no doubt. No dissing.

But dirty hands just ain't her field.

Bettina shrugs. But it's when Katanya and Scarlet lock eyes over the television that things get interesting.

Katanya's hair is slicked back, make-up severe. Something passes between the two dames.

'Lark. What's the M.O we have for Bernadette so far?'

'First she tried to summon the Devil. Then she was playing around with a Rabisu and death spirits.'

Scarlet drums her hands on a desk none of us can see below the range of the camera.

'And her father?'

'*Loads.* Haven't pulled his file in while. Mully and he mixed it up a lot...

But his final big play was to meld with an Archon.'

Scarlet stares at me.

It clicks. Magic is the pattern under everything. It's been there in front of me. Repeating. *As above, so below.* Nod at Scarlet but then look at Bettina. Her father wanted it. She's trying something similar.

Less drastic. But the same basic move.

Breathe in. Tell it true as I can.

'She wants to invoke the destructor goddess utterly. She wants to become a goddess. And then, when Apophis comes... she'll be ready for him. A goddess can deal with an entity like that. That's why she promised the Templars there'd be some goddamn new order for them.'

Bettina don't flinch but she hears the echo of Aristide.

Scarlet goes on.

'We don't know anything about the Old Man and her relationship. We didn't even know they were related until last year but, let's face it, we can make some pretty solid guesses as to what he was like as a father.'

'Well, maybe,' interrupts Elliot. 'That's a big conclusion to draw.'

Scarlet puts a hand on his hand. Goes on.

'She pulled him out of death, carved up his soul. Offered it up. That's a huge sacrifice. Vast power.'

Katanya nods. 'Woman like that. Powerful. Really powerful. But she'll know terror in her life like you can't understand. She made herself powerful for a *reason.*'

Shrug. This is out of my expertise. Don't need to know motive.

Blossom talks. The lawyer with the wire framed glasses. Damnit. Forget he's there. So slick and bland.

'This seems highly speculative.'

'Yes,' says Scarlet. 'I'm not saying... I know we're all thinking of a scared little girl and a door opening to her bedroom but it might not have gone that way. The Old Man was a vicious bastard, yes. Mully and I had some meetings after the Scroll affair and he told me stories. She'll want to...'

'She'll want to make herself the biggest badass ever walked the City,' says Bettina.

The three women nod along with her. Elliot looks annoyed.

Scarlet looks at Bettina.

Get me an idea. But Scarlet had it first.

A bad one.

If we're going to lose, we have to lose to win.

'We can help Bernadette bring her goddess to earth.'

Bettina stares at me and the black hole in my brain commences to ache.

Get up.

Walk out.

Elliot screams behind me his stupid, small opinions.

Bettina follows.

Gets to me before the elevator door opens.

'What?'

Lean back against the wall and rest my head.

'Bettina...'

'What?'

'Fierce warrior goddess.'

'What about it?'

'Dreadful lioness. Who does that sound like, baby?'

'What?'

'*You.*'

She goes quiet.

A mystery pattern under everything.

'Bettina… if we can invoke the goddess… we take her from Bernadette. We *steal* her. Accelerate the sacrifice. But the energy of the sacrifice and the invocation won't go to Apophis, won't go to Bernadette, it will go to us.'

She frowns. 'We just… *jack* the ritual with the jars?'

'Yeah.'

'So what's the problem?'

'The goddess has to go into a body, lady. Who's the best fit for that, in that room?'

Stare a moment.

'Oh. I did it before.'

'Not like this.'

She leads me back in.

Looks at them all.

Elliot starts to say something but realises quick that fucking no one wants to hear it. Velaszquez doesn't talk. Scarlet and me, we lock eyes. It ain't romantic. She had this play figured. How and why? Do not know but there's something in me screaming that she did.

Katanya just stands and… You don't hug Bettina. Just puts a hand on her shoulder.

'What do you want to do, Bettina?' Scarlet asks.

'Can't say I like the sound of that. Someone already tried to set me up with a god and can't say it was much fun.'

'Alright. We'll find another way.'

Bettina nods.

But Scarlet's eyes grow dark.

'Think of the Library you selfish slap-' starts Elliot. Stops at a cool glance from his wife.

'We'll adjourn the meeting for now. We'll… think of something.' She does a pretty good job at hiding her disappointment.

Bettina hot steps out of there.

Me and Katanya stare at each other. What's to say? No one's asking that. The goddess is just an idea but this facet of Sekhmet is powerful and dangerous, made by Bernadette for her. And how that'd interact with her new eye...

'Lark,' says Scarlet. 'A word?'

'No.'

'Alright. Like I said. Adjourned.'

I I

We make plans. To ambush Bernadette and her father's house. Try and end this with force. Only way open, really. Maybe bring in more Librarians from other parts of the Country. Hell, Elliot tells us he can hire some Mossad guys who freelance now to blow the whole thing.

One advantage. If we hit her now, hard as we can, she won't expect it. She's just been playing with us. Jon killed Mully to fuck with me alone. Me? Just a bit of fun. The real deal isn't cult war.

That's it. We can hit her hard.

Have to make use of knowing what she's doing and why.

Could it all be a trap?

Nah. Bait's too precious to risk. Don't catch mice with good steak.

Back at my joint.

My scorpion-sorcerer eregores are nearly ready. Been six months of attending to them, sacrificing, performing rites to them. They hang from a ceiling, awaiting birth. Long melding of human and bug. Tails twitching, held against their backs.

The Devil. He killed the first batch.

The Devil. Alright.

In my sanctum, draw a proper inverted pentagram in chalk, upside cross on the wall. *In Nomine Dei Nostri Satanas Luciferi Excelsis.* Whole deal.

He don't wanna talk.

Jon's out there, Bernadette's out there. Rabisu's gone from me. Mully's dead. Todd's in custody. Scarlet and Elliot hiding out.

There's one person loose. Foulstone.

First met Foulstone with Blossom. Blossom. Came in around the time we did the Devil case. Upstairs man.

Don't know about his practice. Don't know much about him at all.

Two in the morning.

Walk over to my office, pull up his address and by four in the morning, outside his fancy townhouse.

Cat has money.

Blossom's story is strange.

He was a lawyer for a corporation. One of thirty. You know the type. Cold, sharp, contained. Believe in nothing but money, prestige. Blah. So boring it's hard to remember from minute to minute.

(Should have picked up on that. Details slide away from my mind.)

But he came across something weird and couldn't let it be. For Elliot, ghosts bought him to the Library. For Blossom...

Some guy had tried to sue them. Some weirdo. Blossom was working for publishing and the weirdo was a writer who claimed he was owed royalties on a book from the 80s.

That book was on curses. *Defixiones.*

Blossom was second on the case and his senior partner, a woman named Franzi ran rings around the author and ended up taking the poor bastard to the cleaners. Claimed his suit was, dunno, not a lawyer but ended up, they took his book, wiped out his savings and had the fucker locked up.

Franzi got sick. Franzi got mad sick.

Hair fell out in about three days.

Teeth next.

Doctors found nothing.

Finger, toenails.

She couldn't sleep. Nightmares.

Ten days later she killed herself. Smashed a mirror and slashed herself to death.

Blossom knew this was a curse found in the writer's book.

Went to see him in jail. Offered to help him out if he taught curses.

Sure.

Only thing was... the author got himself shanked a week into it.

But Blossom was good at the hunt and found another cult, a crew of resentful bastards who practiced Roman style magic. Chopping up doves for hints of the future in their guts and getting sprayed with blood? Not his bag.

Library was.

Apparently that's still his bag says his records - curse magic. Malisons and jinxes.

Knock on his door. Young man with sleepy eyes and no body fat opens it. Push past.

Blossom's asleep but march into his joint. The bum boy follows along, asking what's up all waspish. See him off with a look.

Upstairs into a bedroom looks like it's from a film. Huge aquarium against one call, underlit softly. Silk sheets and peach walls. Mirrors. Easy to break in. Easy to catch him as he was waking up.

Blossom's in his bed covered up. Ichabod Crane skinny. He fumbles those razory wire spectacles and adjusts his hair as can.

'I trust you understand how outrageously inappropriate this is, Lark.'

'Sure.'

'I don't suppose you'd wait downstairs while I at least get dressed.'

Say nothing.

'God, you're impossible.' He's a perfect diction, unflappable type motherfucker.

'Do you ever think actively engaging in a human conversation would improve your reputation?'

Say nothing.

'Well in that case... Is Arturo alright?'

Nod.

'I am glad.' And he is, whole body relaxes some.

Pull out a chair from a dresser. Put my boots up on the bed. Blossom watches, not yet ready to put on that no-face mask. Bad manners won't rattle him but he'll think I think that's a good tactic. Cats like this don't rate anyone without a watch costs much as car.

'Not here to fuck up your action with your boy.'

'I'll trust you'll be discrete.'

'No one fucking cares you dig dudes.'

'I care.'

'Not here to blackmail, man. Here to talk.'

'I have an office you could have visited and, might I add, so do you. And the authority to compel a meeting.'

'Fucking hell, Blossom. Think it over.'

He does. *This is all shadow stuff now.*

'Is there any chance we could move this discussion to a room more fitting and allow me to dress?'

'Stay in bed. Won't need anything but words.'

He presses a button at the bedside table.

'Arturo, could you bring up some tea and coffee? Thank you, darling.'

We wait and the boy brings them up.

Good stuff.

'What's this all for, Lark?'

'Foulstone. We need to know where he is. Last card to play.'

'And you think I know where he is? I didn't even know he was missing.'

'Read his files. Know you and Elliot and him come in at the same time. Only natural you all get to talking.'

Sips his tea.

'This is correct.'

'Elliot?'

He sighs. 'Should I speak frankly?'

Say nothing.

'Elliot is a *face*. He's the kind of man who came from money and

will stay with money. Born with a suit on. Handsome, charming, as
capable as asking after a rich man's grandchildren for favour as he is
taking young bucks to brothels.'

'Don't seem that way to me.'

'Lark, we are talking about an entirely different class of man
than... you. Make no mistake, you and he may have clashed but he's the
kind of man *yacht owners* enjoy. A flatterer, a charmer. But the world in
which the Library exists is outside of his purlieu.'

'Sure.'

'Men like that, born to high station, they rarely have to leave
their comfort zones as comfort travels with them. If he had been more
self-assured, he should have been an asset. But he wasn't, and so he's
not.'

'Alright.'

'Foulstone, however... is a different matter entirely. He's a
mercenary, a crook. His concern is entirely selfish and his selfishness is
entirely vast. His skills were far more useful than Mr. Everett's, or mine,
in regard to the more occult matters in which we are engaged but a man
with no loyalty is a man with no use.'

'So he was for sale from jump.'

'I'm sorry?'

'Keep going.'

'Lark... you said to be frank. He and I were both approached by
agents of the Sothic Temple. For me, I have no interest in murder and
depravity and those sent to recruit us into becoming double agents
were... not men to who I felt kinship. Dreary appetites are of no use to
me.'

What are your appetites?

'But Foulstone was always a creature of *Hustler* magazine and
football and meat pies. He was eager to join a cult in which he was
allowed to debase himself. He would find great delight in diseasing
me with his orgiastic reports. I went to report him, but my immediate
superior was Mr. Everett.'

'You saying Elliot knew?'

'No. That is to say, he probably thought Foulstone was not involved in a sinister cult but more a sort of... pornography club? I don't know.'

'So Foulstone got in deep.'

'Just that. The Temple was a sideline I believe. And it wasn't until he met Bernadette he came to me to ask for my assistance. You will... this is where we reach a... more difficult part of the story.'

Say nothing.

'You must understand, Lark. For all his vulgarity, Foulstone and I were allies. He introduced me to Arturo. We were both eager to expand our occult knowledge and both eager to become more influential in the organisation. We rose high, but only because of our connection to Elliot and his ascension was based on money. Foulstone, however, had more ambition than Elliot. He longed for more magic. More knowledge. And some gave it to him.'

Bernadette.

'He never intended to *betray* the Library but he was terrified of Bernadette. He began to assist her in creating his shadowy soldiers under duress.'

'Still did it.'

'He did. But I knew nothing of the extent of the Sothic Temple's atrocities until your reports began coming in after the incident at the zoo. I honestly assumed he was simply involved with another cult.'

Go still. Look at him careful.

Don't think he's lying. Then again, man like this, his pulse wouldn't quicken in hell.

'You're talking a lot more than figured, Blossom.'

'I suppose I am. I tell you this because... you've a reputation, Lark. You do bad things to people who cross you.'

Say nothing.

'I think you should put yourself in Foulstone's shoes. Bernadette is nothing to be trifled with, we've seen. We read your reports. Yes, I know where he is and no, I won't hold out on you. I'm... afraid.'

'You don't look it.'

'Please, Lark. Let's be honest with one another. I have no intention of sitting through any kind of interrogation, nor do I wish to spend a night in your cells, let alone end up in your monster's belly. I simply want you to be understanding of Foulstone and in turn, of me.'

'Fucksake, Blossom, you talk too much. Just tell me where he is and leave the rest up to me.'

He sighs.

'I dislike being forced into - He was a... not friend but...'

'Stop. Talking. Tell me.'

He does.

Should tell you. He's sent me into a trap.

I I I

Bettina picks me up in Aristide's old hearse.

'Didn't figure you'd have much use for any of his stuff.'

'You jiving? Threw out all his shit and had it cleaned. Figure I rent out his rooms for nine hundo a month.'

'We need to talk about all that?'

She shakes her head as we drive through the last of the night.

'Sometimes I think about it and I commence shaking. Fear and anger like nothing else. I had me some feelings off him, for real. And then, him kinda hollowing me old like shoes for someone else to wear? Hard to shake that shit off, you know? *Scandalous.*'

She sighs.

'But then I just think he's just the next cat in line who didn't come correct at me. Just another dog. Just a magic one. I'm a shut up shop for a long time after this.'

'Sure.'

'As ever, Lark, your righteous insight into the human condition is fucking *invaluable as shit*, man.'

'Figured.'

'No. I'm not *okay*. But I got work and work cover it all up. And one day, it won't be like this. Not the first time I took a punch, man.'

She shrugs.

We move in silence through the City like a shark.

Pull in down in Crowton.

Fucking slum.

Pre-dawn and the homeless cats are still here. The winter will be here in a few weeks and a lot of these poor bastards will die, or go into the shelters, where they'll only wish they were.

Old government housing flats. CRIME SCENE DO NOT ENTER tape across the front entrance, waving like ribbons in the wind. She parks the hearse.

Open the apartment block door.

Little kid on the stairs in the dark staring at us with no one home eyes. Bettina goes to hand him a few bucks but might as well be giving it up to a statue. Tags on the walls.

Gangs signs, dicks, up on the second floor, one door surrounded to make it look a demon's mouth. Third floor, flickering lights and the tags get weird.

PUT BULLETS IN UR BABIES

MELT ME

SHE IS IN THE PAINT NOW

IF IT BREAKS BREAK IT

QUIT

SHE IN PAINT AND CEMENT

Ghosts thick in the air but two of us are so loaded down with apotropaics these days we sting them and they fuck right off.

Bettina puts hands on a flat door.

'Lemme try. I think I can do something new.'

First, second, third, fourth -

'This one.'

'How you know?'

I know. Can feel the protections on the other side. But her?

'Getting stronger, man. New eye, heart blood of a man tried his hand at Judasing me. Can *feel* living things now.'

She's been living dead awhile now.

Evolving. Teeth sharpening.

'Bettina.'

'Sup?'

'This door has plenty magic on it. We open it up, ghosts are gonna step to us. Can put the hoodoo on it. Or. You can try out the Eye.'

'Fuck yeah, man. Let's do it.'

'Alright. Calm yourself down. Just relax.' Shit, she don't breath less she wants it. And she's dead. Hitting gnosis won't be shit to her.

'You go the Ra information in you. Ra's a sun god. Master of Sekhmet, the Destroyer. He's dangerous, man. You step to him, you get one shot, don't miss. But. He's alright. He's not fucking psycho. He's alright. He's got our back. Think about that. For really real. *Think* about it.'

She does.

'Fire. Sun. Power. Command.'

'Yeah.'

'Feel that in your belly, in your throat, in your puss, in your chest. Images, thoughts, feeling, to do with those words, baste in 'em.'

'Yeah!'

'Now think of that sun coming out of you like a fucking flood of fire.'

She kicks open the door.

Bound dead men screech and reach for us. Hungry Ghosts. Pretas. Addict creatures. Jesus Christ, ancient ones, too! Ragged things, twisted by life and unable to move on to other lives. Bound and tortured by scum like Foulstone. Poor fucking things.

Honestly didn't know Foulstone could get himself such powerful allies so quick.

Defences come up quick but they're at us with fucked up scary speed.

Watching Bettina in gnosis. Slow at first but then it comes. You looking at it in the real world, nothing much. But in gnosis, fire, fury, force. Ghosts scream and Foulstone screams as his creatures burn away like spit on a hot sidewalk.

Bettina stops. Stares at me.

'The fuck was that!?'

'Magic. Powerful magic. Those ghosts... couldn't take them easy.'

She offers me a fist to pound.

Tell you now, should have picked up that these ghosts were serious, too serious just for security. That they wanted me here. But the thing with Bettina's eye just... got my attention.

You'll know it too when we talk about Blossom more soon.

'That's sweet.'

'Yeah. But we still got work.'

She takes open the door and in we go to see Foulstone.

I V

Foulstone's been a decoratin'

Magazines with big titty girls in hot pants and bikinis. Page 3 from the papers. Pile of microwave meals for one and a stack of cheap larger cans.

He done feel asleep with his TV tuned to late night infomercials. He's staring at us now, tracksuit open, hairy belly swelling out. Ghosts cower at his feet like mist, afraid of Bettina's fire.

'Hey.'

He just stares at me and doesn't say much in return. Sleep in his eyes. One hell of a way to wake up.

Studio. Not much room. Bettina closes the door, stands guard, arms crossed. Take the bed myself. Sit down.

'Blossom gave me up.'

'Sure did. Helps? He told me to go easy.'

'Did you know he was a dinner-masher?'

'Fuck does anyone care?'

'I just didn't know. Tried to get his bum boy to dob on him for me but apparently it's for real. Poofs, eh?'

You trying to rile me up over Jon?

'No percentage in getting on my tits tonight, Foulstone.'

'I were you,' says Bettina, 'I'd be trying real hard to leave this room alive and with limbs as still work.'

Foulstone adjusts the dick in his track pants, sits up straight.

'You shouldn't have come here, Lark. She's been waiting. She got me long ago. Soon as you killed her dad, she set it all up. She hated him, you see. The Old Man. She fucking hated him like poison. He was *hers* to kill.'

Bettina nods. She gets it.

'I helped with the shadow surgeries, yeah. But what she really needed was someone fucking dumb.'

'Elliot.'

'Yeah. We worked together a lot. He fucking hated you. Gave me access to the Library when I told him I'd help him see you off and make sure you weren't around his bird.'

'What did you do?'

The television flickers.

'Back doors. Traps. All of it. Fucking... *had to*. There's no moves none of us make she doesn't know about.'

Which means she might know we're planning on raiding her.

'What about Blossom?'

'Who the fuck is Blossom?'

Bettina snaps her attention to me.

'What?'

'Simple fucking question, mate! Who's Blossom?'

'The lawyer.'

Darkness at the corners of my eyes. *What's this?*

Room seems to come in on me. Television flickers on and off and on and off. Bettina walks over to it. Yanks it the fuck outta the wall and it goes dark.

Heart beating fast now.

'If you're lying to me you fat fuck I'll send you insane and let Bettina eat you alive. Are you telling me you don't know who Blossom the lawyer is?'

'Don't know the cunt!'

Bettina puts her fist through a wall.

'The fuck are you talking about, Foulstone.' Her voice is a hiss.

'I don't fucking know any fucking Blossom!'

The television flicks back on. Turn to kick it or some damn thing.

There's a woman on it. Black blouse, broach and pearls and real tasteful make-up. Long bob, dark hair style. Matrician kinda face.

'Oh, Lark. Here we all are.'

Bernadette. Upper class accent. Vowels shot out like bullets.

'You've moved faster than I'd have liked. But here we are.'

'Fucking hell. Look, ma'am, I'm sorry. They came at me. Dunno how they found out...'

'I sent them, you grotesque. Either your ghosts would take care of them. Or they'd eliminate you.'

'Bettina. Hide!' Whisper it while Foulstone struggles not to cry. My girl steps into shadows and behind the television. Don't want Bernadette to know about the eye if she don't.

'How'd you get to Blossom?' Make a fist to keep me brave. She's got a shark's charisma.

'Well, that's the thing, Lark, there never was a Blossom. He's an eregore of mine. He was. Now he's done his work I've let him go. Soon he'll vanish from people's memories.'

Can't match this kind of magic. An eregore is a spirit familiar like my shadow puppet. But mine's a creature size of a kittens. Herr's, a man with a boyfriend and credit history.

She is straight up leagues better than me.

'When you fed my father to that Wick creature, I watched, you know. I was desperate for my father to ascend. I wanted it all so very much. I had plans for him myself, you see. *Traps* for gods prepared. You took that opportunity from me. So I started work the next day on your wretched Library.'

'Jesus Christ, lady, seems to me I did you a fucking favour.'

'Seems to *me* you're a chancer who blundered into something you never should have. I shall take all you love. All I loved was revenge,

Lark. And now, you've given me access to the Library.'

'The fuck I did.'

'Did you know I made Blossom from the blood you lost when my father's man Ludo was put to beat you?'

'No.'

'And more, Lark.'

'No.'

'You've got that slave creature inside you. There's a black hole in your brain. '

Silence. Fear sparking into my hands. Stand up from the bed.

'What's this?' Bettina mouths.

'You think of them as scars. But they aren't wounds. They're *spawn*. You think they're remnants of your death but they aren't. *They're its children.*'

Say nothing. *Say nothing.*

'My father taught me about the Rabisu. I mastered the creature in Lark and have been looking through its eyes.'

No. No. No.

'You took what was mine, Lark. I've had months to walk around in your house. Tonight, my shadowy men will destroy the records in Israel Island. They'll murder Libretto. And as we speak, Jon, once your brother, now my *son*, can walk into the Library and murder all he sees. Your books will burn and your allies will die. Those allies I've not long since turned.'

Stand, get up, Bettina falls in. As we leave, Bernadette laughs like a happy woman. TV goes dark.

'And when I'm finished with that, I'll finally come for you, Lark.'

TWENTY-THREE

I

Didn't even murder Foulstone. Don't matter.

We hit the hearse and move like bastards through the streets. Dangerous fast. Dunno the fuck what to do. We're just moving.

She's been at me since day one. She's been planting eregores, powerful constructs. *Those allies I've not long since turned.* Katanya, Karel?

Scarlet?

Jesus Jesus Jesus Jesus Jesus.

'Go faster.'

'Shut up. Dunno even where we're going.'

'The Library. She ain't saying fuck all to us unless she's ready.'

Realise suddenly that my automatic breathing shut down and there's motes in my eyes. Have to move my lungs in my body like you move a hand. Pounding in temples. Force myself not to vomit.

A few blocks away and the smoke comes clear in the night sky. See the fire before we turn the street. Flame colours the streets.

Library is burning.

Jump out the door before the car's even stopped.

Flames pouring out the top windows. Spreading down from fifth floor to fourth. *No.* The rarest of our books. *No. No.*

The Library is on fire.

Shadowy men line the streets. Last of the Sothic Templars. Wrapped up in their own souls. *Sheuts.* That's the surgery. That's what they were doing. Inverting their own souls into weapons.

Bettina run ones down. He goes smashing up into the windshield, crashes it. We get the fuck out.

Five more move to surround us.

Heat from the building rushes down over us.

Kira's amulet around my neck. Tattoo burns. Ready to throw down.

'Wait!'

Voice rings out over the fire and the sound of destruction.

Turn.

Karel's body comes flying down from the main entrance, down the stairs, to the street. Lands on a security guard's corpse.

Standing there, illuminated in the door. Throwing a shadow down over me and Bettina.

Jon.

'It's time, Lark.'

There's still something of the fevered illness about him. But nothing of the weakness.

Bite the inside of my mouth for focus.

His gnosis.

The Rabisu is inside him. Empowering him. Feeding him. It looks at me from out his eyes with avid cruelty. Weaker than before, much weaker, but not a inch less cruel. In me, it hides, curling around it's young.

Looks like Jon got a better part of it. No demons children in his brain. His is animated and snapping.

Almost stumble back from his... malice.... like it was a fist. The wounds and punches and sorrows from the last few days crest. Break. Fall back against the car.

So tired.

He notices us. Calls out.

'I'm gonna kill you now, Lark. I didn't want to make it hurt but the... what's in me *wants* it to hurt. I'm sorry. But I gotta kill you.'

Car door opens.

Bettina steps out.

'What's up?'

II

Jon comes at her like a storm. He seems to leave shadows behind him. Behind his eyes, the Rabisu stares and it stares at *me*. Hungry. Vile.

Bad move.

Bettina leaps across the car and Jon swings his attention to her. Too late.

She hits him like ain't never seen. Force of it makes me want to puke. Jon's hand shoots up to deflect it and the sound of it breaking won't leave me with any quickness.

But he's still Jon and the Rabisu has returned to him what he's lost. His other hand hooks around to take Bettina in the throat. She stumbles back and he snaps a kick at her, then another, taking her in the ribs. Back up against the hearse, Jon starts in with a series of vicious jabs. She lowers down to charge him and don't see what happens next.

Got my own problems.

The Sothic Templars are on me.

Seems to me these are they cats that got away from our raid. They wrap themselves in shade and line themselves up in a wedge.

Guess it's time to measure staves and snakes, then.

Magical duels aren't lightning bolts and that. You could see this from the outside, you'd be unimpressed. But you had eyes to see with, into the ether, the astral, the half-world, you'd see some wild shit.

One of them takes a doll. Fucking thing looks like me. My skin, my jacket, my hair. Another takes a length of black rope. Goes to hang the thing. Could have done this any time but they wanted to watch.

First thought it to use Egyptian style sorcery. Kinda been deep in that for a week and, not bragging, you can learn a hell of a lot in a week, if you're motivated. But that's *their* current. Their trip.

Gotta play this my way.

Feel the sympathetic magic attack my defences. Kira's amulet burns my skin.

First time we scouted out the temple, the first one, bought a pack of smokes and matches. Still in my jacket pocket.

Take it out.

Unwrap it.

Through my sentries and the curse doll working at my throat.

Sirens in the distance.

Bettina grabs Jon by the arm and spins him into the side of the hearse with force enough to smash windows, dent the fucker deep. Punches him in nose with force enough to smear it across his face. Doesn't seem to feel it and snap kicks her in the knee and something grinds.

Flick a smoke free and take it out with my teeth. This is my magic.

Can't breathe real good.

Spark the match.

This is banishing. This is my Dedication.

Hear my own breathing saw. Noose feeling at throat.

Bettina and Jon start circling each other, sending jabs. Jon's quicker, better at boxing, so Bettina limps backwards across the street. Jon, trailing blood from his nose, a man who should be in pain enough to bring him to his knees, brings his knees up to my girl's ribs and hips. She's on the back foot, limping. She goes up the Library stairs and they vanish into the building.

Hear myself choke.

Drag my smoke anyway.

Oh God that's good. Fills my lungs and my blood with the dark pleasure of smoke in the lung.

Part of me down under everything else thought *I could help myself.* That what was in my brain was... medicable. Went to Kira. Got that tattoo. Listened to people trying to make me a better version of Lark.

But that's not my life.

That ain't me.

Jon is killing my friend. These fucked up maniacs are killing me.

A monstrous thing is coming and the fuck knows what's gonna happen to the whole goddamn world when it does.

Men like me don't die from wounds in the brain. *We don't save ourselves.*

Why fucking pretend otherwise?

Mully is dead. Jon lost and soon he or Bettina will be too. Scarlet, lost to me in every way I want her to be found.

I trow I hung on that windy Tree
nine whole days and nights,
stabbed with a spear, offered to Odin,
myself to mine own self given,

The Rabisu killed me once. A trap Bernadette lured me into. Probably won't beat her when this is said and done. *Why pretend otherwise?*

Smoke from the burning Library wreathes me. Like being inside a storm. Black and grey and orange and the sick feeling of not enough breath.

In the spit flecks hacking up from my closed up throat, spell out the secret names of my eregores, the scorpion-sorcerers, who fade into being around me.

Sirens grow louder.

They are not yet at their full strength, my own eregores, but all they have to do is distract. Which they do. They attack the man holding the doll and his attentions wavers. My breathing gets easier but these fuckers aren't new to this either.

The Templars summon their own creatures and spirit allies. Crocodiles and jackals.

Not Egyptian. Anything but Heka. That's not gonna save me.

Scorpion mudra. Tibetan technique. Magic you do with your hands. Fucker with the doll of me first.

Concentrate *Mully is dead. Jon lost and soon he or Bettina will be too. Scarlet, lost to me in every way I want her to be found* into my hand. Give it some juice and think of Latin names for the fingers.

Digitus minimus and digitus secundus pointing forward, digiti annunlaris and medius distal phalanx touch the pollex, volar facing up. Those words clash with the formulation, the Tibetan spell *sDig pa ra tsa ru can mGo srin*. The derangement of thinking in one foreign language, speaking in another, neither native. Power there.

Tibetan cannibal scorpion spirit. That's what I conjure up.

Dig scorpions, me.

It appears around me, like... armour. Translucent, glass and Wrathful.

'Save me,' I choke to it. It walks out of the smoke. The Templars aren't expecting a scorpion size of a horse to make a dramatic entrance. Swift, it strikes.

Psychic venom spikes behind the Templars' eyes and he screams, dropping the doll as hand goes up to his face. Good luck, fucker. Thirty plus years of ill feeling spit into his head.

Fuck yeah. That turns the tide, gets me free. Struggle up to my feet.

But the scorpion-sorcerers are new and weak and really ain't ready for this. The Templars link hands and their own spirit creatures start tearing my allies apart. A whirl of white-robed monstrous theriomorphs and fanged reptiles, whirling, killing, a spirit war.

Streets of the City home to warring monsters by the fire light.

Then.

The Templars, four left, the best of Bernadette's crew, shadowy and sadistic, link hands and stare at me. My mudra scorpion curls its tail. It will get one shot, then they'll banish it. Then I'm done.

From the second storey of the Library, which is burning now, a smash and Bettina falls, falls, falls and hits the ground with an impact that I can't even talk about now.

A fire truck races down the street like they can't even see us, taking out the hearse. They can't come here. This is no place for things of the earth.

Templars filling me up with suicide thoughts. A cloud a darkness surrounding me. They want me to... this is Bernadette's thing. They want me to stick thumbs in my eyes, after stubbing my cigarette into them. Strangle myself. Smash my own head into the road. Go and burn.

It pours into me, black water into a broken cup. *Every humiliation and regret you ever felt is burned out of you by death. The pain will be worth it. Siren song.* So tempting. To let it all go. To be done with this whole ludicrous fucking world.

Heh.

Wrong choice, fuckers. Wrong move.

Told you I had a cigarette in my hand.

Light it up. Drag in.

Stupid fucks.

I'm already dedicated to my own death.

I've never wanted to survive all this. I want to die a sorcerer, doing sorcerers work! I came back here to the City to do it.

The tattoo on me. Black solar energy. Paradox. Concentrate it. They're wrapped in their shadow soul selves. A black sun has no need for *shadow*. Shadow cannot survive when the light itself is black.

Pour that information into the local reality.

One of them, turns out to be a woman, shrieks as her shadow armour begins to ease, to weaken. Then it's gone and her soul is exposed as the skin under fingernails.

You know why we banish before every significant rite and Operation? Helps with gnosis. Gives you an awareness that you've enterer ritual space and that helps you, you know, do fucking magic.

And it gets rid of any entities that might be lurking about all astral and like that.

She sees something this woman. This is outside the Library. Course there's *things* hereabouts.

Magical battle like this is a fucking dinner bell.

She goes to run. Falls. Commences to spasm. Have to look differently to see what's feasting on her, more than just gnosis, but from the way she's screaming, ain't nothing pretty to see.

Three Templar left but I'm outta tricks.

Fall to one knee, exhausted. They move to surround me. They

could just kick me to death but gotta figure they got much worse in mind for me. Bernadette ain't gonna let me just motherfucking *die*.

Jon's back on the ground and is at Bettina. They're grappling, to the ground and pound now and looking like it's over. Jon's got her in an armlock. Her arm snaps. First time ever, hear her scream in pain.

There's one way she can win, though.

One way.

Took choice away from Bettina once. Her eye. Made up for it, but swore never to do it again. She looks at me, through smoke, the both of us linked through pain and despair. Can see it clear in her eyes. When it was the Library telling her to make the sacrifice, she says *no*.

But she's wrong. She'll die if I don't save her. So I offer her up to the Lion Goddess of War.

I I I

> '*Hail to You, Gods there,*
> *Khaytyu Who stand in waiting upon Sekhmet,*
> *Who have come forth from the Eye of Ra*'

Prayer to Sekhmet. Lion goddess. Desperate invocation. Warrior queen. Blood drinker.

Told her and the Library it was a big rite. But here, the both of us dying, what do we have to worry about? That it'll go wrong and kill us?

> '*The attack of those Who are among the Shemayu will pass over.*
> *My enemy is under my footsoles, life is at my nose!*
> *My heka is the protection of my flesh, so that I am kept whole.*
> *My border is allotted to me according to my wish.*'

She'll be fierce as fire, potent as murder. She'll be...

The Templars keep trying to fill me up with suicide but that's going nowhere.

Bettina glances over at me.

This is it.

She's saying goodbye. She goddess will either take her or she'll die at Jon's hands.

We walked into this unready and unprepared and the thing that killed me once is fit to kill her. Jon's on her back. His hands move around her head.

He's gonna snap her neck.

Goodbye.

Unless the goddess sits in her bones and transforms...

No.

No.

Me being another man who made her a Goddess, not a woman, being a man who hurt her thinking he'll make up for it down the line, making taking her choices away because I know what's good for her?

What's the point of winning that way?

Let the spell fade.

.

I V

Time to take what's coming to me.

Look up at the shadowy Templars around me.

Strike up a chant in Ancient Egyptian, Demotic. Whatever the fuck it turned out to be.

Ancient Egyptians got a lot of curses. Seth's animal, the donkey, might fuck you to death. No lie. Raped by spirits is a curse. Bit less dramatic? Strangled like a goose. Attacked by hippos. Never have kids.

But...

Oh Christ.

From the sudden rush of heat in my belly, on my skin...

Incinerated in a furnace in execration rites. They see self-slaughter ain't happening and are just gonna burn me to death.

Throw up some protections but they're too good, too many and *oh fuck this hurts oh fuck-*

My clothes catch. My sleeves. Pat it out.

My hair catches.

gnosis starts to fall but hold it. Try to die like a sorcerer.

But not like this. The pain is... Hell. Try not to scream but it'll come. Try to go out like -

Then.

The Templar's aren't there.

'Get up.'

A woman's voice. A woman's touch.

Scarlet.

V

'Libretto. They'll ...'

She nods. The entire Library is aflame now.

Her eyes glow with it.

She's let her hair turn red again.

The three Templars have collapsed. They're... asleep.

She's poured sand on them. She waited until they were busy and... a simple charm to send babies to bed.

That's how she saved me. Scarlet's eyes are wild with victory.

'Fucking *Granny Magic* that, fuckers. Spell I get Jet to sleep with. They were protected against every *high* theurgy in the world.'

And Bettina *sees*. We're not alone and we've ways to win.

Jon's twisted her so she sees. He's got her by the neck. He's trying to snap it

She screams. Primal and defiant, not pain this time.

She's not a woman. She's not human. She's a fucking *ghoul*. She's a dead woman walking the earth, empowered by necromancy and driven by sorcery to protect. Me. Herself.

Bettina looks over at me. She forces herself to her knees. Her feet. She screams again. Jon's tearing through the muscles in her neck. The bones and vertebrae are creaking so loud we can hear them over even the inferno. She spins three sixty.

She leaps backwards, ten feet, right across the road, knocking him against the smashed hearse.

Fucking *crash*.

He stays on. She does it again.

And again.

And finally he loses his grip.

She turns. Grabs him by the shirt. Lifts him. Smashes him down on the bonnet. Left, right, left. Jon's fast and Jon's deadly but her strength is not a human thing.

The Rabisu screeches from out of his mouth. She grabs Jon, one hand at his throat. Hurls him like a sack onto the road. He leaps back up to his feet, grace of cobras. Tries that combo of jabs again but she's ready. She sways back.

Jon steps in.

She throws a haymaker.

Jon steps into it, strikes her in the throat with the force to kill. He can't help himself. She's left the opening and in another fighter, that would be the end.

Her trachea crumbles. This would kill any mortal thing.

But...

And now, Jon is unable to evade Bettina's return punch. He's too close, thought he'd won, no defence.

His neck *snaps* as she hits him in the temple. The force is sickening.

And just like that.

It's over.

She hobbles to me and for the first time, we put arms around one another. We both wince. We both look like hell.

Arms around one another, we look up at the Library for the last time.

Just ash now.

Scarlet says 'Come on. We've got a safe place.'

We ignore her for a while.

Then, propping each other up, arms around each other's

shoulders, hers shattered and mine burnt, we leave this place behind us.

TWENTY-FOUR

I

Israel Island. A few hours later. Dawn is minutes away and it's quiet and cold. Me and Bettina ache but this needed to be done.

Dead bodies burning in a pile. Liberetto's white hair is wrapped in a dark scarf, eyes behind darker sunglasses. She's been busy, defending the Archive from what can only be hoped is the last of the Sothic Templars.

'All this time and you thought I'd learned nothing? We've defences here, Lark. Your enemies are lost forever.'

Scarlet hugs her. Note that.

Bettina's fucked all the way up. Soon she'll have to feed. She eyes off the burning bodies, unwilling to get in on the breakfast buffet while there's half a dozen people watching her.

Her Ra eye has turned *yellow*. Looks more like a lion's.

'You look like a badass, now.'

'Hell, man, always did.'

Her voice is a whisper through a ruined throat and that eye is in a mash of bone and tissue and cuts but she looks pretty great to me.

Hold me phone up to her so as she can see herself on the video phone thing.

She takes a long look. Hands it back.

'Cool,' s'all she says.

Who's left?

Karel, Libretto, Elliot, Me, a security guard, one of the scryers. Velasquez died in the attack.

Too many dead.

Scarlet called an ambulance for us. We had to light out quick but now we need to get looked at. Sit there waiting for it.

Scarlet comes sits by me as me and Bettina smoke, apart from the crowd. Elliot stares daggers in her back.

'I think Jon's dead.'

She nods. Glances over at her husband. Takes my dart from me and drags once.

'God that's good. I miss smoking.'

Nod at her.

'We'll have to sort things out soon. Everything.'

'Bernadette's Operation is still going on.'

'Yeah...'

'She's got us on the ropes, Scarlet.'

'Yeah.'

Ambulance pulls up.

'Clear these people out. Bettina has things to do.'

She glances over at my girl. Bettina gives a ghoulish grin. Scarlet fights away a shudder.

'These guys cool?' Gesture at the paramedics.

'Vetted, yeah.'

Stand up. Flick the butt on the ground. Scarlet wasn't lying. Smoke fills me up, gives me the buzz. Dedicated to my own death. Time to stop trying to stay alive. Time to win.

Paramedics help me in. Scarlet sits by me as they check me over.

There's something living in my brain. Some infant demon. Wonder if they'll find that as they ask me their stupid questions.

'We have to get it together, baby.'

'Please don't call me that, Lark. Not here.'

She stares down at me as they close the doors.

'But we do. Yeah.'

II

Days in the hospital are boring. Amuse myself by stealing pills and convincing nurses out of morphine. Man takes his fun where there's fun to be found. But in the end, just sleep a lot. My neurologist comes to visit, tells me to get another MRI. Treat me for strangulation wounds but there's not much to do but rest.

Real tired.

Try to commune with what's in my head but it ain't talking.

They send a psych around. Scarlet's idea, no doubt. Guess how that goes over.

One night, late, in the spooky quiet of the ward after midnight... draw the curtain and switch on that overhead light that throws harsh shadows over my bed.

Hold my hand like a claw and resummon my shadowy familiar.

Kinda missed it.

Shyer than even before. Four legs, long neck and head, my hand all acrawling. Pat it kinda like you might a cat or a dog fits in a mug. Pull my drip out and feed it. Nurses get pissed at that one.

Three days later, they check me out.

Bettina's waiting. She's wearing dark glasses in the morning light. Winter's coming on soon. One of them crisp Autumn mornings lets you know the sun you're in won't last so long.

'Eye kinda freaks folk out.'

'Sure.'

She hands me a fresh pack of smokes and we get into her hearse.

'We'll hit your joint, then tonight, big meeting.'

'Pass.'

'No. You're gonna want in on this.'

'Reckon so?'

She starts the car. Looks long at me with two eyes and one's a God's.

III

We sit around the long black table of the hotel conference room. Igle's there, the peace sorcerer. Libretto, who apparently decided to step up. Katanya. Elliot. Me.

Hotel fucking conference room.

That's what we're reduced to. Laptops are open with seniors from all across the world video conferencing in. Drawn on the table, a ritual circle for those who want to remote view the thing.

There's water for us all. Feels more like a corporate retreat. Elliot's doing no doubt. He's got one of his business mystics taking notes. She don't look comfortable.

He's still the ranking cat for day-to-day operations.

Bettina's outside, not wanting to get involved in this shit. Not a one here complains. Her rep. is solid as can be. She beat Jon. She beat down the Hollow.

Opening incantations are made, corners erected. Spells laid down all around.

Funeral air to it all. No one feels anything but worry. We're on the mat and the ref has started the count.

Elliot's in a cream coloured three piece that, for some fucking reason, makes me want to kick him to death.

'First order of business, to revoke the position given to Frater Lark of Special Executor. Can I get a second, please?'

No one raises a hand.

He glances at his wife.

She meets his gaze and raises not even a goddamn finger.

First time since it started, some chill goes out of that wind blowing in me.

'Scar, what?'

She turns away from him.

Seems like an execution.

Then again, she doesn't look at me, either.

'For God's sake, Elliot,' murmurs Igle. 'This is not the time for it.

He stays.'

Nods around the table. Gets me suspicious.

'You haven't even opened up the... this isn't how we do things.' Igle keeps on.

'I am under no obligation to -'

Scarlet cuts him off.

'Please. Stop. We are here to talk about the future of this Chapter.'

Over a video, one voice, German accent like from the dream, says

'Elliot, we're considering revoking the entire Chapter and cutting our losses. This is not time for a personal issue.'

This fucker must slag me to the entire organisation.

Katanya raises her hand. Irritation clear, Elliot recognises her.

'In the last years, we've had our security compromised by the Blossom entity, we've had sorcerers throughout the City killed, many of who relied on us to protect them and finally, our Sanctum destroyed by enemy action. We've lost *friends*.'

Nods all around.

Katanya and Scarlet lock eyes.

'And this is under the proctorship of Elliot Everett.'

'Oh fuck you, no one could have done better!'

'I disagree Elliot.' Katanya's voice is mild but her meaning is not.

'Who then? Him?!' He points at me.

'No. Her.'

Katanya looks at Scarlet.

Scarlet stands.

'At the risk of sounding immodest, it was *my* plans that discovered Bernadette's action and my agents who purged the Sothic Temple. It was my actions that got us out of the Library. I accept nomination for Proctorship.'

Actually, was mine. She knows that. She also knows I won't steal her thunder. Not if this is going like I want it to go. Clever. Clever Scarlet.

'Scarlet, what the fuck, babe?'

Elliot turns on her, face slack with this.

She don't even look at him. *Now* she looks at me. Nothing but ice. Know that feeling. She's remote. She's inside herself, watching this happen. She's planned this. She knew it would come to this.

'Baby? What's happening?'

'All those in favour of promoting Scarlet to proctorship? *Soror Primaris?*'

Katanya, Igle, Libretto, Elliot, the others.

Don't need to raise my hand.

'Motion passes with one abstention,' says Igle. 'Eirene blesses this motion. So mote it be.'

They repeat that back like church goers.

'The fuck *is* this!?'

Katanya looks over at me.

Scarlet's gaze never drops.

Elliot isn't occult. He's never been truly in the world. He can't be trusted with a demotion.

I have a vision for the Library. I have plans. I know how I want us to be go forward and that's all under attack. Bernadette is scaring the people I need to do things. Messing up my timetables and that stuff.

That's what she said to me and got to figure she meant it. She *prepared* for this. She kissed me in the graveyard and told me this.

Elliot can't die. Elliot can't be taken out of the order.

She knew.

Scarlet's eyes never leave mine.

Elliot goes quiet. Begins to realise what's happened. Or least he thinks he does.

More than anything this: I need Elliot's money and that means staying married to him. I'll never leave him because if I do, the money goes and that's a resource I cannot lose. She said that too.

'So that's it?' whines Scarlet's husband.

'One mistake and you throw me out. Well, I paid for this room so fuck it. *You* get out.'

No one moves.

'I said get out!'

All he has is money. That's becoming clear to him.

'Alright. Fuck all of you. You!' he turns on his wife like she weren't anything. His voice goes quiet as poison.

'I'll have the kid. I'll have the house and I'll leave you on the street.'

Some cats lose bad.

He stands. 'Head office wants to shut you down and you're throwing me out now!?' he rants on for a bit. Then. 'In short, fuck you all.'

He walks out.

Take a cigarette from the pack. Put it in my mouth. Don't light it. Scarlet nods.

Get up. Follow him out.

Bettina's outside the door.

'Need back up?'

'No.'

I V

Scarlet and me walk through the hospice grounds.

Elliot's happy as can be for a man who suffered from a sudden and dramatic sleep disorder that's made him effectively a vegetable. That's what they say, the doctors, anyway. They're having a hard time pinning down the pathology.

It's demon children inside him, though.

From my head to his.

Me?

Can live with something like that.

Him?

Turned him out like a light.

Nurses wipe the drool from his lips while the little girl Jet shyly waves goodbye at the ruins of her father.

In time the demons will grow but that's something to worry

about another time.

Cold winds now. Winter's here. The trees we walk under rake at the sky, leafless and cheerless.

'You communicated with Wick, I read in your report.' Her child in her arms.

'Yeah.'

'Gonna follow that up?'

'Maybe. Wick's pissed, though. And scared. The Apophis entity frightens her. Bernadette said some shit about god traps. Gonna work on that first. And the Old Man's souls. The four jars. She'll have relocated them by now.'

'Alright.'

We walk towards the gate real quiet.

She stops a few steps away.

'I know what you're thinking. You and your scorpion of a mind. No. I didn't... plan for it to go down like that with Elliot, not *exactly* like it did. But you know... Bernadette... *He couldn't save any of us from her.*'

I just look at the Kid. She'd do anything for the Kid.

'Let me have this conversation for you, Lark. Were you manipulated? Yeah. Yeah you were. I couldn't rely on him anymore and so I let him look stupid coming at you. Here's the flattery I know you want - I always knew you could take anything he threw at you. And I knew you'd back my play.'

Which means something to me. Which she knew it would.

'And so long as I visit once a month or so, his family will keep the money coming. You know he gets thirty thousand a month, from family trust, as *pocket money?* Not to mention businesses and investments and Christ knows what else.'

Say nothing. Straight up do not believe her. This was a plan and she let the guillotine fall right where it needed.

'And now I have a free hand. I did have dreams for the Library. Still do. You can be part of that if you like.'

Pat down my jacket. Pull out a smoke.

'Not near the baby.'

Put it back. Leaves crunch as we walk to the car park. The sky is very blue.

Bernadette's out there. Apophis is coming. The Old Man's soul won't die easy but when it does, the world can't be the same. Won't be skeletal cities and monsters ravening. But when Apophis comes into the world, there'll be a thousand little armageddons inside every head.

'Sure.'

She smiles thanks at me. Relief. Kids stirs in her arms.

Wasn't gonna ask this. Swore it wasn't happening. *Just... just watch this. Fuck sake.*

'Any of this change things for us?'

Give her this. She doesn't sigh or get angry. We keep walking a bit longer and come to the gate. Her driver gets out of the town car, opens the door.

'You want to come live in my apartment? You saw it. That your scene? Help me get this kid ready in the morning and clean up after? You want to plan out nutritious meals? Child of a man you don't have time for... want to raise her? Want to help me host parties? Go to galas. Want to put down your books when it's time for dinner? Sing songs? Spoon feed, help her use a bathroom?'

Say nothing.

'Of course you don't. I don't blame you. There's a big part of me wants to go back to our old place and just dance and drink and listen to Rod Willis on mushroom and all that. But there's things I want *more*, Lark. I'm not going to tell you to grow up or get a job. I'm just going to ask you to understand how it is for me.'

The kid wakes up. Turns to look at me. Elliot's eyes and nose. She's gonna take after daddy.

Scarlet leans in, kisses my cheek.

'Mind you, I'll probably call you up horny or something one day, so that's something to look forward to.'

Kinda smile at that.

'We have things to do together, Lark. Big things. *That's* how I want you now. A different kind of partner.'

She gets in and drives away.

I'll come at you straight. She told me that in her house but she didn't come straight at all. She was always looking out for this kind of situation. She used me.

Finding it hard to care with that warm kiss on my cheek. But that don't mean she can ever be trusted a damn ever again.

Spent twenty minutes or so planning how to thank Bendis, goddess of the hunt, who still figure is owed silver and respect for helping me kick all this off. Some debts can't be ignored, no matter what. A madhouse ain't a bad place to contemplate a lunatic goddess, neither.

Bettina picks me up when that's nearly done.

Gets out of the car.

Lights my cigarette for me. Click clack of a zippo.

'You let her go?'

Slowly, nod at her. Closest person in the world to me.

'You did the right thing. Ain't nothing but blood where we're walking now.'

Don't know how right she is.

END